We Can Still Be FRIENDS

Also by Kelly Cherry

Fiction

THE SOCIETY OF FRIENDS
MY LIFE AND DR. JOYCE BROTHERS
THE LOST TRAVELLER'S DREAM
IN THE WINK OF AN EYE
AUGUSTA PLAYED
SICK AND FULL OF BURNING

Poetry

RISING VENUS
DEATH AND TRANSFIGURATION
GOD'S LOUD HAND
NATURAL THEOLOGY
RELATIVITY
LOVERS AND AGNOSTICS

Nonfiction

WRITING THE WORLD
THE EXILED HEART

Limited Editions

AN OTHER WOMAN, a poem
THE POEM, an essay
TIME OUT OF MIND, poems
BENJAMIN JOHN, a poem
SONGS FOR A SOVIET COMPOSER, poems
CONVERSION, a story

Translation

OCTAVIA, in SENECA: THE TRAGEDIES, VOLUME II
ANTIGONE, in SOPHOCLES, 2

Kelly Cherry

We Can Still Be FRIENDS

A NOVEL

SOHO

Published by
Soho Press, Inc.
853 Broadway
New York, N.Y. 10003

Library of Congress Cataloging-in-Publication Data
Cherry, Kelly.
We can still be friends : a novel / Kelly Cherry.
p. cm.
ISBN 1-56947-323-4 (alk. paper)
1. Rejection (Psychology)—Fiction. 2. Separation (Psychology)—Fiction. 3. Triangles (Interpersonal relations)—Fiction. 4. Single mothers—Fiction.
I. Title.
PS3553.H357W4 2003
813'.54—dc21 2002044653

10 9 8 7 6 5 4 3 2 1

acknowledgments

A thousand thanks to my agent, Elizabeth Sheinkman, and to my editor, Laura Hruska, for their expertise and enthusiasm, and a thousand times a thousand thanks to my husband, Burke Davis III.

for **Burke**

You can't kill a minuet de la cour. You may shut up the music-book, close the harpsichord; in the cupboard and presses the rats may destroy the white satin favours. The mob may sack Versailles; the Trianon may fall, but surely the minuet—the minuet itself is dancing itself away into the furthest stars . . .

—Ford Madox Ford, *The Good Soldier*

Ava

■ LOVE. It's not for weaklings.

She thinks: It ought to be. It was meant to be. The meek, the mild, those in need, those who succored those in need, love was meant for them. But that must have been B.S.: Before Sex.

And now begins the time of being assaulted by fury, of being suffocated by despair. Yet she already knows what it means to be a woman scorned. What woman doesn't?

What female, she asks herself again, twisting the telephone cord until it is as convoluted as a strand of DNA, over the age of goddamn thirty give or take a year or two, doesn't?

And since she already knows everything she is about to feel, she thinks perhaps she should simply feel it right now, all at once, like ripping a Band-Aid from a cut, and be done with it.

She has no time for this, for a broken heart. Is she not a hotshot scholar? Her schedule overflows with classes, papers, conferences. She is in Memphis only for the semester, and only because back home in Chicago, where she is tenured at highly ranked Midland University, her salary reflects a stupid bias against Women's Studies—and women. Thus, this semester she is Visiting and Distinguished, not to mention better paid, and also—but how can this be?—crying her heart out, in Memphis.

Muted February light from the windows behind her, where she sits on the couch, makes everything bleak. Her whole life feels rented. She is in a makeshift apartment, a makeshift life. All she has to do to realize that there will never be anything permanent for her is look around.

She wonders if she had known even before she left Chicago that this was coming—this telephone call from Tony that he would begin by saying, "I need to tell you something." If she had taken the job here to make it easier for him to do this to her. Or to avoid having to show him her face when he told her. She could imagine the jumble of emotions on her face. She could imagine his face, every careful calibration of feeling, never too much of anything, no more distance, anger, tenderness, distractedness than the exact amount of each needed to make his point. You wanted that kind of control in a surgeon. You didn't necessarily want it in a man.

But you wanted his dark sexiness, his bravery.

She will not stand for this—for the way he is making her feel. She is not going to *carry a torch, yearn, sigh, sob into her pillow at night. Wait all alone by the telephone.*

Love. It puts life on hold.

She shifts the receiver against her shoulder. His words pour into her ear like a medicine or poison, something both Shakespearean and pharmaceutical, something flooding.

He had called to tell her that he had found intuitive love with—and been put in touch with his inner self by—the beautiful art-historian wife of a movie producer, an amazing woman (but since when did being blond become amazing, she was tempted to ask) whom he'd met in San Francisco two months previously, though he'd not mentioned this fact before, and immediately things that had seemed encoded, such as his arriving late for her birthday dinner and saying it was because of a "last-minute phone call," became as clear as skywriting, and—this was what had to be said, he said—to explain that he could not, therefore, continue his sexual relationship with her, even though he did care deeply for her as a good friend and he hoped they would go on being friends—though exactly how they were going to do this, when she asked him, he didn't seem to know. As he rushed on, she kept an eye on the dead wasp.

The wasp had been dead for a couple of weeks and was disintegrating on the pale green carpet, becoming smaller and translucent in a slow fade. At first she had planned to get out the vacuum cleaner but that would have meant rummaging through the crowded closet, which was surely stuffed with the skeletons of former visiting professors. Then she kept thinking that soon she'd overcome her squeamishness and pick the poor dead thing up with a paper towel and flush it down the john. At some point, she had become fascinated with the process of decomposition: it reminded her of the ending of that movie, *The Incredible Shrinking Man*, where at the point of disappearance the hero merges with the cosmos. She thought wistfully of merging with the cosmos.

"Beautiful?" she said.

"I'm not talking just about physical appearance," he said quickly, a lurch in his voice like a roller-coaster. It was tricky, she thought: when you broke up with someone you had to work in all your justifications and excuses without being too cruel to the other person. She felt sorry for him, having to take all these curves at high speed.

She didn't believe that he was not talking about physical appearance. When she thought about his physical appearance she felt vertiginous, urgent. His welcoming eyes, knowledgeable hands, Arthur Ashe good looks were a drug to her system. Besides, he had managed to mention the word "blond" before almost anything else.

"I think I should tell you something about her," Tony was saying, "if you can handle it."

Could she handle it? Could she handle the electric current running at high voltage through his low voice, something like a charged fence meant to keep her out? She knew she could not handle hanging up. The minute she hung up, it would be over. Of course, that was what he was telling her, that it was over.

She started to cry but she was not going to let him know that. She bit her bottom lip, but then that reminded her that he had once said he wished her bottom lip could be an all-day sucker. She bit harder. "It doesn't really have that much to do with sex or even intellectual stimulation," he was saying. "It's just that she's taught me so much about myself. She's put me in touch with feelings I haven't had since childhood."

What feelings were those? She imagined him as a small boy in a New York ghetto, a lonely, brainy little black boy (*half* black but it had always worried her that he seemed to be passing, he wouldn't lie to a direct question but he was willing to let friends and colleagues assume he was white, maybe Lebanese or Saudi, when half black was the same as black so far as the world was concerned). She was feeling maternal toward him!, and he was going on about the difference between *love*, which was what he felt for this movie-producer's art-historian wife and was easy and natural and above all something called "intuitive," and *affection*, which was what, he now said, he felt for her.

Maternal indeed. As he continued to talk—all this talk; it was what men replaced feeling with (he had never talked this much before)—she began to realize that the meeting with the amazing blond married woman in San Francisco had taken place at almost the very moment when she, then back home in the battering cold of Chicago—all the colder because he hadn't suggested that she come along to his medical convention, she could ride the streetcars! visit Fisherman's Wharf! eat Chinese! but No, he'd said, No—was miscarrying his child.

Her only pregnancy. She'd kept telling herself that she couldn't be pregnant, not for the first time at this late date, but could she? Her breasts were the most sensitive they'd ever been, full and straining against her bra.

"Ted and Yvonne"—also from Chicago, also attending the convention, why wasn't she invited, well she must have known, she must have sensed even if she hadn't admitted it to herself, and she was admitting it to herself now, that he had been sending her a message by not inviting her—"introduced me to them"—to the art historian and her movie-producer husband—"and they say this couple is the most exciting, glamorous couple they know, and as you know they know a lot of people," he went on, while she remembered the would-be baby leaking out between her legs, *sneaking out, skipping town heading south taking a detour around life straight to death, that last stop, it was supposed to be a last stop not a first stop*, a tiny nameless blot, not even a fully formed clot—a clotlet.

She'd been wrong, she'd told herself—she wasn't pregnant, she was getting her period. After the lab tech had punched her arm to draw blood for the serum test, she'd stopped in at the hospital gift shop to stock up on *Women's Wear Daily* and *Working Woman*, pop-culture she as a feminist professor of modern American literature in the Women's Studies Program was supposed to be above reading yes, but she *did* wear clothes almost every day, she *was* a working woman, she *believed* in Women's Studies but she was in need of a long-lasting mascara that would not run down her face when her boyfriend informed her that he had fallen in love with an art historian, and while she was paying the cashier, she felt the warm sticky liquid pooling in her underpants. This had felt, at least for a moment, like the end of everything. It had felt as if the blood had come straight from her heart, some artery connecting heart to womb. The body weeping slow red tears. She had bled all weekend, her stomach cramping, her thighs marbling like a cake against the toilet seat. On Tuesday, the nurse specialist called her and said the test was positive. "It can't be," she'd said to the nurse; "I'm having my period." There was a long silence before the nurse spoke again.

She couldn't help wondering if worrying about why Tony didn't want her to accompany him hadn't been a cause of her miscarriage. Maybe her body had intuited that he was having intuitive sex with the blond woman. When events were that coincidental, it was hard to believe they were just coincidental. While Tony elaborated on the blond woman's virtues, she thought of a baby she might have named Carlos or Carlo or Maria, something to reflect Tony's complex ethnicity, little wasp (but one-fourth black) crinkling into a papery nothingness like the wasp on the carpet. Merging with the cosmos on a tampon, a minipad thrown in for good measure.

She had told Tony about the miscarriage when he got back from San Francisco. Now she wondered if that was why he had not told her about the married woman then. Maybe if she had not immediately blurted out her own news he would not have waited until now to tell her his.

He had come to her house straight from O'Hare that Sunday evening, and if she hadn't told him right away he would have heard about it at the hospital the next day. After she told him, Tony corrected her terminology. Like the other doctors at the hospital, he informed her she'd had a "spontaneous A.B." She had lifted the tea kettle from the stove and joined him at her kitchen table. She reached across the table for his hand. "How come you're so cold?" she asked.

He shook his head.

She rose and looked out the window. The Chicago neighborhood was bandaged in snow. Here and there, holiday lights were already strung and shining.

She had felt stronger addressing him from there, standing next to the counter. It was a position that she was comfortable taking, the position of a teacher lecturing to her class.

"It was a *miscarriage*," she had said, arguing strenuously for some semantic point that she knew seemed silly to him. But to her, "spontaneous" sounded like a choice, and she had not had a choice.

She came back to the present to discover that she had moved from the couch to the hallway floor and now was sitting with her back against the wall, the telephone cord looped around her wrist like a bracelet. She was telling him she loved him, and he was telling her he cared for her but that it wasn't intuitive love, but at least he didn't know she was crying, she was sure she was managing that. He had had one night with this woman plus one weekend—he'd flown all the way back out to California after telling Ava he couldn't free up his schedule to make the short hop down from Chicago to Memphis—and he was saying that he knew it was unlikely to last "given that she lives so far away and is married" but that he also now knew that when he did marry again it would be to a woman for whom he felt this "intuitive" kind of love.

Ava wondered if intuitive love was any different from the kind that had prompted him, in the beginning, to call her once or twice a day; that had made him unable to stop touching her—her hand or her face or the back of her neck; that had caused him to smile and say that she made his heart beat faster so it was a good thing, wasn't it, that he was a heart surgeon. He pointed out that they had not been communicating very well for the past couple of months. She did not point out that his leading a secret life would tend to put a crimp in their communication. "I thought we were building something special," she said. "A bond. I thought every hassle or problem we had and solved was actually something that strengthened the bond."

She could hear he hated her saying that: there was a sharp note of disagreement in his voice just for a second—he had said he wanted to be friends but clearly there were limits to friendship, things you didn't say to a friend such as never tell a man he's been living a lie, pretending to be something he's not, this is not what a man means by friendship—and it was sharp enough to cut. A knife in your chest, this is what a heart surgeon does. She wanted to win him back. Trying to flatter him with her jealousy, she said, "I hope I never meet this woman." She laughed, lightly. "I'll strangle her." She unwound the cord from her wrist and looked at it.

And then when he said, "That would make me very unhappy"—as solemnly as if she had not been joking—she knew she had lost him.

With an odd objectivity she wondered what she was going to do first when he hung up: call her shrink or her girlfriend. She supposed she'd better call the shrink first; it always took time for the answering service to get hold of him. She could call her girlfriend in the interim.

"I care about you," he said again, this time with finality. "I care about what's going to happen in your future."

"Me, too," she echoed softly. There was a pause like arrhythmia, followed by the sound of his hanging up.

The click of his receiver disengaging from hers seemed to ricochet around the room like a bullet. This must be what people meant when they talked about a parting shot.

In the last moments of their conversation, she had sunk completely to the floor, which, she realized, had not been vacuumed at least since the previous visiting professor, who must have been a smoker. Curled up on the carpet, she saw that the figured roses were dusk-colored with cigarette ash. It was so interesting lying here on the floor, on a bed of roses. She rolled over and found herself face to face with the incredible shrinking wasp.

Tony

■ ANTHONY G. Ferro, M.D., had already been sick once earlier in the morning, just thinking about the call he knew he had to make to Ava. Heaving into the bathroom sink, he'd been tempted to blame Ava for the awful, pained way he felt, and though he knew he was being unreasonable that had just made him even angrier toward her. He'd been in his new place only since October and was proud of the way the co-op reflected *him*, his personality, not his ex-wife's or his son's or Ava's. If he was puking in the bathroom, what did this say about his ability to order his life?

But it was Ava who had thrown everything into disorder, however innocent or unknowing she portrayed herself as being. Women did that, feigned innocence to avoid responsibility. They were always complaining about how men never accepted responsibility in a relationship, but they did their own running from it. For a couple of months now he'd been giving her loud and clear signals that things between them were not going to go the way she wanted them to, and still she refused to read him. You couldn't say it, but it sure as hell seemed to him that women must have some sort of hormonally wired short-circuiting, something that allowed them to tune out reality whenever it didn't accord with their wishes. That was why he had dreaded this call: he had been afraid he was going to hurt her, he didn't want to hurt her, but Jesus Christ!, she was making it hard for him not to hurt her.

Listening to her hesitant, hypocritical responses—the tactful modulations, which permitted the pointed digs; the soft, low voice, which sheathed barbed words—he imagined his heart a pendulum vacillating between guilt and anger, between wanting to be kind and needing to be clear and resenting her for making him feel these things.

It was true that earlier on he had made some rash statements about the potential their relationship had. He even said once that he might want to marry her after his divorce came through, "though I can't," he remembered cautioning her, yes he was sure he had said this, "say for sure." And at the time he really had thought he might want to marry her but now he knew what love was, and it was not, finally, any of the things Ava thought it was.

He knew this because he had learned from Claire what love was. If he felt a little foolish at having taken so long to learn what love was, he was also exhilarated to have learned it before it was too late.

What Claire had taught him, and what he was in fact rather proud to have been able to learn even at this late date, was that love was liberation: a freedom from conventional expectation, a freedom from assumptions about the self that led, if you dared to follow it where it took you, to self-discovery. He was discovering himself and why not, why not he thought, leaning forward over the edge of the bed where he was sitting with the receiver hot as a mouth against his ear, Ava crying, he was positive she was, long distance, he had spent a lifetime fulfilling his responsibilities to others he had a responsibility to himself too, it was time he dared, time he stopped running from that particular responsibility.

Everything with Ava was always so full of meaning—he could feel himself filling with anger again at the thought of this—so black and white, so life-or-death and goddammit to hell life and death were what he had to deal with every moment of the day and the rest of the time he'd just like to be having some fun, yes, fun, not a meaningless term even if it went against the millennial zeitgeist and even if the sexual revolution was long over, he had been in med school when it started then years of being a husband father good citizen in Marshfield before the separation and his move to Chicago where he'd accepted a position—a city of universities and hospitals, Chicago was, the hospital had been after him for years: he could do research, they offered; he could teach. That was what was wonderful and different about Claire: she knew how to enjoy life, how to laugh.

"But we laughed a lot too," Ava was saying, in the sad, pinched voice that he knew was supposed to solicit his sympathy and did, dammit, did. And of course Ava could laugh. But he always had the feeling that she was laughing for his benefit, to keep him interested in her. It made him feel too much at the center, too much the cause, as if she depended on him for her very life or at least for her pleasure in it. And sure enough, in spite of all the emotional prophylactics he'd tried to employ from the beginning of their involvement, it was, in the end, all his fault, exactly as if he had given her a sexually transmitted disease, namely the fatal infection of expecting someone to behave, feel the way you wanted them—him—to behave, to feel, but plainly she had had this habit of expectation long before she ever met him.

"But I don't see," she said, "how what we had can be compared with one night and a weekend of messing around with a married woman."

"It's not *messing around*." Tony was relieved to have his anger legitimized. "If it were just *messing around*, I wouldn't have felt the need to call you. I think we are good enough friends that we owe it to each other to be honest. It wouldn't be honest of me to keep sleeping with you. And while I know it's unlikely that this other relationship can last, given that she's married and lives so far away, it has had a profoundly significant effect already. She's taught me what I'm capable of feeling."

For a half-instant, he remembered having said to Ava, in the first month of their affair, "You have the capacity to make me both sadder and happier than anyone I've ever known." At the time it had been true. The sadness? That had been what he felt lying beside her on the waterbed in his cheerless apartment before he bought this co-op that was all his, near the hospital. No matter how much medication the psychiatrists gave her, she still could not sleep. Night after night, she lay awake, motionless at his side. He'd doze off for a while but then some dream of anxiety would thrust him back into the dark room, and always she was awake, her eyes burning into space.

It was not his fault that he had not known how much *more* he was capable of feeling—more even than that dark sadness, much more even than the first satisfaction of letting her depend on him, knowing he could help her, could stay beside her through those long sleepless winter nights.

"We can still see each other and do things together," he said. "We can still be friends."

"But not sleep together."

"No."

"Tell me one thing," she said.

He sighed and glanced at his watch. They had been talking for two hours.

"You've had two months to think about this," she said, as if she'd read his mind. "Almost three. I only just heard about it today, remember."

"I realize that."

"Are you convinced you won't ever want a future with me? That you will never change your mind?"

Did he know the answer to that question? If he did, could he injure her with it? *First, do no harm.*

A siren keened in the distance. In Marshfield, home had been a place of silence, snow and silence. Silence falling like snow in the widening rift between him and his wife of eighteen years.

"I won't answer that," he said. "I think I've been as unsubtle as I can be. You think about what we've said. If you want to call me back, I'll be here this afternoon. Call collect."

"Collect," she said, as if trying out a new language.

Was she mocking him?

"I love you," she said.

"I care about you too," he said, and he did feel enormous affection for her but he also felt that if she were a *lady* she would not assault him with the word "love" like this, it was a kind of weapon, a way of making sure he felt her pain as she registered the difference in their vocabularies, and yes, it was he who had spelled out the difference in their vocabularies, she didn't have to hit him over the head with it.

Hanging up, he thought about calling Claire, but he decided he'd better keep the line free in case Ava called back.

He made a list of items he needed to pick up the next time he found himself in a shopping center. He set up his computer.

The afternoon wore on, and Ava didn't call back. God but she was a difficult woman.

Yvonne called to say that she and Ted had planned to go to the symphony at Orchestra Hall that night but Ted couldn't make it. Would Tony like to join her?

He started to say no, thinking he owed it to Ava to be here if she called back, but then he realized that the day had dribbled away while he waited and he decided if she hadn't called back by now, she probably wouldn't, or maybe she was waiting to leave a message on his machine sometime when she knew he'd be out, it would be like her to do that, and he said yes.

What his call to her had meant, he reminded himself, was that he did *not* owe it to her to be here. It was not his *job*.

Changing into a shirt and jacket for the evening, he carefully folded the sweater he had been wearing and shelved it in the bureau he'd bought—he was still finding furniture for his new place. The television set, next to the bureau, he had borrowed from Ava when she rented out her house in Chicago for the semester in Memphis.

The bedroom had narrow, horizontal windows placed high, the walls holding the bed in a secret embrace. Ava had commented on how good the sweater looked on him; he'd been wearing it the day he put her on the plane to Memphis. "Russet cashmere," she said. "Imagine. Was it a Christmas present?"

"Yes," he said. He knew that if he said nothing more she would assume it was from his ex-wife and would be careful not to ask any more questions.

He'd wanted Ava to have a Christmas, and so they had celebrated together in his new digs, with fresh coffee and leftover cheesecake, before he drove north to Marshfield to spend a couple of days with his son (and Ry, too, of course; they were still the same parents of the same child, divorce or no divorce). Ava opened her presents gleefully, as pleased as he had known she would be. Yes, buying earrings for her, a blue jar, a candlestick, a brass letter-opener edged like a ruler, a miniature lucky elephant, he knew her smallest desires. "You must have spent hours finding all these special things," Ava said, a bit breathless. "Not really," he demurred—and, in truth, it'd taken no time at all and that made him feel guilty. He knew her so well that making her happy cost him nothing.

Making her unhappy, however, cost him plenty, he felt she had taken him for all he was worth, made him pay and pay until he felt bankrupt around the heart, he should not have to feel like this, though he of all people, he supposed, should know that the heart's economy could crash without warning.

Boyd

■ SIX weeks earlier Boyd Buchanan had been leaning, as he had on many such occasions, against the cash bar. The occasion this time was a medical convention in San Francisco, and the bar was swagged with gold tinsel. The cocktail napkins were red and green. With Christmas only days away, the caterer had aimed to be festive without offending conventioneers who might prefer to celebrate Chanukah or Kwanza.

He was watching his wife zero in on her latest conquest. She had picked a Mediterranean type this time, Syrian or Lebanese maybe. If he were younger and an actor, an agent could pitch him as the next Al Pacino, though Pacino was all about energy threatening to blow up in your face, and this guy was letting nothing out, was the kind of guy who waits for the world to come to him. When Ted had introduced them, he'd said he was a surgeon. Someone Yvonne worked with in Chicago—did some kind of research with. Well, he'd bet the poor son of a bitch didn't suspect that just now Claire was scrutinizing him with the same kind of intensity a medical researcher might bring to bear on a new virus.

The room was crawling with medical researchers. It was, he felt, a curious place for a movie producer to find himself in. Curious and, to tell the truth, unfitting. Even after twenty-five years of marriage to a professor, he felt awkward around the degreed, the professionally professional. He was too dumb. He never understood what they were talking about.

Claire, of course, could talk with anybody. They had come to this medical convention in San Francisco to see old friends from college days in Chicago—Yvonne and Ted Cassidy. Claire and Yvonne and a couple of other students had shared a house when they were in graduate school at Midland University; the absentee landlord turned out to be Ted, who, when he got back from his leave of absence, fell in love with Yvonne. His other tenants moved out; Yvonne moved into the master bedroom. "It was my room the year he was away," Claire said the third time Boyd took her out. He had taken her to one of those beer joints with sawdust on the floor and peanuts in shells in bowls on the tables, intellectual aspirations, and tapes of bands like The Grateful Dead and The Rolling Stones. The sixties! Boyd had been a film student at Midland U., by then (for way too long) driving a cab and writing scripts that piled up in his apartment. They had met at the espresso machine that had replaced the popcorn machine in one of those movie theaters that had shown French and Italian films all through the decade. He'd taken one look at her and seen how smart she was. He had seen that she could rescue him from, on one hand, the drama majors with their hair styled by Paddy Chayevsky and, on the other hand, the cheerleaders who intended to be models, with their brains styled by Classic Comics. His plans and Claire's plans dovetailed. She was headed to Berkeley for her Ph.D., he to La-La Land to look for a job.

He liked Ted. You could talk to Ted about ordinary stuff, real life, cars and football and fishing. (But not about how a woman says one thing to mean another, and not about how this could make a man feel both stupid and flattered.)

It would have been embarrassing to watch Ted watching Claire hitting on the surgeon if they hadn't all known one another for so long by now that they hadn't any secrets. There was nothing secret about Claire's affairs.

Nothing. Her blue eyes were as bright as high beams. (A law should be passed obliging her to dim them within five hundred feet of an oncoming male.) Boyd could tell that the poor bastard, the poor Syrian or Lebanese or Greek or Turkish bastard, thought she was wonderful.

And she was. She was, she was.

Boyd was not without sympathy for his wife's need to be unfaithful to him. He sighed when she sent out sexual signals that were about as subtle as traffic signs, but he knew that people have to define themselves and that this was part of her way of defining herself. Or maybe, he thought, this was part of his way of defining himself.

He fetched himself another drink, tonic-and-tonic with a twist of lemon. The noise in the cavernous ballroom was getting to him. Voices, ice clinking against glass, the piano player in the background. . . . Someone was speaking to him, a woman. Her words floated toward him on the sound waves like a little fleet of ships. Maybe one of them was his ship, coming in.

"What do *you* do, Dr.—"

"Mr.," he said. "Buchanan. I'm here with my wife."

"Oh."

Immediately, he felt contrite. She was simply trying to include him in the conversation, and he must have sounded as if he were putting her off. "I take an aspirin a day to keep the doctor away," he said by way of apology, smiling at her. He had heard that aspirin was good for the heart. She was wearing a name tag that said she was from Michigan.

"But your wife is?"

Ted appeared at his side, put an encouraging arm around his shoulder. "Boyd's a filmmaker," he said. "Hangs with stars."

The woman's eyes subtly brightened, as if a stagehand had supplied glycerin drops. She had been ready to dismiss him as unimportant, and now she was ready to assume he was much more important than he was, really. He wished Ted had stayed out of this. It made him uncomfortable, this assumption other people had that what he did was interesting. All he was, was a money man. He put together deals. He was a goddamn wheeler-dealer.

Green-lighted projects or rerouted them to development hell, protected the bottom line.

Ted tightened his grip on Boyd's shoulder, released it. There was a message in this: So Claire's launching a new affair. You start one too.

But he didn't want an affair, though the woman was attractive in a quiet, dark-haired way. He never had affairs. That was one secret he did keep from Ted: that he had no desire to sleep with anyone except his wife.

He knew that Ted assumed that he did. This was another of the assumptions people held about movie producers, that they had affairs all the time, with Marilyn Monroe or Dietrich, women who didn't even exist anymore but they were eternal and eternally young in the American psyche. Had them in your office in positions you'd give yourself a heart attack if you tried to get into. Making movies was incidental, even wheeling and dealing were incidental, people thought or wanted to think and wasn't it odd (and annoying) how people wanted you to live out their fantasies for them.

Ted had disappeared again, no doubt thinking he should get out of the way so Boyd could make his move on the woman from Michigan, and had joined Claire and the surgeon, and now Yvonne was headed their way. They seemed so complete over there, the four of them, self-contained, like a string quartet or an island, that for a moment Boyd felt as if he'd been stranded. Or put out to sea on an ice floe, the way Eskimos launched their old people into death. He was older than Claire, Yvonne, Ted. A good deal older than the woman from Michigan. He looked down at her, her small hands wrapped around the paper napkin that made a kind of white heel on her glass, trying to think how he could extricate himself without disappointing her. At the first lull in the conversation, he said, "You have lovely eyes." The inappropriateness of the statement rendered it all the more effective. She flushed, as if he'd surprised her with a present. (It would start now, he knew, the missing checks with unitemized stubs that represented a gold tie-clip, golf clubs, an art book, a cashmere sweater.)

"Excuse me," he said, nodding in the direction of the little clump of people that were, in one way or another, connected with him. "My wife is expecting me to take her to dinner along about now." He smiled as graciously as he could and edged off sideways toward the assembly of pals . . . maybe he had gotten it all wrong and Claire was only trying to be nice to a friend of Yvonne's, it was not impossible that he'd gotten it all wrong, he'd gotten plenty of things wrong at one time or another, that much was for sure. He wished he could manage a few days soon on his own at the ranch in Santa Fe.

But as it turned out, Claire was not ready to leave the reception. He wound up in a lengthy conversation with Ted, and when he looked again for Claire, she wasn't to be seen. Nor was the surgeon.

Claire

■ THREE days after the convention, standing at the window of her office at school, casting her gaze beyond the sculpture garden, Claire Buchanan had seen one of the aging exiled Russian dissidents crossing campus. She knew he was one of the aging exiled formerly-Soviet dissidents because he wore sunglasses and a leather jacket and carried a purse. Even in December, students in Los Angeles went barefoot or wore Nikes or Portuguese-fisherman sandals; they wore jogging shorts and vintage-store T-shirts that were left over from elections they had been too young to vote in and that said things like VOTE FOR BOSCH (as an art historian, she enjoyed that one), or were apolitical and said things like VANNA FROM HEAVEN, or were neither political nor apolitical and said things like UNIVERSITY OF MOSCOW (Idaho). The dissident wore serious trousers and a turtleneck sweater and walked with his shoulders hunched, as if trudging across the tundra. Claire felt a sympathetic pull in his direction—he did not belong any more than she did in L.A., this city where smog rimmed the horizon like a sweatband, where the palm trees seemed like a reproach to anything less than excellent posture.

There was a knock on the door. Tony Ferro. She had been expecting him. She had invited him to come down from San Francisco after the convention was over.

He was as sexually hypnotic as she remembered, and she remembered that the longer Boyd had watched her with him, the more she wanted to escape with Tony to some private place. When she and Tony slipped away from the reception and teased each other into an empty hallway, it had felt to her as natural as a dance step.

He was waiting for her to acknowledge him. She said hello. This business of having to say one thing when you meant something else, this softshoe everybody did, this dance where he bowed and you curtsied but if you didn't take the right steps there was no dance. She showed him in, pointed out the prints on the wall, some of the books in the bookcases.

She turned off the computer. She had been entering data for the plate illustrations for her forthcoming book on erotic-religious Bhakti art of the medieval period but she would not say "erotic-religious" to a man, it was not a joke, her work was *not a joke* but men always tried to make it one. All those allegorical phalluses! Krishna's powerful lingam!

No joke.

It was in India that she had begun to have affairs, far enough away so that Boyd couldn't feel other men were trespassing on his property—not that she was his property!—in a country where her blond hair and fair, scented skin were as valuable as gold. In L.A. she was nothing but a blond nothing, a beautiful blond nothing where gold was the standard. In India she was more than beautiful—she was American, the Beautiful American, she was bullion, and when she returned to the States she discovered that her time over there had changed her perspective on herself and that American men, too, as long as they were not from California, thought she was more than beautiful, thought she was *something*, artists from Taos, engineers from Tennessee, heart surgeons from

Chicago would do anything for her. And still would. But she would not allow any man to misunderstand her work.

He was looking at the illustrations in one of the books, his face deliberately expressionless. She could tell he was shocked, that he was working hard to keep expression away: there was blood in his face, a flood of it beneath the skin, his tenebrous complexion. So much anatomy, he must be thinking, so out of context. He was a man who liked to be in control and he was also, she would stake her fucking diamond earrings on it, a man who was dying to be out of control. He put the book back on the shelf.

"I want to show you my house," she said to Tony Ferro.

"Your house? What about—?"

"He's at our place in Santa Fe."

She would take him home, see if they made each other happy. One thing life had taught her was not to take too lightly the pursuit of happiness. It was a serious business, much more serious than most people realized—not so much the happiness part as the pursuit part because what else was there but the darkness closing in on you like windowless walls. The gods knew this, or at least the Indian gods knew it.

"I checked into a hotel," Tony said.

"Check out."

There had, of course, been a reason she was drawn to the East. Claire felt there was a truth about the East, an honesty, a refusal of sentimentality, that was lacking in the West. The East knew that forces of generation and dissolution were impersonal, and inescapable.

Tony

■ CLAIRE let him know that he would have to leave before Boyd got back on Christmas Eve, but for the nonce Tony leaned his head back onto the rim of the hot tub, feeling the sun reach down through eucalyptus and pine trees to caress his face like fingers (how he had first known he was going to become a surgeon: he was good with his hands, could fix anything even as a boy). The sky was so blue it was like water as if he were standing in sky and looking up at an expanse of water. Through lids almost closed, he glanced over at Claire. Her breasts white as water lilies, fragrant too. He liked coming between a woman's breasts, liked going to sleep with his head on a woman's breasts.

He would not say that to her, of course; she would be offended. She would think he was crude or shallow. The ends of her hair had gotten wet and clung to her sides of her face like seaweed, tendrils of something flowing and algal, golden as Botticelli's beauty on the half-shell. She smoothed her hair behind her ears, laughing. Drops of water had snagged on her eyelashes.

The water was so hot that at first he had thought he was going to faint and then felt at home, as if he'd just discovered his proper element, not the bone-splitting cold of Marshfield, not the disorderly, rioting winds of Chicago, it was the tropics warm and moist and heavy, must be the Colombian blood in him if not the Italian.

For the first nine years of his life, he had assumed that the light-skinned woman with the lilting voice that had seemed to him like the voice of an angel was his mother. Desirée told him stories about Jamaica, an island where everything was always dazzling bright and clean because the sea made it so, an island like a piece of plaid cloth she told him, blue and yellow and green, washed by the sea and hung out to dry in the sweet salt air. After he knew she wasn't his real mother, he sometimes imagined that Francie was; he had an all-black brother, Francie's son, and if Norbert was his brother why wasn't Francie his mother? But when he was thirteen, Francie took him to bed, possibly at his father's direction, and from then on he believed the story about how Desirée had been unable to have a child and his father, collecting on an unspecified debt, had impregnated the daughter of a business acquaintance, and the child had been given to Desirée to raise. Which she did, in a distant sort of way, moving elegantly through the big house in Harlem, with, somehow, a subdued swirl to her step, nothing too showy or theatrical but letting you know, anyway, that here was a star, here was where stage center was, humming "Begin the Beguine" as she peeled potatoes at the wooden table in the kitchen.

He remembered sitting on the tall stool by the counter, trying to make alphabet letters out of the peels. On warm windy days, the curtains at the window above the sink stirred. Desirée said God had a big spoon and sometimes liked to stir up a pudding kind of day, a warm, swirly day, not quite eggbeater weather. He wanted to know whether God was making rice pudding or bread pudding or chocolate pudding. Desirée laughed. When she laughed, her face seemed to glow from inside, as if a lamp had been turned on just below her skin. "Your light came on," he would say to her, not knowing how to say it any better than that.

His real mother—he had thought she was a maid or babysitter but she was his real mother—would visit him on weekends. Sometimes she took him home to her apartment to spend the weekend with his half-brother and half-sister and grandmother though at first he hadn't known they were who they were, his relatives.

His real mother seemed so grateful every time she saw him. She was a small, timid creature, self-effacing, easily pleased. Too easily pleased, like Ava, it made him feel guilty, he would have preferred it if she, his mother—but perhaps Ava too—had occasionally complained or scolded him, had let him know that more was expected of him.

His father had fled Colombia as a child, entering the U.S. illegally near Miami. After a few years, he obtained papers—he'd never spelled out how—and wound up working for the water utility. Some more years, and he was a contractor; whatever, Tony now wondered, that had meant. Exactly for whom had his father worked?

He never asked. His father wasn't the kind of man who tolerated questions, and even if he had been, Tony loved him too much to ask questions that, he somehow knew, he seemed to have been born knowing, would upset him. Tony had never wanted to see his father upset, about anything. When they went downtown—that would be midtown to the white people—the sales clerks thought Desirée and Tony were white, Desirée in her teasing, elegant hats, her head held high, her profile queenly, but when they saw his father their attitude changed. It had filled Tony with anger that he did not know how to express because he did not want to upset his father, so he pretended it wasn't there. Look: no anger. He had wanted the world to treasure his father the way he did. And he made up his mind that when he grew up, everyone would like and respect him the way he wanted them to like and respect his father (small too, almost as small as Desirée, bald, his skin tight over his cheekbones so that looking at him you had a sense of skull as scaffolding, his fingernails wide and spatulate and startlingly pale as if the tips of his fingers had been left unfinished, unpainted). As Tony grew up, he made a practice of doing things for people—favors for friends, assistance for colleagues, the occasional free pacemaker for a special patient. He was seldom angry, and when he was, it was always at bureaucracy or institutions, never individuals. He could be counted on, so people counted on him. Nobody ever omitted him from an invitation list. He was elected to committees. His first wife had wooed *him*—she the all-white daughter of an aristocratic family from Louisiana. And he was bedded down by all the lovely women, not least among them, a *fait accompli*, Claire, with her lively eyes, blond hair, buoyant breasts, yes she was lovely, a woman of taste and intelligence and discretion but open to life.

Claire had asked for nothing. All she wanted from him was for him to enjoy himself. He knew that would change; there would come a time when she would ask for something, because people always did, but the point was, he told himself, she made him feel that she cared about *him*, that she was not employing him to achieve any objectives or to validate herself. And the way this made him feel was thankful. He had the feeling that something he had waited for all his life was now finally happening for him, and he kept wanting to thank someone. In all likelihood, he thought—the sun warm on his face, wind soughing, languid as a sigh, in the eucalyptus and pine trees—he was falling in love.

"I want you to come to Chicago," he said. "I want to spend time with you." He was startled by the inkling of chagrin that showed in her eyes before she looked away.

"I can't just do that," she said. "I have obligations . . . students . . . ."

But he knew the routines of academia now; he had learned them from Ava. "What about spring break?" he asked.

Ava

■ AFTER Tony hung up and she had left a message with her shrink's answering service, Ava called Marilyn in Chicago and wept her eyes dry. "I never trusted him," Marilyn said. "You know that."

"I wanted to marry him," Ava said.

"Hush," Marilyn said. "You hurt now—let it out. But I'm telling you it's for the best."

Once Ava had no more tears, and she could hear her voice becoming calmer, she agreed to call Marilyn whenever she felt the need, and hung up, and called her girlfriend in Los Angeles. "Listen," Phaedra said, "whatever you do, don't write or telephone him."

"But I want him back!"

"If he's going to come back, he'll do it on his own. Tony is not a passive man. Besides, you may find you don't *want* him back. He sounds a bit immature."

"Maybe he is," Ava said. "Sometimes I think he's still a kid trying to climb out of the ghetto."

"So what he thinks is that the ladder you climb out on is a white woman?"

"It's more complicated than that." She decided to tell Phaedra: "His birth mother was Italian. His grandfather offered his daughter's child up as payment to a man who'd done him a favor. The man's wife, Tony's adoptive mother, was West Indian but looked white. She couldn't get pregnant. Tony always thought of the young black woman, his father's mistress, who did the real raising of him, as his third mother."

"No wonder the guy's confused. *I'm* confused. What kind of favor did his father do for his grandfather? It must have been some favor."

"I don't know. Tony doesn't know. He used to hear his grandmother talk about the Mafia now and again."

"Ava," Phaedra said, "I don't quite know how to put this, but has it occurred to you that Tony may be crazier than you are? Not that I think of you as crazy, but that's how you always refer to yourself."

Ava looked out her window. There was a park with a zoo across the street, and at night peacocks broadcast shrieks as long and loud as banner headlines. She liked to joke that it was hard to tell them apart from the students, who partied in their frat houses all weekend. She had been on the telephone ever since morning and now it was night. "I realize it seems like a bizarre upbringing," she said. "But I always thought Tony was the sanest man I ever met. Who else do I know who gets up at the crack of dawn to go make rounds? Here's an example, just an example. His son didn't do so hot last semester and Tony spent a whole week—in between fourteen-hour operating days and meetings of the Medical Board that go on almost as long—seeing deans, engaging in various high- and low-level encounters, and talking with the boy about what he really wanted to do. He got him back into school, too."

"That's an example of what? He was just doing what any parent ought to do. A man can meet the minimum daily requirements for parenthood and still be a shit."

"Someone suggested I should write to him, to keep a door open."

Marilyn had at least sort of suggested this; at least, she hadn't suggested *not* writing to him.

"He knows how to get in touch with you if he wants to. Besides, you can't reason with someone in the throes of an infatuation. Let him get over it. As I say, you may not want him then."

"You know what I want?" Ava said. "What I want right now?" It had come to her just now like something that had been there all along waiting for her to recognize it; she could see now that this was what she *had* to want, it was the only thing that would make sense of what had happened. "I want a movie producer."

Phaedra laughed. "Caspar and I know one or two," she said. "We can do something about that."

"Yes," Ava said, confirming her idea as it began to make itself clear to her. "Why shouldn't I have a movie producer of my own?"

"Why not?"

"Tony said *wife of a movie producer* as if her being the wife of a movie producer was as important to him as her being who she is, whoever that is."

"That should tell you something."

"It does," Ava said, doing a double take. "It tells me—"

Wait, she thought, *was* that what it told her? Was she hearing her own mind correctly? Could she be thinking what she thought she was thinking?

Sometimes the workings of her own mind shocked her. She wondered if she had ever really been crazy or had just been in a state of shock, unable to make what she thought jibe with what she thought she was supposed to think.

"It tells you what?"

"I just realized something else," she said. "I don't want just any movie producer. I want that movie producer."

"Oh, no, Ava. No, you don't."

"Oh, but I do!"

"Maybe you are a little crazy, just the tiniest bit."

"What's crazy? Would I be behaving any crazier than Tony? I don't think so."

"You can't be serious. Can you?"

Ava said nothing.

Phaedra sighed, and Ava felt it like a wave of the hand, an absolution. "Can you find out his name?"

"Marilyn can. You know, my girlfriend in Chicago."

Ava now heard in Phaedra's voice that tone that meant she was organizing, prioritizing, planning. It was how Phaedra could put on makeup in five minutes in the morning and it would still be perfect after a day of board meetings and fundraisers. "Call me back when you get it," Phaedra said. "Plan to come for a visit. Don't worry about Caspar; he's spending most of his time in Santa Monica, getting ready to go to trial. We'll have the apartment to ourselves. Even if you don't get anywhere with the producer, it'll be good for you to have a vacation. In fact, we'll have such a good time maybe you'll forget about the producer. Maybe you'll forget about *men*. You're a feminist, Ava. You're supposed to know that you don't *need* a man."

"Feminists are people too."

"I said *need*. I'm not against love, or sex, for that matter. But you neither love nor are hot for this movie producer you've never met and whose name you don't even know."

Ava's heart went on high alert. She didn't believe love could exist without need. That was group-therapy talk, not reality.

After they hung up, Ava stayed on the couch, gazing at the picture window though the only thing she could see was her own image hung like a painting against the black night. She was making a mental list of the mysteries Tony's affair with the married woman explained: his sudden concern about his receding hairline, for heaven's sake, not to mention his brilliant new stroke in bed, a sweet but prolonged upward movement, confident and unfrantic. It explained the sense she had had for two months now, even before his telephoned confession, though she'd tried to deny it to herself, that he had broken the connection with her, the invisible thread that tied them together across a room full of partygoers, and explained why when friends remarked on what she was wearing, how she looked, he stepped back as if disowning her. She guessed he'd have felt guilty if he had acknowledged those compliments since he had already transferred his allegiance to the movie producer's wife. His lovemaking that last month had been comparison shopping.

Tony had made her the legatee of all the unexpressed anger he felt toward his wife, while the married woman in California got to be the beneficiary of the guilt he felt toward *her*. He had to be in love with the woman he left her for, didn't he—it was the only way he could justify his behavior. And what was safer than falling in love with a married woman? Now he would redefine his relationship with her, Ava, making her the friend for whom he felt *affection* but not *love*, and he would start to believe in this redefinition but that redefinition wasn't accurate. He had loved her—even if he hadn't dared admit it to himself because his divorce hadn't been final yet and he wasn't sure he wanted to remarry right away—but she was sure that in spite of what he said, he *had* loved her, calling her in great excitement the day he "managed to go five minutes at a time without thinking about you!" She wondered if everything would have ended this way if she had not miscarried. Even if it had, she wished she had not miscarried. She would have had the child on her own. She would still have something of his, then. And then she realized very precisely what she did want.

And why not? She was owed. A woman stole your boyfriend, the man who would have been the father of your child, and she owed you something, she owed you big-time. No one ever got anything for free in this world: if there was one thing Ava knew, it was that. Tony's grandfather had known that! He had paid with a grandchild!

So there were precedents. There were precedents for everything in the world.

Was she crazy? In her life, she had never done anything for which she would have been called crazy if she did not live in a culture that confused sadness with craziness. She had been sad, that's all, and she was not going to live her life in the darkened halls of sadness, afraid to answer the door.

Boyd

■ BOYD threw himself into the leather armchair by the fireplace. He eased off his boots and socks and rubbed his feet. He was tired; he would have a hot shower before scrounging something to eat.

Through a long stretch of glass that functioned as both window and wall, he could see the sun taking a nosedive into the west. The sunsets in Santa Fe were spectacular; they were one of the reasons he loved this place. Not that L.A. was any slouch when it came to sunsets, either, but the smog in L.A. got to him; it was like you were seeing everything through a dirty window.

This was where he liked to unwind from business. He had just finished putting together a package deal for TV, all the creative elements had been lined up, even the piece-of-shit screenplay was in place. Claire didn't much like it here—too quiet. Spooky, she said. But he loved the feeling he had that there were ghosts in the hills, that the spirits of Spanish Franciscan friars inhabited the elusive shadows between the small adobe buildings of the town. He loved the morning mist, the cooled-down horses grazing in the fields.

He'd talked with Claire by telephone that morning. He suspected the surgeon was at the house, something in Claire's voice, a faintly manic note that crept in when a new affair was taking off. Why did he put up with this? Because he loved her, that was why.

All the same, it was understood between them—or somehow understood, unspoken but understood—that Claire's affairs would be brief. They would be floaty, not anchored in the life she shared with him.

The more he replayed the phone call in his mind, the more convinced he became that the surgeon had been in their house.

He went upstairs to take his shower. The bedroom was gray: light gray walls, dark gray carpet. A dark green comforter on the bed, one shocking-pink Art Deco armchair. A gigantic skylight opening onto the desert stars.

Loved her and would do anything for her, would let her do anything. If only they had been able to have children. Everything would have been different—not better, necessarily, but different. And better, he admitted. Children give you a reason, a focus, are like tables in the hall where you can rest the heavy package of your heart that you have been lugging around with you all day.

Before he went in to the shower, he turned down the corner of the comforter wanting the sheets beneath, cool and ironed, to be waiting for him when he got out. For a moment, he stood there, next to the bed, looking around, looking up. He cocked his head, as if listening for something. The room was completely silent.

Ava

■ THEY say that people who have decided to commit suicide often suddenly perk up, that the decision frees them to relax. Ava thought something like that might have happened to her. Now that she knew what she was going to do, she was infused with purpose and energy, something rather like self-confidence and zest. Close enough, anyway, that she felt she could call Marilyn now and this time not fall apart.

"Why is it," Marilyn mused, long-distance from Chicago, when Ava told her what it was she wanted Marilyn to find out for her, "that we're all college professors?" *All* being Marilyn and Ava and the married woman Tony was involved with.

"Female college professors are the equivalent of editorial assistants in publishing houses," Ava replied. "How many women professors do you know who earn what the male professors earn? The male professors get the sinecures but someone has to hold office hours for the students."

"Don't you think breaking up with Tony has made you just a little bit cynical? I wish you'd forget him. I warned you he was the world's biggest flirt. He tried to flirt with *me*."

"He can't help it, Marilyn. He thinks he wants to sleep with women when really what he wants is to be liked."

"You should ask yourself why you're in love with someone this ignorant of his own motives."

"He's cute."

"Please, don't shortchange yourself, even with a joke like that. Him, too. If you love him, he's more than *cute*. But IMHO, a man who makes a woman cry is not worth crying over." Marilyn had never had a *humble* opinion in her life. But she was soft-voiced, so that Ava was always surprised to see how adamant she could be about her convictions. Where Phaedra was efficient, Marilyn was tough.

Marilyn was like French bread, both substantial and sweet, with smooth brown skin spread over her high-energy body like all-American peanut butter. Her mother, she had once told Ava, had sometimes called her "Jiffy" when she was little.

"I do love him," Ava said. "*And* he's cute."

"And now you want me to find out who he's involved with."

"Who her husband is. They could have different last names."

"Probably not, if they've been married that long. All right, I'll give Yvonne a call. Or I could just wait until the information finds its way to me? It's bound to, if she's in art history." Marilyn was in art history.

"Be careful not to give her any clues that you're doing this for me. She would tell Tony."

Here I am, Ava thought, actually asking Marilyn to poke around and track down this guy. I am actually doing this. That must mean I am actually going to do what I think I'm going to do. *Was* she going to do it—a drastic, even a dire thing but oh, oh god, oh, she was so tired of being kicked in the face, that was how she felt, she was going to take responsibility for her life, change her world, make lemonade. She was not a goddamn victim. She had been one in the past but she was not going to be one now. "I can't wait that long. My biological clock is ticking away."

"Ava, you'd better face facts. Tony is not going to marry you and father a child for you."

Marilyn didn't know about the miscarriage.

"You already sound so much better," Marilyn said. "Time heals better than any doctor. Just give yourself a little more time—"

"Do you think he'll ever come back?" Ava asked, ashamed for asking and afraid to hear the answer but unable to stop herself. Her friend would have to think of something to say that would give her hope without encouraging her to waste her time, something that would soothe her ego without insulting Tony so deeply that if things did change she would hold against her friend whatever she said now. Ava could kick herself for putting her friend on the spot like this, she should be ashamed of herself, oh she was, she was.

"I think the man is naive about relationships," Marilyn said, coming through for her. "I told you from the beginning he's unstable. But I don't think you can ever know what the future is going to be. Things change. Just don't count on them to change the way you want them to. Even the way you want them to change may change."

"You're right," Ava said. "I know you're right. But everything you say about the nature of change doesn't change the feeling I have, which is that at any moment my sternum is going to explode like there's a car bomb in back of it instead of a heart."

"You remember that report a few years ago that said a woman over whatever age it was has a better chance of getting killed by a terrorist than of getting married?"

"I remember."

"They're the same thing. Men are terrorists, in war and in love. They really do believe all's fair."

"Now who's being cynical?"

"I *did* say you should forget him. Why don't you take a vacation over spring break? Go somewhere *really* warm and nice."

"But that's exactly what I'm going to do. But first, you've got to get me this guy's name."

Boyd

■ SOMETHING had changed between Boyd and Claire. It wasn't just the whispered phone calls that ended when he walked into a room, the E-mail she was working on and sent to her outbox so he wouldn't look over her shoulder and see it. That was old stuff, not new. What was new was that it was the middle of March and this had been going on since before Christmas.

He tried not to get in her way. When it seemed as though she might construe simple breathing as interference, he said he had to put in some time on his current project and thought he'd concentrate better at the ranch. In fact, he made terrific progress at the ranch—a month's work accomplished in less than a week. He rested his pen on the legal tablet on which he had jotted his notes and figures, and then he carried the cordless out to the patio. This early in the morning, the air was as fresh as if God had just called for light. He dialed his home number, carrying the cordless out to the patio. Claire would be up, affair or no affair, moving back and forth between the bedroom and the bathroom in the house in L.A., one pair of anchors or another trading witticisms on the television set while she got herself and her briefcase ready for school. That beat-up old briefcase—he'd thought often of buying her a new one but he never did because the truth was he thought it was wonderful that it was beat-up, not one of those lizard-skin status symbols executive women whisked through LAX with but an honest-to-god briefcase of the kind college teachers were supposed to stuff books and papers in.

Sometimes Boyd thought that what really amazed him was not Claire herself so much as the love he felt for her and for everything about her. He did not know why twenty-five years of marriage resulted in boredom for some people and for others, like himself, intensified almost beyond his ability to bear it, a feeling that in the beginning had been *merely* love.

But when Claire answered the phone, Boyd was obliged to acknowledge miles of highway in her voice, an emotional distance that was like the old Route 66. He had had his suspicions (from which he tried to hide). Then the temporary certainties, like pinpricks, that the surgeon was hanging on longer than the others. Now he knew it in his heart, which was icing over and becoming treacherous. "Hon," he said, "I'm coming back the day after tomorrow. Just wanted to let you know in case you had anything planned." *Or anybody in the bedroom.*

"Oh," she said.

He felt as if he'd already gotten home and climbed into the bed with her, with his cock sticking straight out, and she had said, No, thank you, I'd really prefer a dildo.

"We've got a cattle call out on the cable deal," he said, feeling the ridiculous need to justify his return to his own home. "So I'll be needed at the studio."

"Do you have to fool with that? Those things are such nuisances. They always seem to drain you."

He noticed his palms were sweaty. They were making wet spots on the phone. He wiped his hands, each in turn, down the fronts of his pant legs. "I don't have to, but I'll feel more responsible if I do."

"In that case," Claire said, "you won't mind if I go out of town myself for a few days. There's some research I'd like to do."

"Oh?" Shit, his heart was pounding, it could have been running the four-forty. A man of his age shouldn't have to feel like this, it was a strain. One of these days he would die of this. "Where to?"

"Chicago," she said.

He *could* have been an actor: he kept his voice even, devoid of telltale inflection. "What's in Chicago?" he asked. *Besides the surgeon.*

The grass that came up to the patio was so green. It was so carefully cultivated. The sky was so blue. His chair, he thought, with despair rising in him like a kind of tide, was so wrought-iron.

He wondered why he was fixating on the surgeon. Claire had dalliances; a new admirer restored her sense of herself, made her feel as young and desirable as a starlet, a model, the trophy wives who browsed Brentano's in their Manolo Blahniks before meeting for pasta primavera. Did he think there was something different about the surgeon? Did he think there was something different about Claire? No, Boyd thought, there's something different about me. I'm older, I'm tireder, I'm—he shut his eyes as if that would help him to hear his wife better over the phone and he realized he was beginning to be afraid.

"Two things," she said, as smoothly as if she were delivering a lecture to one of her classes. "It's not all that far from Taliesin, and you know I've been interested in Frank Lloyd Wright since graduate school. And Yvonne."

Not of anything in particular, just everything in general.

"It was so good to see her in San Francisco," Claire was saying, "it made us realize we'd like to catch up on things with each other in a way we never do when she and Ted are out here for conventions. This is a good time for me because it's spring break."

Boyd looked around wildly, past the pool, out toward the hills, the pale blue and pink watercolor wash of sky, as if somewhere out there in all that scenery there could be a clue for him, some hint about how he should behave. The sun had come up over the hills, fast and round and so bright he felt blinded. "Sure, hon," he said. "Why don't you do that? Take a few days and go to Chicago."

Ava

■ "I told you art history is a small world," Marilyn said. "They are Claire and Boyd Buchanan. I met her once at a College Art Association convention. I forget who introduced us. She did her graduate work here. Long before I got here, of course. And just her master's. She went to Berkeley for her Ph.D., which was a smart move on her part considering the quality of the graduate training we offer." Marilyn was not shy about expressing her dissatisfaction with her department. "That's probably why whoever it was introduced us. The fact that she had been here."

"Oh god. This means she understands his life out here and what he's looking for. And he'll find it in her and never come back to me."

"That's making some pretty large leaps."

"Don't tell me what she looks like. I already know. All art historians are wonderfully groomed, like you. Her sweaters will never develop pills. She'll carry a great handbag and it'll be real leather. If she's beautiful, I'll feel plain. If she's not beautiful, I'll know I just wasn't good enough."

"Good enough for what? For a man who's going through a midlife crisis? I wish you'd find someone to go out with down there in the Old South."

"Mmmm," Ava said. "Beale Street has the most beautiful men in the world. A civic attraction, but the mayor doesn't know it. Sometimes I ride the bus just for fun. I like to look at all the good-looking black men. I catch myself staring at them, trying to see *him* in them. As an art historian, you ought to observe for yourself how their upper eyelids leak into the skin over the bone that defines the outer edge of the socket, right above the cheekbone. It's so classy. It's so heartbreakingly pure. But they always turn away after a while. They probably think I'm strange." She felt Tony had imprinted her brain with a model she would spend her life trying to find a copy of.

"When is spring break down there? Soon, I hope."

"I'm going to L.A. to visit Phaedra." Ava watched the telephone cord curl and uncurl as she stretched it out and then let it go again. The wasp had crinkled to a translucency like that of cellophane. "And while I'm out there, I'm going to look up Mr. Boyd Buchanan."

"Ava, promise me you won't do anything crazy."

She couldn't promise that. Besides, she knew that even if she didn't think something was crazy, you could never be sure that other people wouldn't think it was. People had ideas, but what she had was a plan and she would be implacable about fulfilling it. Ideas led to labels; but a plan could lead to life, to a new way of seeing and a new world to see.

"I'm supposed to do something crazy," Ava said. "It's my stock in trade, remember?"

Claire

■ IN the station wagon—left over from his days as a family man, no doubt—on the way to his place from O'Hare, there was a moment when things felt so right that Claire could imagine what it would be like to have reached the final incarnation, when the requirements of karma have been satisfied and no further error remains to be corrected. The unending changing that is the hallmark of apparent reality would have given way to perfection and stasis, an eternity in which truth must necessarily be self-reflective, God's face looking forever on God's face—but would it be as beautiful as this face beside her, as dark and grave? She was sure what he wanted most of all at this point in his life was to let go, just let go for a while, but this was not something he had as yet learned how to do. She would have to help him.

"Yvonne wants us to come to dinner tomorrow night," he said.

"I told my husband that's where I'd be staying."

"I guess he's besieged by starlets," Tony said.

"I assume he does what he wants," she said. "Let's just enjoy our time together."

Her suitcase was in the back of the station wagon. Probably he had had to drive his son around to friends' houses, drive his wife home, groceries in back with his tennis gear. "You like to play tennis," she had said, pleased to learn anything about him.

"The trouble is," he said lightly, "because of my work I'm always late for my tennis dates, and there's never any time to warm up my jock strap, which is always ice-cold from being in the back of the station wagon."

Snow was piled along the sides of the street—gray snow, as if it were ill, or had aged. It made the entire city look a smudged black-and-white, like old newspapers.

And the buildings—thick-trunked, stocky as if they needed to keep from being knocked down by the wind. At least until they had driven far enough out to find themselves among houses.

She thought of the colors that Tony, surrounded by this monochromatic, eye-numbing snow, did not have a chance to see. Had he never seen, for example, the colors of the chakras, the seven sources of human energy? Even this midwestern noncommittal gray: had he never seen the veil-like smoke color of the chakra of the heart, despite all his close observations of that organ? It was as if there was a darkness in *him*, obsidian and rich, waiting to make itself visible, a part of his emotional spectrum desperate to be realized, released, *seen*. A heart of darkness that needed to be found out, brought into the light, and, viewed, would reveal itself as marvelously vital, nothing to be afraid of. Maybe that was what was different about him: not anything he could give her but what she could give him. *Visibility*.

And again she touched him, this time on his face, his face that seemed to carry night around inside it, his face like dusk.

Tony

■ WITH Claire's gloved hand in his own gloved hand, Tony drove to his co-op (he did not yet quite think of it as home). He could not understand why he felt so guilty. He and Ava had held hands like this when they first met, which was not so long ago, a year, a little over a year ago. But he had told her about Claire, his divorce from Ry would be final this month—he had no obligations to anyone except himself and there was no point feeling guilty about Boyd Buchanan, Claire was an adult and could make her own choices.

Ava could call this messing around with a married woman but Tony called it learning to live for yourself—-and not, for once, for the dozens of people who surrounded him, daily asking him to do something for them, support them, take care of them, save their lives (Ava had been chief among them).

He had to let go of Claire's hand to wipe the inside of the windshield, which was fogging up with condensation. The defroster no longer worked efficiently. It occurred to him that Claire was probably not accustomed to being driven around in dilapidated station wagons with deteriorating defrosters, and he felt a bit embarrassed that this was all he had to offer her. Maybe he should buy a new car. As he cleared a circle on the windshield, he looked up at the sky. They were on Lakeshore Drive, the colossal structures to their left an anthem to American commerce. There was a pink glow over the Drive, caused by street and building lights reflecting on the ice-covered lake, a kind of aura. It was very beautiful, the pink glow and the frozen lake and the snow blowing like white smoke across the street. He really should take more time to look at the world around him, he thought, and as he thought this, he looked at Claire, who was now the world around him, and it seemed to him that she was his New World, a paradise, a place of ease and joy and belonging. The pink glow fell on her, too, her profile, sculpted in the light from the dashboard, gently blushing. But was that the glow of the lake shore, or had he made a mistake referring to his jock strap?

Boyd

■ HE was in his office skimming the trades when the receptionist announced that a friend of his wife's, one Ava Martel, was waiting in the anteroom. Since it was a personal and not a professional call, he told Sally to send the friend in even though she had made no appointment.

She stood in the doorway, with Sally's office behind her like the view into the distance in an Old Master painting, a prospect of ebony furniture and indirect lighting and filing cabinets, and she made him think of art and truth and beauty, of high ideals and the nobility of the human heart, because her silhouette was so pure and sweetly defined, so glowing, like a cool unself-conscious heat, that he instantly recalled his own youthful allegiances and—he could not deny it—his deepest continuing beliefs, underground but ongoing, in the values both of artistic representation and communication among creative minds through history.

He pulled his glance away, glad that Ava Martel could not know how extravagant his response to her had been, feeling foolish that he could overreact like this. When he looked at her again he noticed her long slim legs, the narrow waist, the square-set narrow shoulders, tantalizingly naked—could shoulders be thought of as naked? but hers seemed so, edged cunningly, as they were, by a sleeveless open-necked white shirt . . . . Cunning because so candid . . . .

He rose from his chair.

"It's good of you to see me without an appointment," she said, thrusting out her hand as she entered. He shook it.

"Have a seat."

She was good-looking, with short wavy dark brown hair, thick eyebrows, a kind of feminine precision in all her features and movements, precision in her profile. The kind of easy elegance that comes either through privilege or suffering, though now that he thought about it, he supposed that suffering might just as easily result in sloppiness. Maybe the more a person suffered, the more he backed away from the myriad little decisions each day demanded, the tasks of drawing distinctions and setting standards, knowing how futile it was to fulfill them. Was he thinking of himself, he wondered.

"Sally said you're a friend of my wife's."

"Claire."

"Where do you know each other from?" he asked, hoping to get a handle on why she had looked him up. He began to move things around on his desk: nameplate, scratch pad, pen. He looked at her again, this time in the eye.

"We don't."

She was sitting up very straight, and she had said that without moving a single facial muscle. *Remarkable.*

"I'm afraid I don't understand," he said, carefully.

The minute hand of the clock on the wall behind her moved soundlessly to the next stopping point. He always liked a clock on the wall facing his desk; it let him control the length of appointments without unsettling visitors.

He was suddenly convinced that there was a trap laid for him somewhere in this conversation. "If you are not a friend of my wife's, why did you say you were? And how do you know her name?"

"I didn't say I knew her. Your receptionist assumed I did because I said that I live in Chicago, as your wife Claire once did. I teach at Midland. Actually, I'm in Memphis until June, though my home base is Chicago. At any rate, I mentioned to your receptionist that your wife used to live in Chicago."

"And how do you happen to know anything at all about my wife?"

"Because she's having an affair with the man I had hoped to marry."

He stepped around to the front of his desk. It was true that her eyes were clear and rational, true that her eyebrows were a Declaration of Independence. It was true that she looked like the Enlightenment, but maybe she was only a French Revolution, a Bastille gone crazy with demands. "Let me guess. Would this man be a surgeon?"

"Yes."

"Then, Ms. Martel, you are not telling me anything I don't already know. Moreover," he said, "I suspect you've been misled by your own feelings into thinking that I would have welcomed this information, had it been new, which it is not, because I would want to act on it. I have no intention of acting on it. My wife is entitled to live her life as she sees fit. Does that surprise you—that I would say that?" He heard his question in stereo: directed toward his visitor, and inside his head. *Did it surprise him that he would say that?* But there had never been anything else he could say, Claire had left him no options—not short of leaving her, anyway, and if that was an option, what was a marriage?

And what was a marriage if someone could walk into your office and within moments you were admitting, at least to yourself, that you were afraid of losing your wife, that you were jealous of a man you knew almost nothing about, you were on the verge of naming grievances, worries, insecurities—none of which were the business of the mysterious visitor who had walked into your office.

For what? What was it she had come for? She wanted something. People wanted things, didn't they. Didn't he.

He kept staring at her, thinking that sooner or later she'd give herself away. He was beginning to admire her self-possession, her Mona Lisa sense of centrality, although a woman who thought she had the right to reveal a wife's secret, or what she thought was a secret, to the wife's husband, was probably a hysteric.

He had told her she was not bringing him any information he didn't already have, but to hear—to have it confirmed—what was wrong with him, anyhow? A sharp pain was working its way up through his chest. It was like being filleted. He took a deep breath and the pain eased.

"Mr. Buchanan—"

"Boyd," he said (almost cavalierly, he noted to himself with satisfaction). "If you're going to call my wife, whom you do not know at all, Claire, you might as well call me Boyd."

"Boyd, I do not give a fuck what your wife does with Tony—"

The pain again, stabbing him. He would have preferred not to know that name.

"—or what you do about it. That's not why I'm here."

"Then I must admit to being confused. Why, if I may ask, are you here?" It seemed to him that his jacket was tight across the shoulders, he should have it let out.

"Tony met your wife, Claire, at a medical convention in San Francisco just before Thanksgiving."

"I know. I was there," Boyd said, dryly.

"Then you know that I wasn't. I was in Chicago. This was before Memphis."

"What does all this geography have to do with anything?"

"At almost exactly the same time Tony was getting involved with your wife, maybe even on the same day, I was having a miscarriage."

Boyd was trying very hard to figure out what he was supposed to say next. Who announced something like that? Bare shoulders—forget bare shoulders. He felt as uncomfortable as if she had shed all her clothes and was waiting for him to give her a gynecological exam. There was nothing sexy about it. No, there was. He lived among people who disguised themselves with personas. Everyone in Hollywood had a persona. For a woman to reveal herself so completely, without prologue or hesitation—it was seductive, after all. As was her mouth, source of all these startling words, kissable lips a natural pink, no added paint, stain, or gloss; none needed. But the lips trembled, turned downward, then pushed outward as she blew a small breath in his direction to get hold of herself, but that puff of air seemed also like a gift she was offering him, a personal, even intimate transfer of biological energy.

He didn't want a hysterical female on his hands, but he still didn't get the connection she was trying to draw. Why *was* she here?

"When Tony got back from San Francisco, I told him about the miscarriage. He called it a *spontaneous abortion*, by the way. That's the medical term. He didn't, of course, tell me about your wife. I didn't find out about her until February. He waited until I was in Memphis—so he wouldn't have to tell me in person, I guess—and told me that he was in love with your wife."

"In love."

"Oh yes," Ava said. "She's taught him that real love is intuitive. She's put him in touch with his feelings. It's been a profound experience for him. He's learning so much about himself."

The jacket was definitely too tight, so tight he couldn't breathe. No lobbing back of a breath-ball for him! No anything from him! "I don't want to listen to this. I think you should go."

For a moment, nothing happened, and he thought she was getting ready to leave. And although she had not yet left, he already missed her. He knew he would never again in his life be so surprised. Never again would he be able to look on her fineness, her—elegance was not the right word because it suggested sophistication, and perhaps the delicatest overlay of cynicism as must accompany self-knowledge. Claire was elegant. The woman he had just lost—had actually told to leave—was fresh, Edenic—not innocent but unconcerned with appearance and presentation. Already the day seemed longer, threatening to drag out into a lifetime of loneliness.

"I don't like that kind of talk either," she volunteered then. "I think of it as California hot-tub talk. But I thought you'd be used to it, living out here."

"One thing I'm not used to is having women barge into my office on false pretenses in order to detail my wife's peccadilloes."

"I wanted that baby," she continued. "Do you realize it's even possible that my worry over Tony's not writing or calling when he was in San Francisco may have contributed to the miscarriage? Maybe I was being *intuitive* too. Now I may never have a baby, because the likeliest father is busy discovering himself with your wife."

"I'm sorry. Nobody ever said life was fair."

"Exactly. Which is why we have to do what we can to obtain justice where we can."

"What do you mean by that?"

"I mean I want to have your baby, Mr. Buchanan. You owe me one."

■

He returned to his side of the desk, removed his jacket and hung it over the back of his chair. Then he detoured to the window. Despite the trimmed woods he could look out toward—planted trees kept free of underbrush—the road that ran behind the building swarmed with traffic of one kind and another: messengers on bicycles, security cops in a car, parking cops in a car, cars traveling to or from the parking lot, one of those little white vehicles that looked more like a robot than a truck (he didn't know what the guy in it did), and a garbage truck that resembled Godzilla. The intense sunlight, falling so equably everywhere, exposed the lack of significance of every object in this scene. The people were carbon, and the people's lives, experienced with such warm emotion, mere arrangements of energy, temporary and ramshackle.

Then he remembered another window, long ago, how it had been open to a spring day and how he had stood there looking out at a yellow warbler in a chinaberry tree. He remembered that the small bird, as pretty as an ornament, flew from branch to branch, and that the leaves shook and shimmied as if doing a fan dance.

Two men climbed down from the garbage truck and fed it the contents of several large trash containers. He could view the scene but he couldn't hear it, because the building had been designed to muffle noise.

He could hear only the clamor in his own head. He couldn't even hear himself think. What *did* he think, he asked himself, of what this woman had just said to him?

He turned around to face her again, walked back to his desk, sat down.

"How about a walk-on?" Boyd Buchanan said, when he'd finally absorbed what she had said. "That's what most of the crazy ladies out here want—a chance to be in the movies. Would you settle for a walk-on?"

"A baby," she said.

The clock was still marking time. No doubt the garbage collectors had moved to the next building. In his mind, the warbler became a baby—a baby in a chinaberry tree, cradled by boughs. Boughs break, babies tumble and fall.

He could buy a little more time to think by doing dialogue shtick. "I owe you what?" he could ask, and she would say, "A baby" and he would say, "I owe you a baby" and she could say, "Of course" and they could mix it to a rap beat, but he was not into shtick.

"You can't be serious," he said, wondering why he didn't buzz Sally and ask her to call security.

"I wouldn't be here if I weren't."

He guessed he knew why he didn't buzz Sally and ask her to call security. It wasn't every day that a woman walked into your office and said she wanted to have your baby.

"And what," he asked, "would you do with this baby?" Hang it in a tree. Let the wind blow.

"Raise it."

"By yourself?"

"Of course."

"You don't think a child needs two parents?"

"Many children manage with fewer."

He'd had his aunt and uncle.

"Babies become kids," he said. "Kids are a handful. Kids become teenagers, many of whom are monsters. Teenagers become adults. A lot of adults you wouldn't want to have to spend any more time with than necessary." It was the speech he had sometimes given to himself, telling himself that he and Claire were perhaps fortunate not to have had children.

"That's not your problem," she said.

"My problem is you. Why?"

She shrugged. "Luck of the draw, I guess. Claire might have slept with someone else. Tony might have taken me to the convention. He didn't."

"Would you like some coffee? I can buzz Sally."

She shook her head no. Now that she had said why she was here, her face had softened. You let go of a secret and it let go of you, that was one of life's truths though not widely known by people in the business. Her shoulders had relaxed, she looked younger and even sweeter.

"You can't have a baby just because you want one," he said.

She blinked. She blinked a whole series of rapid-fire blinks, to make her point. "I can't? Why else does anyone have a baby, except by accident? Do you mean I can only have an *unwanted* baby?"

"You know what I mean," he muttered, feeling like a dope.

"You mean I'm not married."

He rolled his pen between his palms and nodded.

"That's why I'm here," she said, slowly, as if explaining that it would not be a good idea to play in the middle of the highway, it would not be a good idea to eat your chemistry set, it would not be a good idea to practice swinging your baseball bat in the living room. "If I were married, I wouldn't have had to come here."

"Maybe, maybe not."

She looked at him sharply. "You and Claire don't have children?"

He said nothing.

"Then," she said, "maybe you need me as much as I need you."

"Oh"—he dropped the pen; it rolled briefly and stopped—"no, I don't think so." But this was a tactic, he knew, and not one of life's truths.

"That's a tactic," she said. "You're saying that as a way of preserving your high ground, but I don't believe you."

"Believe what you want."

She crossed her legs. The red skirt seemed to brighten, as if it were a fire flaring up. He didn't want her to believe what she wanted—he wanted her to believe in him, that he was wise, powerful, gracious, compassionate, and uncompromising. Could one be both compassionate and uncompromising?

"I could take off my clothes," she said. "That might persuade you.

I know by West Coast standards I'm a little on the flat-chested side, but then again, what I do have is all natural. No silicone, no saline. Plus I have great legs." It was as if she were playing a scene he had previewed—and now he felt guilty as hell, as if she had said those lines only because he had wanted her to.

"Jesus. You really are beyond the pale, aren't you," he said.

"It's never been put quite that way before."

"What if I call your bluff and say yes, I want you to strip?"

"Do you?"

"God, no. Please, no."

"I was kind of sure you wouldn't call me on it." She lowered her eyes and plucked at her skirt, and he was astonished by how quickly she looked demure as a nun. "It just seemed like something that would be in a movie."

"And were you joking about the baby, too?"

"What do you think?"

"I think you must be a couple of croutons short of a salad."

"I would never joke about having a baby."

"What made you think I wouldn't call your bluff?"

"You seem nice."

Claire had once told him that when a woman tells a man that he seems nice what she means is *You aren't what I expected*. "What did you expect?" he asked.

"I don't know. Slicker. Smarmy. Brutal."

"Brutal?"

"I don't mean physically brutal."

He was quiet, thinking what in her life might have brought her to that word, that phrase.

He set the pen down and flicked it, and it spun briefly.

"You really like to manhandle that pen, don't you?"

He looked at the stopped pen lying on its side on the desk.

"Someday I'm going to buy myself a nice pen," she said. "As it is, I mostly use ballpoints with red ink. To mark up papers— We have to pay the department for them. Can you believe that?"

Claire used a fountain pen. And carried her papers in that wonderful old beat-up briefcase. . . . "Look," he said, "I don't know how to break this news to you, but I don't cheat on my wife. It's just me. I don't like the idea."

"That seems generous of you," she said, "considering."

"I don't use sex as a way to even the score with anyone, for Christ's sake. Neither does my wife."

"Are you sure that's not what she's doing?"

"Aren't you an educator? A liberated woman? Don't you believe in equal rights and opportunities for women? Don't you think a woman should be able to make her own choices?"

"Midland U. would knock those ideas right out of you." She didn't know he'd been a student there; she didn't know everything about him. "You can't teach at Midland U. and go on believing women will ever be treated equally. Not by the administration, anyway."

"Really," he said, amused in spite of himself, "you and Claire have a lot in common. You should hear her on that subject."

"Now we'll have even more in common."

"You're crazy, aren't you," Boyd Buchanan said. "Really crazy."

"It depends on what you mean by that. If you mean *out of touch with reality*, the answer is no, I'm not crazy. Inventive, that's all."

He laughed.

Ava

■ "IT'S just me," Buchanan said. "I don't like the idea."

But he was entertaining it or he would have had her thrown out by now.

It wasn't easy, sitting here in this sterile box of glass and ebony with, she could tell from the way his glance kept veering toward it, a clock on the wall behind her, pretending to be cool, commanding, leading this man to a conclusion by the force of her certainty that it was the right one. She was not an actress. She could put on a little show for her students, entertain and educate them, but they were students. Most of them came to class actually wanting to believe in her.

Did he even begin to guess how scared she was? She knew he could have her thrown out at any moment. She had seen the white car slowly, confidently, patrolling the grounds. Suppose he decided to complain to the president of Midland U.?

But that was a silly thought. But—she felt like a college kid herself, in this room. Maybe because she was on the wrong side of the desk. Maybe because he was older, distinguished-looking. Even the way he was dressed let you know he was a man who controlled other men's lives: there was nothing corduroy, flannel, tweed, or khaki about him. He was not an academic, infantilized by years of trying to please the departmental father figures and achieve tenure, promotion, a grant, ultimately a sinecure. His sense of self had not been eroded by committees; by chairmen who had passed over him for nominations, handing them to cronies or team players instead; by never having the right to decide on anything unilaterally or the responsibility for the consequences of his decision.

She had expected—she was a snob!—schlock, something phony and corrupt, the suffocating, sickly odor of too much luxury, too little concern for the welfare of others. Boyd Buchanan surprised her with layers.

Ava was never afraid to admit she had been wrong. She was not a grudge-holder. She did not feel she was the center of the world or had to be. She loved her friends, her field, her ardent advisees, the bike path that ran through Lincoln Park, and Tony.

Lost to her forever now.

Her breath seemed to snag on the thought, caught there and unable to go in or out. She thought she would die in Hollywood, someone named Sally in the front office. Her hands were clammy, and she tried to wipe them inconspicuously on the sides of her skirt, wanting him not to see how nervous she was.

She even loved herself for having come so far, out of the dark and tangled woods of her psyche to a life of action, in which she was not afraid to offer to others the love she felt, but she had not escaped her own desperation and she *was* afraid the man on the other side of the desk could see it, would know that the only thing that could bring her to him was time running out, catching up, passing her by. And did she altogether love her books, her students? Didn't she want something more from life than books and students?

"I want to have your baby," she had told him, then waited while he paced to the window and back, took off his jacket, sat down again. And when he had snapped back, "You can't have a baby just because you want one," she had countered by saying that she thought he needed her as much as she needed him.

She could hardly believe the things she was saying but that had never stopped her from saying anything before so why now, why not steer straight ahead. It was rather a bonus that he was attractive, a suit type but without a tie, jacket off, hazel eyes, clean-shaven, his hair going silver. She had to admit he'd taken her aback when he said he didn't cheat, she thought everyone in California cheated rode a surfboard belonged to a sect.

Boyd

■ HE laughed. He knew he probably shouldn't—wasn't laughter a kind of complicity? even a surrender?—but he couldn't help himself. And there was something weirdly flattering in all this too, not discounting the deflating fact—could she have made it clearer?—that she was interested in him only because he was married to Claire. But what else was there about him to interest anyone? He was, after all, a realist. If your business was fantasy, you'd better be.

Ava

■ PHAEDRA had driven to the beach house in Santa Monica to spend a few days with her husband, Caspar, leaving Ava to sun herself by the pool at the condominium on Wilshire. It was a large, rectangular pool, and the water was cool although it looked hot in the Los Angeles sun. Ava lay on a chaise longue, applying sunblock to her legs. She untied the halter strap around her neck, letting the loose ends trail down her sides. Her sunglasses were two crossed tennis rackets, the handle of the white racket ascending above her left eye, the handle of the black racket rising above her right. She pulled the rubber raft over to the ledge and climbed onto it, paddling with her hands to propel herself out to the center of the pool. There she floated in a haze of serotonin, the sound of rushing traffic as distant and soothing as surf or tranquilizers.

Tony

■ AT the last minute Ted had flown off somewhere as he frequently did—smart bastard, he must have known what this dinner would be like. Across the table Marilyn and Gordon were side by side. Marilyn was facing him. Gordon, from Ava's department—that was how she knew Marilyn—was facing Claire. Tony contemplated Marilyn, her cornrowed hair ornamented with flashing sequins. She looked like some compactly chic creature, but from another planet. He hadn't meant anything by it, by his long look at her—staring, he'd been staring—but she glared back at him as if he had just violated the First Amendment, infringing on her freedom. The freedom to despise your girlfriend's ex-lover. The freedom especially if you were black to despise your white girlfriend's black but white-looking ex-lover. He wasn't really sure whether she knew he was black. But probably Ava had told her. There was no telling what women talked about when they got together. Or for that matter, what art historians talked about, when *they* got together. It turned out that Marilyn already knew Claire, which he supposed was not surprising but it sure as hell made things uncomfortable.

Someone should write a book called *How To Do What You Have Done Many Times Before But With Someone Else Like Eating And Holding Hands And Yes Of Course That Too Without Feeling Like a Self-Conscious Shit.*

Tony had gone to people's houses for dinner with Ava two dozen times in the past year. He remembered the time they attended a Passover seder at Steve Rubacher's house in New York. Steve had handed out haggadahs with passages underlined for each dinner guest to read in turn.

Reading out loud always made Tony nervous. He had skipped a grade in school, and it had turned out to be the grade in which you got good at reading aloud. When his turn to read came, he sought Ava's hand under the table and held onto it as he stumbled through the paragraph. *Let my people go,* he read. He hadn't known that that was in the Jewish service.

It was not that he didn't want people to know, nobody who knew him could accuse him of that. Hadn't he loved his father? But tell him, would somebody please tell him, what were you supposed to do when you didn't look like what you were, was he supposed to go around grabbing people by the collar pushing his face into theirs, saying Look! I'm black! I just happen to look white! That would be pretty goddamn stupid, wouldn't it, would make everyone uncomfortable, so he wasn't trying to pass he never had never would nobody did that anymore but neither could he be responsible for advising everyone he met of his racial heritage. His own son was more white than black, for that matter.

During the seder, Ava had talked with Steve on her right while Steve's mother, on Tony's left, whispered into his ear, trying to convince him not to rush into another marriage as soon as his divorce was final (he and Ry had chosen to wait until their son graduated from high school). "Take your time, play it safe," Mrs. Rubacher had whispered in his ear, conspiratorial as the CIA. "You don't have to hook up with the first woman who comes along."

For an instant, he considered telling everyone here what Steve's mother had said. Some people think safe marriage is as important as safe sex, he'd say.

During dessert, Tony felt Claire's hand wandering into his lap under the table. He held it and squeezed it, and then he returned it to her lap. This wasn't the Golden State. This was the Midwest. There were proprieties. But one thing that had never ceased to awe him was how bodily all bodies were, how they had shape and size and density, how they occupied space, and also how they were whatever color they were and how they sometimes resisted direction, had a will of their own.

Claire

■ WHY had Yvonne invited Marilyn Henegar to this dinner? Did Yvonne really not understand what was happening? Or did Yvonne honestly think that Claire would never be thrown off balance, would always be in control? Or was this some way, unconscious perhaps, of expressing her anger toward Ted, since Yvonne must know that Ted was having an affair, was always having an affair, was in fact an expert in the art of the far-flung affair, and it was possible that despite their long friendship she was angry with Claire for doing exactly what her husband was doing. As this thought occurred to her, Claire felt it as a judgment, a condemnation, and felt anger warm her face like wine, felt herself rushing to her own defense and she raised her chin—she tossed her highlighted hair back from her forehead—she smiled and she smiled and she gazed brightly across the table.

Across the table, Marilyn Henegar's boyfriend, Gordon Somebody, had a gift for mimicry and had been doing Politicians of the Past. "Read my lips," he said; "I do. I move them all the time, especially when I'm reading."

By comparison, Tony's repartee fell flat. Tony's tone was too cutting, was somehow surgical, and his low laugh seemed timed to an audience's heartbeat, was stethoscopic, unspontaneous. Claire was discovering that Tony memorized jokes, mentally cataloguing them for various occasions. That he wished never to be without a joke when he needed one, like a life preserver or a flashlight or a dental dam or pessary, for crying out loud, made her feel protective toward him.

But dinner was long, and Claire found it harder and harder to keep her smile in place. Every time Marilyn Henegar turned her head, the light from the overhead fixture bounced off the mirrory sequins in her cornrows. Glasses were drunk from and left to litter the table, napkins crumpled like candy wrappers in a park.

"It's too bad Ted couldn't be here," she said to Yvonne, watching her face to find out what she did or didn't know.

"If I waited for Ted to stick around before I gave a dinner party," Yvonne said, presenting a platter of cheese and fruit, pouring cups of gourmet decaf, "I'd never get to see my friends." Yvonne had developed crinkles around her eyes that deepened when she smiled. Watching a woman age, Claire thought, was like watching a portrait being revised line by line.

"The thing about modern relationships," Marilyn said, "is that you have to make reservations or else there's no room."

"Careers take more time than children," Yvonne said. "Is this the way it should be? You have to nurture your career, look after it, give it a good talking-to now and then! Our mothers should have warned us what would come of losing our professional virginity. Home Ec should have prepared us. What to do with a colicky career, that's what we needed to know and what we've had to learn the hard way. He's going to Siberia next winter." Ted was a geophysicist.

"When I get out of here in the winter," Gordon said, "I always try to go someplace that is not Siberia."

"*Make* reservations, or *have* them?" Tony asked Marilyn.

"I guess it depends on where it is you think you're going."

Boyd

■ IT was a crazy idea, but it had its entertainment value. He let himself be entertained by it, then he began to entertain it. The more he thought about it, the less convinced he was that it was such a crazy idea. Sure, the woman who had thought it up might be crazy but that didn't mean the idea itself was crazy or couldn't hold water or was entirely without merit. He kept seeing miniature images of himself—babies with close-cropped gray hair, hazel eyes, lined faces, and tooled boots. Babies that kept themselves in shape at the Athletic Club. Wheeler-dealer babies.

Claire had had some early infection, PID they called it these days, he remembered she had told him that not so long ago, and it had left her Fallopian tubes scarred. Maybe if they were trying now, they could fix her up—they could do so many things these days, these doctors, these—oh, shit—surgeons. But it was just a little too late for that.

Once upon a time he had tried to talk Claire into adopting. She would have none of it. If it wasn't her child, she wasn't going to raise it. There was her career. He had been disappointed, but he had understood that none of these stated reasons was what her decision was based on—her decision had been based on her hurt feelings and she had a right to those feelings. If it had been hard for him how much harder it must have been for her, a woman.

The thing about a child, or anyway one thing about a child, was that it was one thing that would last through the end credits.

Not much in his life would.

Not that he'd done badly. In this town, you could be up one day and flushed down the toilet the next, but he was still on top. In this town, everything was temporary, but he still had the same wife and intended to keep her. Some of the movies he'd put together hadn't been total crap. He knew good product when he saw it.

He could do something very Cassavetes, he thought, mocking himself, a film called *Fathers*. Shots with the fathers in the park, their kids riding piggyback. Shots with the fathers attempting 2 A.M. feedings, testing the temperature of the formula against their hairy wrists. Shots of the fathers when their wives wanted to make love: Sorry, dear, I'm exhausted. *Cinéma vérité*.

He supposed it was middle age, this awareness of mortality, of one's personal shelf life. Time's winged chariot had more horsepower even than his beloved Jags and was more capacious than anybody's stretch limo, making room for everyone he knew. Even Claire had taken to staring at herself in the mirror. She would stand in front of the mirror, pulling her skin up behind her temples, letting it fall again. She was always so quiet when she did this. It was almost eerie because he had the feeling she had completely forgotten about him, her focus on her own face was so intense. What if this surgeon decided to give her a face lift, or anyway get one of his friends to do one since the guy was a heart surgeon, not a plastic surgeon (he knew they traded favors like that). And most of the time she wasn't even tugging on her skin like that. She was just staring in the mirror, only her eyes moving, like reading a book *he didn't want her to change her face he remembered what she'd looked like when he'd first met her, bright and blond and a little hyper with eyes of a blue that Chuck Yeager could only dream of and oh indeed with great great titties and a mouth that was always in action smiling or talking or kissing if they'd had a kid back then, it'd be in college by now.*

Ava, now. Ava. You take a woman like her, she's too old for fantasy, she's old enough to know what's what in the world, her mind is furnished with a lot of interesting stuff, you could learn something from her, hell, he wouldn't even mind learning about feminism, the theory and history of feminism, he believed in feminism, it was an important subject, but she looked as if she had only just graduated from college herself. She looked so *new*. He could imagine her newness, her modernity. He could imagine that her lingerie was the new, minimalist, frill-less kind you saw in magazine ads these days, sheer cotton, briefs cut high on the sides, backless camisoles. He could imagine that her thighs were soft and strong, her breasts high, her nipples as pink as her lips. Her skin would be as smooth as . . . Jesus, he didn't know. As smooth as the satin ribbon on a gift.

Claire

■ "DARLING," Claire said when she and Tony were back at his house and in bed, her head sunk in the crook of his arm so that she was speaking into his naked side, his side that was so vulnerable, a carcass, like meat; she could feel her blocked breath blown back into her own mouth, hot and peppery, "the most crucial thing in the world is self-actualization. I realize that I may sound irresponsible or callous, saying this, but I'm neither irresponsible nor callous. You don't think I'm callous, do you? No, of course not. Because I'm not. But I do believe that if you let your life pull you—I don't mean just you, I mean us, everyone—in different directions at once, fragment us, the jagged edges of our personalities will work their way into the people around us, impinging on *their* integrity, causing wounds. And humanness oozes out of these wounds like blood, like lifeblood. We owe it to everyone who is a part of our lives to be the fullest integrated expression of ourselves that we can be. It is the only way we can avoid hurting other people. I would hate to be like Marilyn Henegar, convinced that we all have to be in competition for something. For what?"

"I don't think that was the problem," Tony said. "It's just that she's a friend of someone I used to see."

"But that's the same thing," Claire argued. "People assume that, because the material world is finite, we are emotionally and spiritually finite as well. But we're not. Darling Tony, we are infinite, infinite, infinite," she whispered, heady with the scent of his dark skin, the meaty, unvegetarian scent of him.

Tony

■ HE felt her breath on his skin like a sedative, something that would carry him into a healing sleep, a dream of life. Something curative or at least consoling.

Boyd

■ ON the other hand, he had encountered his share of crazies, he knew crazies. They came at you from all sides and one day the West Coast would sink under their combined weight. Over the years he had witnessed, among his own good friends, more crack-ups than the San Andreas fault could dream of.

He knew crazies and he knew crazy and he did not truly think this woman was it. Willful, plainly. A bitch, no doubt—no, he did doubt that. He wasn't convinced she was a bitch. People did things when they were hurting, he knew that. He knew that! Stubborn. Stubborn she had to be—refusing to surrender to reality, reality being that her surgeon boyfriend and Claire had left her out in the cold (but if he couldn't understand that who the hell could) and yet, or because of that, there was a graceful, unimposing definition in her demeanor and she knew, he was sure she knew, what she was doing.

Ava

■ IT was like lying on Tony's waterbed, this floating in the pool, on the rubber raft, with the sun on her sunglassed face. It made her think of what it had been like to make love with him. A cock like a scalpel she used to tell him, a corny thing to say really but if you couldn't be corny in bed where could you be. It was, in fact, amazing to her that he had been so good in bed, because he was so secretive about everything else having to do with his body. The shower would be running and then she'd hear the john flush and realize that for the past five minutes he'd been taking a dump and had the water going so she wouldn't hear him. In a year of going with him, she had never heard him fart. At first she had thought this was splendid self-control, and then she had decided that what it was, was a good little boy from the ghetto determined to have the best manners in the world.

It was interesting, wasn't it, she asked herself ruefully, how he could be so circumspect about his own habits and yet expect her to give her body over to him without reservation. He had assumed he was welcome in every one of her orifices. She had liked going down on him, but she had not liked swallowing his semen: There was always so much of it, milky and thick and sour and salty and too much to swallow all at once, a flood. It dribbled from the sides of her mouth like drool and she felt both sick and ugly and had to hide both feelings from him, and of course having to hide her emotions had made her feel distant from him just when he was—at least she had thought he was—feeling close to her. She had always hoped he'd change trains at the last minute and come inside her but he never did—if they started that way, they finished that way.

There was that time in New York, after the Passover seder, when she'd let his semen run out of the side of her mouth and make a huge puddle on the sheet. She remembered lying with her head turned sideways, staring at the glistening damp beside her as if it were something of scientific note, a spilled specimen maybe. She felt as if she had failed him terribly, she had dropped the test tube, she remembered feeling as if she had done something he might fire her for. He didn't say anything, but he got up and got a towel from the bathroom to put over the puddle, which was on her side of the hotel bed. (How did the cleanup crew stand it, the biology of their work, the endless evidence of bodies that could mean nothing to them beyond numbers of sheets changed, towels folded over racks, rolls of toilet paper to be replenished? She would goddamn kill herself.) She remembered thinking that maybe they could just ignore everything. If you ignored something, it usually got bored in the end and went away. Maybe you could even ignore hate she could feel him hating her, putting the towel over the puddle and hating her, and eventually it would just turn on its heels and head out of your life, leaving you still in love, as much in love as you were in the beginning. "Tell me something," she had begged, speaking into the dark.

After a long pause he answered, "When you say things like that to me, I feel like you're trying to get me to make a commitment."

"It doesn't have to be that," she said. "Just anything." She wanted him to acknowledge her existence, that really was all she was asking, unless she was fooling herself, and, of course, psychiatrists always said you were fooling yourself.

"I don't know what to say," he said, resistant as aluminum siding. Sometimes talking with a man was like playing handball! You bounced the ball off the face of the wall and it came right back at you! "At times like these," he went on, "my mind goes off in about six different directions at once."

And she gave in. "It's all right," she said, now feeling guilty that she had put so much pressure on him. "You don't have to say anything."

"That's good," he said. And then he fell asleep—same thing as if he'd gotten back up and walked out of the room.

She had stayed awake *always so hard for her to sleep that fear of what might happen when she closed her eyes* feeling bad about gagging on his gism *he saw it as a rejection* and about being too small for him to enter by the back door *but didn't all those magazines tell you that was dangerous now* and about not understanding what he was trying to do when he had had her sit on him facing him and then instead of letting her slide down he pulled her up and she'd felt so stupid sitting on his face, how could anyone think that was sexy except it was sexy to Tony and probably to everyone else. She wouldn't be surprised if no one ever slept with her again she was so sexually untalented, in fact if she were a man she'd probably refuse to sleep with herself and what was Boyd Buchanan like in bed?

Boyd

■ NO, no, he could not be so foolish, so irresponsible. He could not, having managed so carefully for so long, crash and burn his life on L.A.'s free ways, ways of narcissism and greed. You didn't father a kid for the vanity of it. And certainly not by a crazy woman out for revenge.

But he could imagine, too, that it could be a greater crime to refuse life where life was possible. He could provide. He had something to offer a child—love, which Claire would have shared if she had been able, parental love. Was it crazy, was he crazy, to want to hold a child in his arms even this late in his life, was this emptiness he felt something that was supposed to belong only to a woman, was he an anomaly—an aging anomaly, at that?

In his arms. Experimentally, he cradled air. He crossed his arms over his chest as if to pat an invisible baby on its back. He was pathetic, wasn't he. A man old enough to be a grandfather and he was imagining himself doing what mothers do—crooning lullabies (a little Ella Fitzgerald thrown in); putting his ear to the baby's chest while it slept, to make sure the watch of its heart was keeping time; carrying the baby in a sling under his chin (he'd have to make sure he was smooth-shaven). If he had a baby he would never sleep again, he would stay awake twenty-four hours a day to make sure it was doing okay, and he would not dare to breathe on it but all the same he would find a way to kiss it just fucking nonstop.

Claire

■ TONY took her on a tour of the hospital. He was like a resort director, showing her the tennis courts, the cocktail cabaña. There should be a round chocolate in gold foil on every waiting pillow like money, complimentary champagne in a bucket by the bedside, shampoo and body lotion in small, pretty bottles. If you didn't like the way your vacation was going, you ought to be able to bail out and buy a ticket to Hawaii.

In one room, a researcher was performing microsurgery on a female rat. Claire stared at the soft pink fruitlike flesh, the hips splayed and the delicate pelvis exposed. Strong white lights lent an aura of unreality to the scene, making the colors too bright to be believable. The rat's small forepaws rested one on top of the other; her whiskers were stiff as a hairbrush. Her little rat tail lay undefended between her spread hind legs. The male researcher was sitting at the table, operating under a magnifying lens by remote control. When Claire peered through the microscope, she was startled to see the fine sewing, like needlepoint stitching. All of a sudden, the rat twitched. Claire asked if she didn't need more anesthesia. "She's fine," the researcher said, "a real trouper. This is her third operation in two days."

"Will she die?" Claire asked, meaning: are you going to kill her?

"Some of the rats have long and happy retirements," Tony said. She could tell that he recognized her discomfort but he didn't know it was more than that. She would not tell him, not tell him what it had been like to want a child and find out you couldn't have one, it had been her fault not Boyd's though sometimes she thought she blamed Boyd for not being at fault if that made any sense and of course it didn't, it was plain insane.

"Without ovaries," Claire said. "A long and happy retirement without ovaries."

"If it makes you feel better, we certainly don't have to worry about the rat population dying out because of sterility," the researcher offered.

Claire kept seeing herself on the table. She must have been exposed exactly like that. Maybe there'd been a green drape or two, but her pelvis had been open like that, tubes and ovaries in plain view of the doctors and nurses *so one woman couldn't reproduce, nobody had to worry about the human population dying out because of sterility someday she too could have a long and happy retirement without ovaries.*

She wanted a refund. A trip to Hawaii.

Ava

■ ANOTHER reason for staying awake at night was that if you didn't keep an eye on it the third dimension could go missing, it could just disappear, leaving everything around you flat as flatware. This made it hard to walk, if you decided to get up. You had to hold onto things. And then the third dimension might suddenly decide to come back and pop up in front of you and cause you to stumble. For this reason, it was sometimes necessary to curl up on the floor, since you could not fall off a floor. But then very likely someone would come into the room and tell you to get up, and even if you wanted to, it would be hard to answer because everyone would be talking to you from a great height, as if they were all superior. It was difficult to know how to answer such superior beings. There you were, the lowest thing on earth, the proof of that being that you were lying on the floor, and how could you explain any of this to people who towered over you like skyscrapers, a city of faraway, high-up people?

Boyd

■ MEETINGS, all day nothing but meetings, meetings. If you asked him, God had never said *Let there be light*. No, He'd said Take a meeting. And on the seventh day, God had lunch at the Polo Lounge.

As Boyd walked through the door he knew heads were turning. Even heads that didn't want to turn did, unable to resist the pull of invisible strings, the torque of power. If he wanted, he could get the turning heads to say words they had no intention of saying. This was what you could do with power, this was what power was. You could get people to sit in your lap, ventriloquized, and they would be compelled to do whatever you told them to do.

The lives of at least some of the diners, it was not too much to say, he held in his hands—or they thought he did, which came to the same thing. Maybe he was having a midlife crisis, but it was driving him crazy, this hierarchy of influence built on nothing more than people's basic perception that they themselves did not count. It was driving him crazy, knowing that he was still one of the ones they figured counted and for no other reason than that he acted as if he did. It was their faith in you that prompted other people to put up hard cash, to sign on the dotted line. That was what you were selling: yourself.

As he'd said before, everyone in this business was an actor. So it was only hardheaded business sense and not vanity that urged him to say to himself as he strolled through the restaurant that he was doing all right, he looked good, he was moving. A mantra for our times, he thought. My very own feel-good tape.

When he'd first come out here, they'd tried to get him to *be* an actor. "You look a little like Newman," they said.

"Newman will not be flattered," he said.

Eric Harrold, young upcoming star of stage and screen (but Boyd didn't think he would last, he couldn't keep his powder dry, kept inhaling it), extended a hand across the butter plates.

It was impossible to be natural with actors. They were always trying to tap into their emotions, but they never asked themselves why it was they had to work so hard to do something that other people had to work hard not to do.

The waiter brought their salads, and Harrold excused himself. *Yes, using*. While he was gone, Boyd had a telephone brought to his table. He had not known he was going to do this, but as soon as he dialed the number Ava Martel had left on his memo pad, it seemed to him that it had been inevitable that he would do it. She had said she was staying with friends, and he expected one of them to answer, but it was Martel herself on the other end of the line.

"It's Boyd Buchanan," he said. "I'd like to discuss further the subject you brought up in my office the other day."

"Sure," she said. "Go ahead."

"Not *now*," he said. "Jesus, I don't mean now."

"When, then? I'm not going to be out here all that long, you know. I have to get back at the end of spring break."

"Wait just a minute, Martel. You're supposed to be the one who's hot about this idea. Now you're telling me to operate on your schedule."

Her laughter was a rippling sound like water rushing into his ear. "I wish you'd avoid the word *operate*. That's what Tony does. That's not what I do."

"You may think this is all some kind of kick or lark or whatever, but what you were talking about in my office is serious. You don't appreciate that, scratch the deal right now. It's okay with me if you're crazy, the world is full of crazies, but irresponsible is something I don't go for."

Eric had returned to the table and was crunching croutons between his unnervingly white teeth.

"Does that mean you're willing to do it?" she asked.

"It means I'm willing to discuss it."

"Why don't you come here? This afternoon?"

"What about your friends? I mean, I wasn't exactly planning to put this on teletype in Times Square."

"They're out of town till Tuesday."

"Give me the address, then."

She recited it while he took it down in the little address book he carried in his inside breast pocket. He wrote it on one of the back pages, leaving off her name. Then he signaled for the waiter to take the phone away. Boyd refused to carry a cell phone. In his opinion, cell phones were detrimental to manners and suits.

"A friend?" Eric asked, smiling broadly. Those teeth were like klieg lights. Boyd wondered how much they had cost.

"A deal," Boyd said, decisively. "You know about deals, don't you? Or has it been that long since you cut one?"

"Ow-ow," Eric said, shaking his hand as if it'd been burned.

Boyd motioned the waiter back to take their orders.

"Speaking of deals," Eric said, "I've got a friend who's got a property

I want you to look at. You'll love it. It's magnificent, incredible. It's so incredible it's unbelievable. Have I got your attention yet?"

"Let me tell you something about myself, Harrold," Boyd found himself saying. "I'm a simple man. I like movies. I really *like* movies. And I also like fast cars—I favor Jaguars—nice clothes, and horses. I like to get outdoors on the weekends. Anybody can call me up, I'm in the book. Every four years I go to the polls. I cry at funerals and smile at christenings."

"So what?" said Eric. "You sound to me like a man who's having an argument with himself, you know that?"

Ava

■ PHAEDRA and Caspar's living room was designer-decorated in muted greens and grays, the colors of frosted grapes, without the chill, for the grays seemed to hint at lavender. Ava plumped the pillows, moved an ashtray half an inch to the right.

She sat down to wait. From where she sat, she could see the patio and the pool. Or she could turn the thin vertical blinds against the view and instead quietly contemplate the Ming vase, the Lalique vase, the Steuben glass, the Steinway. Deciding it would help Boyd Buchanan to feel at ease, she drew the blinds. A sense of cool shelter descended on the room. Outside, the world was lit up like an apocalypse, bright as nuclear warfare, an atomic glare glancing off the billboards and the hoods of cars, four stories down. Outside, it was like the end of time, but here in this room, it was like being inside a time capsule, it was like waiting for something to happen, to come along to open you up so *you* could happen. So you could happen again.

Tony

■ WHEN Tony's phone rang in the middle of the night, he knew it was bad because he did not usually get called out of bed anymore. There were residents, interns, junior colleagues to take care of after-hours crises. He rolled over and picked up the receiver before he was fully awake.

And Claire said she was coming with him.

He tried to tell her that might not be a good idea. "If you found the rats upsetting—"

"They were rats. I'll be all right. I want to see you doing what you do." Her face in the lamplight looked feline, Egyptian, exquisitely enigmatic.

He was pulling his pants up over boxer shorts. His son razzed him about the boxer shorts *Jesus, Dad, only old men and dorks wear those things anymore* but Tony preferred them because they made him feel less conspicuous in the surgical locker room.

He reached for his beeper, which was on the floor, being recharged, and unplugged it and attached it to his belt.

There was a door from the front hall of the building to the residents' common garage. The garage door lifted complainingly, groaning at the inconvenience. Claire at his side, Tony backed the trusty station wagon out into the wintry night. It had been through a lot with him, this station wagon, had been through a significant part of his life with him not to mention how many trips to the grocery store, how many times he had had to drive his son here or there. Yes, he could afford a BMW or Jaguar or Alfa Romeo or what have you but he was not in need of a fucking status symbol, he wanted to be taken for who he was and not what he owned, or was owned by, as—wasn't it Emerson?—had said, and the wagon still got him to the hospital and the tennis court.

The March air was like ice, so brittle it could crack, it seemed it would break up into floes, it made breathing like skating on thin air, and it felt strange to be outside like this with Claire after lovemaking rather than before lovemaking. Tonight he had *already* felt her feathery trembling. He had *already* heard *her* breathing take on that magnificent selfish note, become a series of greedy little gasps until she got what she wanted and said so in a short semi-scream, not really a moan, more like a held note, followed by a sigh that was almost an afterthought.

It felt unnatural to be out here together at this time of night. Or maybe—the thought just appeared in his mind; he had the very peculiar sensation of reading his own mind—it was that what had come to seem natural was to be at home with Claire. Which meant marriage, didn't it.

Ava

■ WHEN Boyd Buchanan arrived, she offered him a drink. Phaedra had told her to feel free to use the liquor cabinet—or the bedroom.

"Nice place," Boyd said. "Do you have mineral water?"

Ava was drinking vodka gimlets. "Don't get serious about him," Phaedra had warned her. Phaedra knew she was trying to seduce him, but that was all Phaedra knew. Ava still had not told her that she intended to get pregnant by Buchanan.

He was wearing a coat and tie and slacks, but instead of shoes, he wore boots, probably he started that years ago as an affectation and by now it was just a habit.

"I think I saw mineral water in here somewhere," she said, opening the bar refrigerator and scouting around. The light inside the refrigerator made the food look waxy, made the bottles and jars look like medicine. "You don't drink?"

"No," he said. "Listen, Martel—"

"My name's Ava."

"Let's get something straight right from the jump, here. I'd want you to sign a paper saying you agree never to hit me up for support.

No child support and no palimony. I've got my own problems, I don't need Lee Marvin's." His voice softened. "We need to do this right, for everybody's sake."

She handed him a bottle of Perrier. "Do you want a glass?" she asked. He shook his head no. "You surprise me," she said. "I guess I didn't really think you'd agree."

"If you want to back out, say so. But say so right now. I don't have time to fritter away on a *fantasy*."

"Now you wait a minute," Ava said. "This is too important to be classified as wasted time. Whether we do it or not, we're going to talk it out. First of all, I want *you* to sign a paper for *me*. One saying that you're not going to appear on the doorstep of my life someday out of the stupid blue arguing that you've got a right to your kid six months of the year, or something. Is that understood?"

He laughed, a sound surely, she knew, like that of a heart breaking. "So you're feisty as well as crazy."

She held out her glass, nodding at the bar. "Fix me another drink, will you?"

"No," he said. "I don't make drinks."

She raised an eyebrow inquiringly but refilled her own glass. She thought she ought to have all the drinks she wanted now, because as soon as they started trying to get her pregnant, assuming he went along with this, she would quit drinking even wine. She would start drinking mineral water. "I'm also not certain of the psychological complications for me," she admitted. "I mean, if I carry your child for nine months, I might develop some kind of weird fondness for you. Then what?"

"I can't answer that. That's a question you'll have to answer for yourself. I have no intention of breaking up my marriage. I don't even have any intention of carrying on an affair with you. All I am willing to consider is impregnating you. If that's too heavy for you to handle, maybe you shouldn't have suggested it."

"Would you please sit down?"

He sat down on the couch. She sat down in a chair across from him. The room was dim because of the closed blinds, the dusky colors that seemed to be first one shade, then another.

She gazed into her glass as if there might be tea leaves there, but there was only a quarter-moon of lime. "Doesn't it bother you," she asked, "that your wife is sleeping with someone else?"

"Sleeping around is the norm out here, even today." He stretched out his legs. He sighed. "I don't know," he said. "Of course I mind. Don't you suppose I mind? For crying out loud, I grew up in Little Rock, Arkansas. Sure I mind."

"Little Rock," she said. "Why, that's practically Memphis."

"Yes. I remember once when my aunt and uncle and I drove over to Memphis. Memphis was the Big Time. We sat in the lounge of the Peabody Hotel and watched the ducks march in and out of the fountain." The ducks lived on the roof of the hotel but put in scheduled appearances in the lobby.

"Cybill Shepherd is from Memphis," she said, as if describing a tourist plus. "Tennessee Williams lived there for a time. You could come visit me. And it will still be the Big Time."

"I have a better idea," he responded, leaning back into the couch. "Come to Santa Fe."

Claire

■ THEY had scrubbed her in and put a gown and mask and hair net on her, and slipped long, latex gloves onto her hands. She watched from the side, against the wall. There was blood on the floor. The room was packed with people—she had never realized so many people would be milling about in an operating room.

She had been worried, in spite of her pretended savoir faire, that she would get sick, but she couldn't even see anything. It was not at all like seeing the little rat with her stomach sliced open and all her female organs bright as paint under that high-powered, pitiless light. Of course, it wouldn't be. Tony was a heart surgeon, not a gynecologist.

Tony

■ AS a kid, he'd gone through a phase when he kept bringing home stray or sick animals. Each time he brought one home, his father would tell him to get the animal out of the house. "This isn't a hospital," his father would say. "If you can't take care of a creature properly, you've got no right to interfere. Let it die a dignified death."

One day Tony had found a pigeon with an injured wing. It must have been hit by a car, because it was lying on the curb in front of Sammy's Red Beans and Rice Restaurant. He didn't interfere. That evening, at home, when his father came in from work, he told him about the pigeon. "Dad," he said, "I didn't bring it home with me. I let it die, just the way you said I should." He thought his father would praise him. Instead of praising him, his father put his hand on top of Tony's head as if he were going to pat him and then let it just rest there, an abandoned benediction, as if he'd changed his mind about patting him or had forgotten that he'd been about to pat him, and then after a moment his father had walked away, and Tony stopped feeling proud but without quite knowing why.

Tony's father was older than most of the other kids' fathers. He lived to see ninety, a small, twisted licorice-stick of a man. He spent the last twenty years of his life fretting about his will, but in the end all the money went to lawyers. Tony promised himself that he'd never worry about what was going to happen after he died; it would be his son's concern, not his.

Funny, how much he had loved his father. His father had not been an easy man to like. But he had been the center of so many lives that not to love him would have meant finding another center. And where would that have been.

They had closed but his hands still smelled of iodine. He washed them again and dried them under the hot-air blow-dryer. He had told one of the nurses to be ready to hustle Claire out of the O.R. if she got sick. He wondered what had been going through Claire's mind as she watched him work—she would be impressed but she could be repelled too. She was difficult to read. Her stylish laugh, her lively blondness, her energetic professionalism, her sexual playfulness—he felt that these were somehow disguises, whereas Ava, with all her shadowy grace, had been essentially unsubtle, a plate-glass window with all her emotions on full display. It had not been possible to give himself over to Ava: because her transparency had required of him an endlessly vigilant self-consciousness; because he couldn't escape his knowledge of how everything he said and did and felt reverberated in her psyche. With Claire, he knew nothing. With Claire, he was freed of responsibility, it was like being giddily lost in the middle of broad daylight on a street corner without signs; he couldn't be expected to know where he was headed.

"You okay?" he asked her.

"Fine," she said.

Tony remembered his first surgical procedure, when he was a med student. It had been an episiotomy. When the OB/GYN handed him the knife to make the incision, he felt he was going to faint, but he didn't.

Boyd

■ "I guess I could come to Santa Fe," she agreed. "It's a good thing I have some mileage accumulated. Probably not as much as your wife and Tony are accumulating, but some. Just think, if it weren't for Frequent Flyer tickets, we might all be leading chaste lives."

He liked her wit even though he could hear the gaps and hollows behind it, the places where a cold wind tore through, the silent, secret shrieking. The more he got to know her, in fact, the more he liked her. She didn't have Claire's polished shine, she had a shadowy side, but that only made him curious about her and he was also fascinated by the soft curve of the back of her head, her long neck with its bones that seemed to pronounce themselves when she turned away; fascinated by the thick eyebrows and high cheekbones.

When she read the contract his lawyer had drawn up and was ready to sign, he gave her his pen to use. It was a gold Mark Cross pen that had been a present from Claire. She signed her name simply, each letter legible. She folded up her copy and put it in her handbag.

On their way to his car, he said, "Now what?"

He had not intended to sound so brusque. He felt terrified and excited, and on the verge of tears, though he would not let anyone know that. To father a child—to create a human being. This would be green-lighting a production, all right. Could something so fabulous—no, so real—really happen to him at this point in his life?

"Now we go to bed. Here and now. Santa Fe later."

"I have to warn you," he said. "I can't guarantee it's going to work, under the circumstances."

"If at first you don't succeed, try, try again."

"I can't believe you said that," he said.

"Sorry," she said, refusing to meet his eyes. "The truth is, I don't know what to say."

Ava

■ BACK in Memphis, she taught her classes, standing at the front of the room and looking hard at her students, trying to discern what they looked like to their parents *were they not all of them creatures of transcendent beauty in their parents' eyes, even in surfing shorts even in Speedo costumes even with multiple earring holes tiny shiny golden hoops in a row as if their ears had been planted with a new variety of flower or on the contrary did parents necessarily view their children through prisms of criticism and self-dissatisfaction as her father had*, trying to discern what they had looked like as infants, what magic had transformed them into the shapes and sizes they were today. They had been helpless babies in christening gowns (darling larvae!). Now they were a whole different life form, with pierced body parts.

A storm blew up and a spring rain scatter-shot the old-fashioned French casement windows, dripping down the cement window ledge, and the tulip tree's leaves blew upside down like little umbrellas, and she turned the lights on, which made everyone in the room feel oddly close but restless. Lightning silhouetted the stone statue in front of the library. She dismissed class early, dashing across the green campus to her apartment.

Each day she woke expecting some change in her body, some magic of her own that would tell her she was pregnant. That she was about to become a different life form, large and waddling and eager, the embodiment of expectancy. Slipping her nightgown on as she got ready for bed, she glanced at her breasts, hoping to find they'd gotten bigger since morning—and then quickly glanced away, as if to look would be to ask for too much.

When her period started, she called Boyd's office in L.A. and left a message for him with his secretary, Sally. "No go," the message said, and she worried if even so pithy a statement could be taken as a complaint or accusation.

But she didn't want to expatiate on the situation. She might end up saying how she felt, which was scared and depressed. Men never understood that emotions were just something you *had*. A man confused emotions with motives and thought that whenever a woman had an emotion, any emotion, what she was really trying to do was get him to take responsibility for it.

He called her back to say he would meet her at the airport in Santa Fe in two weeks.

She was beginning to realize how broke she was. The reason she had taken the visiting position in the first place was that it paid a living wage, which was not what she earned at Midland U. But she didn't make enough to join the jet set.

"I'll buy the tickets."

She had not foreseen this; she didn't want to take money from him.

He misread her hesitation. "Sorry," he said. "Maybe you thought I'd have a private plane." He spoke softly, but there was an amused note in his voice. "I'm just a movie producer," he said. "I'm not Steven Spielberg."

"You shouldn't have to pay. I didn't mean to cause you this kind of trouble," she said.

"Of course you didn't. You never meant to invade anyone's life in order to accomplish your own complicated aims, which included revenge. I understand completely," he said, laughing gently. "I can afford a lot of plane tickets," he said.

"If you're sure."

"It's no hardship to make love to a pretty professor."

"I know you're partial to professors."

"Hey, no fair," he said. "I'm only trying to be helpful, remember."

She started to cry.

"Easy with the waterworks, Martel," he said. "We made a deal. This is not a relationship. And unless it's a relationship, you don't get to cry."

She stopped. "You're right, I know," she said. "I was only crying because I happened to think about the wasp. I mean, here I am on the phone, and—"

"The wasp?"

"It's gone now. A dead wasp. It kept shrinking until it just vanished. Like the incredible shrinking man in—"

"I love that movie," he said.

"There used to be a wasp on my living room floor," she explained. "Now I guess it's just shriveled up into nothingness. It's depressing."

"Well, look, what are you talking about death for, anyway? You're supposed to be thinking babies. Martel," he said, "Ava . . . cut the gloomy shit."

Claire

■ SHE was proofing galleys of an article she had been invited to contribute to a festschrift honoring one of her former teachers. The celebratory collection would include essays on the Rembrandt copies of Moghul miniatures, the Jain influence on Hindu art, sandstone sculpture of the school of Mathura, Gupta art and purism, and the mandala in pop art of the American sixties, as well as her own piece.

There were times, now, when no matter how hard she tried to concentrate on her work, she was aware of being both the self she was now and the younger self she had been. Watching a movie she'd seen before, for example, she would find herself both watching the movie and watching herself watching the movie the first time she had seen it, years earlier. Working on her essay, she was aware of herself both working on the essay and, years earlier, becoming the woman who, today, was working on the essay. That young girl with long straight hair—a West Coast girl, California dreaming, but with a secret desire for academic respectability (the only kind of respectability she had ever cared about)—who danced in the park and took classes in Asian art and religion when such studies were thought frivolous rather than, as now, an essential correction of the canon in an era of globalization—that slightly desperate young girl who regularly altered her mind on Saturday nights only to find that it had reverted to its usual intellectual pursuits on Sunday morning—that girl was now this polished, professional woman sitting next to her, next to her watching self, wearing drugstore magnifying glasses and picking her way through proofs.

And if there had been no sixties generation, no sexual revolution, no collective turning of youthful heads in the direction of the East, where might she be now? How much was karma, how much the luck of the draw, how much *sociology*? Had there really been some innate connection between her and the East, or could she be just as readily working on Dürer, say, or God help her, Warhol? . . .

Maybe, moving away from the Western world, she had only wanted to run away from home *how her parents had always worried so about money her sister safely married to a lawyer Claire why can't you be more like your sister why can't you comb your hair you have such a pretty face why do you always hide it.* (To think these voices were still in her head!)

Why all this anxious confusion, this reckless communing with her past? Tony . . .

She had made herself a cup of peppermint tea and was sitting at the oak desk in her second-floor office at home, the PowerBook at one end and a window overlooking the steep canyon road at the other. She had the window open and could smell the sea; there were jonquils and tulips in a clay jug at her elbow, and deep red fuchsia seemed to have been splashed over the lawn like drops of blood. In midsummer, sunflowers would line the driveway like traffic cones. She had occasionally thought about driving straight through the guard rail but not because it was a thought she wanted to have but only because it was a thought that seemed an essential part of any guard rail.

As she looked out over the canyon, she realized how quiet the house was. It struck her now that over the past year Boyd had begun treating

Santa Fe as his principal residence, commuting to L.A. for specific jobs. In his absence, this big house with its gleaming banisters and the artwork she had collected on her trips to India and the electronic equipment in the rec room and in the living room, her ikenoba, floral arrangements illustrating the Buddhist belief that a flower is a reflection of the human heart, each arrangement an organization of three points representing heaven, humankind, and earth, an art form she had briefly explored while in Kyoto on a teaching Fulbright, and the silk taupe pillows on the living room couch, and let her not omit from this list all the unnecessary bedrooms, seemed as lonely as an abandoned movie set.

Tony

■ HE remembered Francie entering his bed. She crawled into it by inches, an animal scouting a cave. She wasn't, of course, that much older than he was. Her face warm in the dark. He said nothing, afraid either to acknowledge or deny what was happening. For a moment, he thought that if he didn't breathe, she wouldn't move, and that what he wanted was for her to stay forever exactly where she was—here in this bed, next to him. But that was in the moment before he knew anything. When she moved, he understood everything. He understood that a woman's body was like a lock, a man the key.

He came almost immediately. She rubbed his sexual fluid on her face in little circles, like a cold cream. She brought her hands down to her breasts and continued to massage herself with his come. He found out later that she thought it would bleach her skin. He wanted to tell her to be sure not to tell his father about any of this, he still did not understand that his father had sent her to his room. He wanted to ask her why she had come into his room and done this. Was she in love with him?

Boyd

■ THOSE days in Little Rock, he and his uncle would sometimes go fishing. His aunt packed a picnic basket for them and they gathered up their fishing tackle, taking off as soon as the sun was up. They had a favorite spot, a favorite for both of them, not far up in the hills.

Under the cottonwoods near the little crook downriver of the bend, they affixed bait and dropped lines. Flashes of reflected sunlight darted through the ripples like a school of minnows. Such brightness everywhere, and moving, moving. The lines floated on top of the water. Buford, as he was still called then, and his uncle each had a tree designated for leaning back against. Buford leaned against his tree, glancing at his uncle now and then but mostly concentrating on his line.

Every so often he'd hear the tornado whoosh of a car heading down the highway back a mile, bound for Memphis. Jays called to one another in the loblolly pines and poplars thick on the opposite bank. A piece of an old pier stuck out into the river, too rotted to fish from; the water that lapped beneath it was dark and eerie. The water in the middle of the river was bright and peaceful; the way it moved, it was almost like a hypnotist's watch that would put you in a trance or daze.

As the sun rose in the sky, light unfolding like a morning glory, his uncle's hat tipped farther and farther forward; it was as if his uncle were engaged in some enormously slow enormously polite act of bowing. Finally Buford couldn't see his uncle's face, only a shadow under the hat, like a shadow below a cliff.

The sun made Buford drowsy too; he wished he'd thought to wear his baseball cap, because he could use something to shade himself with, even under the tree's lushly leaved branches. A fly buzzed in front of him; it seized the sun like a prism or a marble, and its wings shone blue and green. The sun-spangled river flickered like flies, as if a thousand lines had been cast—as if a thousand lures attracted him—lures flicking blue and green in the silver water and golden sunlight—attracting him as if he were underwater, the sides of him cool and slippery as scales, himself a bright and moving thing to be caught on a hook and eaten.

The end of his line trembled, tightened. Something had nudged or brushed it in passing, or the current had tugged at it. A momentary urgency, like dying.

That pressure of the business to be finished and then it was finished, finished for all time, and where was the pressure then, the urgency?

He wondered what his parents had felt, their car underwater, their faces ballooning at the windows like flat, moon-eyed fish in an aquarium. Had fish passed by like people, then, peering in at the odd life-forms in the car? . . . But his father and mother had not been life-forms for long, they had quickly become death-forms. He hoped it was quickly. His aunt and uncle refused to tell him anything but he had seen a newspaper article before they came to fetch him away to Little Rock LOCAL PAIR DROWN IN FORD IN FORD it said, it really said, he had felt the shame and anger of it how could anyone do that, make a joke of his parents' deaths, heat building in his bones as in radiator pipes, something hot and spitting in him, a high, thin whistle in the valves of his heart, his heart that was still always about to boil over, bring him to a dead stop.

Tony

■ EACH day he tried to guess whether Francie would come into his bed that night. Sometimes she did and sometimes she didn't. During the day, he tried not to look at her. It began to be a burden, this having someone love you like this, if this was love, and he didn't understand how something he wanted so much, something he craved, could also be something he wanted to avoid. He thought the junkies on the street must feel this way, wanting and not-wanting at the same time, mind pulling one way, the body another. He would pretend to be asleep, and she'd shake him by the shoulders, and he'd rub his eyes as if he were groggy, a child still—and he was—and mumble something, but she'd put her hands on him anyway, and his body would behave as if it had nothing to do with him only with her and it would all happen just as she wanted it to happen. As *he* wanted it to happen. And yet he didn't want it to happen. He didn't tell any of the guys at school, because he knew something was wrong, they would be jealous but they would also think his family was strange and he wanted his family to be normal.

Boyd

■ THEN the moment passed, that moment of seemingly unendurable urgency. And now the pole was easy in his hand again, the end of his line wavering gently in the water as if something live were circling it, interested, or as if it were itself a live thing or, perhaps, a thing peacefully dead and without a will of its own, subject to the river's sway.

Ava

■ THE ticket was waiting for her at the counter. She had no luggage to check, just a backpack slung over her shoulder. At Albuquerque, she caught the shuttle to Santa Fe, and when she arrived in Santa Fe, he was waiting for her at the entrance to the airport. She let him carry the backpack to the car.

She looked out the window of the leased Jaguar as they drove into the country: mesas and buttes, arroyos, to the east the Sangre de Cristo Mountains, he said, a travel guide. He added that the landscape included "much vegetation not always apparent to newcomers," piñon and ponderosa pine, sagebrush and willow trees, and sweet alyssum. Out of the corner of her eye, she watched him driving. His foot on the accelerator was booted; he perhaps thought he was rustling her back to the ranch, the old homestead.

At the house, she changed into her Nikes, jeans, and a short-sleeved sweatshirt that had a tendency to slide off one shoulder. "You ought to have boots for desert country, protection against snakebite," he said. She smiled broadly. She was always pleased when people outwitted her.

He fixed glasses of iced tea and shoved a frozen pizza into the microwave. They sat opposite each other at the long table, as if they were at a formal dinner except for the jumble of brass-pinned screenplays. "Sorry," he said, sweeping them into a pile on one side of the table. "Looking for properties, you know?" She could see that he was good-natured and unpretentious, gentle in his ways, fastidious, and—it made her sad to see this—easy to hurt. "Why are you doing this?" she asked. "I mean, what's the real reason?"

"Do I have to have a reason?"

"Your wife might not have a reason. Tony, I think, is doing his best not to have reasons, though it goes more against his grain than he knows. You— I just don't believe you ever do anything without a reason."

"I'm afraid of dying."

"Oh."

"That's not a good enough reason?"

"I was expecting something less generic. Everybody dies."

"I'm a generic kind of guy."

"Maybe," she said, doubtful.

"And you're pretty."

"That's not a reason." But she was blushing she could feel her face red and warm like a campfire *oh hell.*

"Not a reason, but a cause."

"Look at that!" she cried, jumping up and running to the window. "It's one of those birds from the cartoons."

"A roadrunner."

"Do you *really* love Claire?" she asked, careful to keep her back to him.

"I guess love alone is never enough to keep somebody living with somebody," he admitted. "There's more to it than that."

"What, then?"

"I respect her."

This was what not what she had thought he might say, though she didn't know what she had thought he might say. She walked back to the table and wiped her hands on her napkin. The napkin was an outsized square of dark red linen, the color, he had said when he handed it to her, of the chili peppers that one saw hanging drying from the adobe walls of houses. The chilis were bright red in fall and deepened as winter progressed such bright colors here it must be the light, a light that seemed to step aside when you looked at something, to remove itself from your line of vision so you could see whatever you were looking at without anything at all in the way.

"I respect you, too, Ava. I wouldn't be doing this if I didn't."

She almost laughed, it was so like the line from high school *Of course I'll respect you in the morning*, but she felt he could be easily hurt that way, by being laughed at. Emotions passed over his face as if it were a movie screen, the smallest feeling visualized and huge.

And when she left Santa Fe on Monday, in time to teach her Tuesday class, she was pregnant, she was sure of it.

Boyd

■ *CHESTNUT hair, a sweet chin, brown eyes, and thick, emphasizing eyebrows* and as she slept in his arms under the immense skylight, the immense sky, he thought how sad in a way that he hadn't met her years ago but maybe even if he had things would have turned out the same: events happened, people just went along for the ride. If he had been married to Ava Martel, she would probably be having an affair with the surgeon right now, wasn't irony wonderful, he said to himself, it could get you out of a lot of tight spots. Starlight flowed down through the skylight and into the room and down her cheeks and neck and spilled onto her sexy shoulders, touching them with sparkle. He pulled the dark green comforter up and tucked it around her. She smelled of pizza and toothpaste. To hold a woman in your arms—it was everything, really. A shame, he thought, that you couldn't get a budget for a movie about a woman like her but she was over thirty.

Claire

■ THE pollution index was up. It made everything—cars, buildings, people—seem slightly out of focus.

She parked the Cimarron on Sunset. Rochelle was waiting for her at her station in the back corner of the room, and Claire sank into the vinyl chair, letting her right hand soak in soapy water while Rochelle worked at the cuticles on her left hand, her bare feet propped on a neon-pink vinyl footstool while plump, presumably happy Yuki roped sinewy cotton in and out between her toes. Rochelle asked Claire what color polish she wanted, and she chose rose. Yuki attacked Claire's feet with a pumice stone. Rochelle scraped an emery board across Claire's nails.

One of the establishment's bosses had come into the room and was having himself done, manicure and pedicure, just as she was, his pantlegs pulled up, his feet sitting in a pan of water. A woman washing his feet as if they were Christ's. In days gone by, Morgan Fairchild had come in, and sometimes Betsy Bloomingdale, and before she'd been First Lady, Nancy Reagan used to come here. Today there was nobody Claire recognized—only other women like herself—unknown—and the boss.

Drifting in the vinyl chair, hand and foot afloat in soap-soft water, she thought of Tony miles from there, his curly dark hair covered with a hood, his face masked, his body draped in greens. Green scrub suit, green long-sleeved gown. He was her Krishna, dark erotic creative and many-armed, hands moving swiftly over the sleeping patient, touching, cutting, sewing, healing.

He had asked her to divorce Boyd and marry him.

She had been shocked. "I can't do that," she had said before she knew what she was saying.

"Why not?" he had asked.

"I love Boyd."

"I thought you loved me."

"I love you both. I love you equally."

"That's impossible," he had said.

"Anything *else* would be impossible," she had argued. "You don't love someone with reservations. At least I don't. So everyone you love, you love completely." With her eyes closed, Claire reran the conversation with Tony—for the hundredth time.

But she had been touched that he wanted to live with her, that he wanted to integrate her into his life. Boyd showed how he valued her by letting her be as free as she wished, but it was, she had to admit, exciting to have someone want to possess you the way Tony wanted to, like a country or a secret.

She had been so eager, for so many years, to detach herself from the world, to enjoy it but at the same time know that she was enjoying it, always aware of who was who, what was what. She wondered: Did Tony imagine how deep her distrust of life went, below the surface of her enjoyment of it? Did he begin now to fathom the depth of her cynicism, how she had learned to let go because she knew there was nothing, no one, she could hang on to or lean on or cling to?

Boyd

■ IF he had met her at the beginning.

He wouldn't be currently wandering through his days trying to ignore the obvious, which was that if loving someone, Claire, wasn't enough to get them to love you, he didn't know what was.

But then, he couldn't imagine what he would have done for all those years, if he had not been married to Claire. History was Claire. Claire on the San Diego Freeway, riding the accelerator with her bare foot, her hair singing in the wind. Claire with her beat-up briefcase. Claire so amazingly, painfully young—in their one-room apartment in Hollywood, her hair tucked behind one ear as she bent over her desk, reading, the goose-neck lamp casting a skirt of light around her, a kind of net in which she was caught; he had reeled her in. Claire older—growing scared. Claire serious or ironic—it was not always easy to know which.

It was not as if there had not been numerous alternatives to the history they had written. After all, L.A. was freeways and free women. You went to work in the morning and somebody offered you free ass with your doughnuts and coffee. You stopped by to see friends, and the friends wanted to share their happiness with you and offered you free ass with your nose candy. You dragged yourself home after a hard day's work and walking out of the studio you were besieged by ass, all of it free and up for grabs. He had tried to live decently during the late Roman Empire but he had the sense that in spite of all his trying he had done something terribly morally wrong, that somewhere along the line he had compromised himself. He tried to tell himself it was inevitable, you lived you got a little dirty your jockey shorts got shit streaks. He still felt he'd messed up somehow.

Ava

■ AT the end of the semester, Ava flew back to Chicago, the house untenanted. So quiet; it needed the noise of personal objects, the small songs of clothes the humming of books. She hauled boxes of dishes up from the basement, liberated plates and glasses from their newspaper wrapping and washed them by hand at the kitchen sink. In midafternoon, she stopped to rest, sitting in a chair on a scatter rug of sunshine, thinking of nothing or trying to. When the phone rang, she expected it to be her former tenant; nobody else knew she was back. It was Tony.

Tony

■ "HI," he said.

"How did you know I was back?"

"I drove by on my way home. The door was open. You were unpacking. My middle name is Sherlock Holmes."

"Why are you calling?"

She was angry, then. "To welcome you back," he said. "Besides, I have your TV, remember? When would you like me to bring it over?"

"Marilyn has a key. She can let you in sometime when I'm not here."

"I thought we'd go to lunch. Talk about things."

"There aren't any things to talk about."

"I think there are. Why can't we just be friends? You know I'm fond of you, Ava. That doesn't change."

"Why not? Everything else does, apparently."

"I'll bring the TV now. I want to talk with you."

"I may not be here."

"I'm bringing the fucking TV over right now," he said. He slammed the receiver down.

Ava

■ SHE thought she would die when she saw him. (It was a good thing he was a doctor.)

She held the front door open for him while he maneuvered the television set inside. Without asking where she wanted it, he carried it up to the bedroom and put it on top of the dresser at the foot of her bed. That was where they used to watch it, from the bed. Ava, Ava, she told herself, you should have realized that was a bad sign. They had had it on, on their last night together—it blared away, oblivious to the competing drama in the room.

It had been a bad day, that last day even more of a last day than she had realized then though *he* knew it, dammit, he knew it. In the morning, he'd been distant, she was exhausted from packing. His distance frightened her. She wanted to extract from him a promise that they would spend the night together, their last night she said not knowing but he said they'd see how things developed. What the hell did that mean she had wondered. He said she needed to pull herself together and she could call him later. Pull herself together? Was she not together? Maybe he just meant catch some sleep? She went to bed at two in the afternoon knowing something was wrong but what exactly? and when she woke up, she called him, he said he'd come over and then she felt better thinking this was evidence that they could work through their problems, all was fine now, and after dinner they went upstairs and turned on the TV and she kept quiet like a fucking mouse while he watched the game. In spite of her afternoon nap she kept dozing off and waking up and each time she woke up he was in a worse mood. When the game was over, the sitcoms in rerun came on, but he didn't turn the TV off even though he had started to stroke her. My skin is in love with your hands she had once said to him, every time you touch it, it says a pledge of allegiance. But he couldn't get hard. "I didn't bring anything," he ventured as an excuse, though they had frequently made love without contraception but then, she knew, he had been half-hoping she would get pregnant, as had been she, no, she had been wholly hoping. She reminded him that she now had a diaphragm—the hospital had given her one after the miscarriage. As if to say, shame on you!

The hospital had been so officious, as if she were a teenager, as if she hadn't known all along that without contraception you might get pregnant, as if Tony, their prize cardiac surgeon, did not also know this high-level medical fact, but did anyone try to give him lectures about condoms?

He nodded, and his cock had now shown itself willing even if he wasn't, so she put the diaphragm in but skipped the cream it was so messy but still he didn't enter her and she asked him to and did not know whether she was issuing an invitation or begging.

So he did—and almost as soon as he entered, he started to quiver, a light fluttering of his limbs and pelvis as if he were falling into her from a great height. This was the way he always came, she guessed you couldn't help the way you came, he always trembled, stirred by some delicate fear. It was as if it happened without his active participation.

He came with a high-pitched groan that seemed to express both his pleasure and his disapproval of his pleasure. She fell asleep, but an hour later she woke again *something was so wrong* and discovered him kissing her on the top of her head. Then he sat up on the edge of the bed, slumping forward, his elbows on his knees. She turned the night lamp on. The light and his posture exaggerated the lines in his face and the heavy cast of his features. His stomach seemed rolled, like dough. The hair on his chest was matted with sweat.

"Will you be very upset if I leave?" he asked.

She was made of glass. Her heart, her brain, her legs were glass. She had to be careful not to move suddenly. She could cut herself. She could cut herself on her own heart. "If you have to leave," she said, "you have to leave."

She would not ask why. If she didn't ask, he would be impressed by her independence, he would feel free and therefore stay attached. This was her hope.

She had walked him downstairs to the door, the door he had just this minute walked back through on this afternoon in June. It had been two in the morning then, that last night. The street was quiet. In the moonlight, the snow heaped on both sides of the street had looked like long, humpbacked creatures, bewildered brontosauruses who had turned up by mistake in an ice age.

Claire

■ "WOULD you care for a coffee?" Rochelle asked, taking the manicure tray away.

"No, thank you."

Yuki plucked the cotton puffs from between Claire's toes, smiling wordlessly.

Claire had often thought of telling her that she did ikebana and that the artful complication and emotional restraint and humanist philosophy of the practice of ikenoba, the oldest of the schools of ikebana, soothed her but that she also enjoyed zen'ei ikebana, a style of the modern sogetsu school that encouraged the free expression of personality in design, and that she would like to thank Yuki's country of origin for introducing it to her, but she had not, because she imagined Yuki would only feel contempt for her fumbling overture, and why not? A revelation like that was only a way to call attention to the self. Look at me: I know something of your culture. It was offensive, and she wouldn't do it.

Zara's station was in a small room in the back next to the restroom, even more removed from the world than Rochelle's manicure station.

It was cramped and dingy—not, one would have thought, where movie stars came to get their legs waxed. Claire lay down on the gurney, her skirt hiked above her knees. She always had to remind Zara to do the knees. Zara leaned over her legs, turning them this way and that under the high, dirt-streaked window, examining them for hairs. Claire had been having this done for so long that to use Zara's words (it must be strange to spend your life thinking about other women's body hair) her "regrowth was minimal," but she welcomed the sensation of sheerness that she had after each session.

The wax was in a metal container on an electric cooking ring on the counter. The container looked like a hot pot for soup or coffee. Zara dipped a tongue depressor into the hot pot and scooped up the wax, slathering it in wide strokes on Claire's calves. The heat seeped into Claire's sore muscles.

"Ready?" Zara asked, after the wax was evenly distributed.

Claire nodded.

Zara plastered Claire's legs with long cotton strips, pressed them in place, and then, one by one, in a series of swift, stinging movements, yanked them off. Claire rolled over, and Zara did the backs. "The knees," Claire reminded her then, just as Zara was about to announce she was through.

Some years ago in Benares, Claire had walked on her bare soles over a bed of hot embers. She had prepared for the exercise with fasting and prayer. She had to admit she did not exactly stroll or amble, you could even say she had hot-footed it, but she made it across, and the bottoms of her feet were untouched by the fire. Not a welt, not a single singe. She had scorched collars more, in the days when she ironed Boyd's shirts. It had not been painless, but her mind had freed her body from cause and effect just long enough for her to do it, and an enormous exhilaration raced through her. That night in the hotel room with a breeze chasing the muslin curtains, and a stray cat she'd adopted curled on the rush mat, she abandoned herself utterly in an endorphin fog, using the young Indian engineer until he tore himself away. Later, she told Boyd about the coals—not the engineer, not even the cat—but he never could believe that she wasn't exaggerating or that there wasn't a trick to it.

After she walked through to the front, waving good-bye to Rochelle and Yuki, and paid at the front desk, she stood at the entrance, deciding whether to return home or go on to the slide library in the Dickson Center.

Her heart began to hurry, as if it were trying to catch up with itself. The palms of her manicured hands began to sweat. She reached into her briefcase for the cosmetic case in which she kept her pills. Five milligrams every four hours for anxiety. A Rolls sailed by in front of her as if it were riding on water. The sun flashed off the silver hood ornament, which was bright enough to attract a school of sharks.

Boyd

■ THE crew was flying out to Tucson tomorrow to film the dog race. Tonight they were shooting the crowd scene at the track. They would have to match the backs of the actors in Tucson with the fronts of the actors here, so he was having the scene Polaroided by the cameraman.

They were at the Hollywood Park Race Track. The ground was damp and smelled of horses. They had put a couple of scrims up on the concrete around the concession stand, and there was a false-front betting-bar. The director, a woman—he still had trouble realizing how many women there were in the business now, women who were something besides actresses and whores or was there any difference oh don't be a jackass he said to himself of course there was a difference—was perched in front of the monitor on a canvas chair that proclaimed her name on the back. She had short red hair. FIFI, the chair said. What the hell kind of a name for a director was that—*Fifi*?

"These are going to be dark," the cameraman said. He held some Polaroids up in front of Boyd.

Boyd zipped up his jacket and plunged his hands into his pockets, trying to keep warm. It was cold out here at night. He hated exteriors. Not that he had to come out here but he didn't like not checking up on a project now and then, it made him feel like something more than what he knew he was.

He nodded at the cameraman, who seemed to take it as a sign of absolution. "What's to drink?" Boyd asked.

"Milk and Gatorade."

"Get me some Gatorade." He watched the cameraman, a fat, agreeable fellow, ambulate (as his uncle would have said) toward one of the trailers lined up next to the set.

What in the name of Jesus Christ did he think he was doing, fathering, at his age—and from a distance which whatever the bonus mileage it earned certainly outclassed his cock—a child by a woman who was not his wife? Would she discard him now that he had served his purpose?

Tony

■ "YOU can't pretend I don't exist," he said.

"No? You pretended I didn't."

They had come back down and were standing in the living room. Ava had stripped the oak molding when she moved in and if you looked closely you could see specks of white paint in the grain. He knew this because on several earlier occasions he had looked closely at the oak trim while trying to decide how to respond to something she had said.

He focused on the white paint-specks now. She seemed determined not to ask him to sit down. She was wearing a fullish blue skirt and a sleeveless white cotton shirt, and she was barefoot. He could imagine a faint stickiness under the soles of her feet, a tiny indiscreet damp spot on the hardwood floor under each foot.

"I figure when someone's pursuing an idea of himself as vigorously as you are," she said, "there's nothing anyone can do except get out of the way."

"If you really wanted to get out of the way, you'd let me normalize this relationship so it could take its place in the regular array of relationships. Let's be friends, Ava."

"The regular array of relationships," she said. "I like that."

"It's a waste of both our time to be sarcastic."

"You know what your basic problem is?" she asked softly. She was fiddling with a button on her blouse, not looking at him.

Oh, fuck. He did not particularly want to know in fact he did not give a flying fuck what she thought his basic problem was did he walk out now or see it through?

"All right," he said. "What is it?"

Claire

■ AFTER a few minutes had passed, she felt calmer. She decided it was not a day for working, not even a day for reading. It was a day for visiting the Colours Salon that Georgianne had told her about. It was a day for being good to herself she needed something she needed a treat she must learn to listen to her heart it would tell her what she needed what she was afraid of.

Tony

■ "YOU'RE afraid to fart," she said.

He sat down on the sofa. He did not know whether he was supposed to take this as a statement that made some kind of sense or leave.

"In front of me," she added.

"Oh no," he said, adopting a tone of great seriousness. "Not just in front of you. I *never* fart."

"You don't? You really don't?"

"Don't be ridiculous, Ava. Of course I pass gas."

"We went together for a year. Never once did you fart. And you always shut the door when you went to the bathroom."

"I was brought up to have good manners."

"I know," she said, sadly. "You were brought up to have the best manners in the world. And the best education in the world. And the most success in the world. And the most glamorous woman in the world. You were brought up to be white. That's what all those superlatives are supposed to add up to, isn't it?"

He looked at Ava but she pulled her eyes away. He and Ava were entering a forbidden zone; they had never talked about how he felt about being black, not really. She was nervous, that was why she wasn't looking at him, her throat muscles had constricted, her mouth had gone tight. He resented that tightness. It was as if she assumed an assault even when it was the farthest thing from his mind, it made him feel guilty even when he was the one getting battered, anyone would have to say *she* was battering *him*.

"Suppose I weren't, to use your word, superlative. Would you have looked twice at me?"

"Drop the most glamorous woman in the world and let's find out."

"I'm in love with her. You know that."

"Why don't you use her name? Claire Buchanan."

What was going on here? "How do you know her name?" he asked. Of course there was an explanation. Marilyn must have carried news of Yvonne's dinner party back to Ava—academia was like a hothouse, gossip being grafted onto more gossip; still, he had not thought Marilyn would do that, had thought she would want to protect Ava.

"I guess I ought to know her name," Ava said. She was looking at him directly now, emotion evident on her face as if it had overcome barriers. "I'm carrying her husband's baby."

Ava

■ SHE gave him a moment to take in her declaration.

He had somehow managed to go white. She could see his dark skin draining, the blood running off into the byways of his body.

"Ava," he said, still using that slow voice, that voice he thought he had to use to keep her quiet, "I don't like it when you act crazy. I don't think your craziness is either glamorous or amusing. I like you to be sane. So don't say things like that for effect."

"I'm not acting crazy, Tony," she said. "I have never acted crazy. I'm not even being crazy. I really am pregnant, and the father really is Boyd Buchanan."

He stood up as if that might offer him a new perspective, a view of the situation that he could comprehend. She felt sorry for him. He was a methodical man, aggressive and systematic, and here he was, having to deal with something that could not be studied in relation to a control group.

"That's crazy," he said.

She shrugged, pretending a nonchalance she didn't feel. "You're repeating yourself," she said.

"Are you going to tell me how this occurred?"

"I went to Los Angeles. Land of movie producers. I stayed with Phaedra. Do you remember Phaedra? And her husband, Caspar? And then later I went to Santa Fe a couple of times, where Buchanan has a house, and on one of my visits to Santa Fe it took."

"Does this mean he and Claire are getting a divorce?"

He had just thought of that. She could hear the horrible eagerness in his voice. "You'd like that, wouldn't you? Not that I know of. You're probably forgetting that they really are crazy out there in California. They really go for all that open-marriage shit you used to say you thought would be swell. At least Claire does. You may think she's in love with you, but I suspect she's only being open with you."

"It's more than that."

"Then why isn't she getting a divorce?" Score one for her.

"Would you marry Buchanan if she did?"

"You probably think a woman doesn't even have to be there to have sex. She can just spread her legs and sleep through it. But it's not like that—"

"You still shock me sometimes, even with all I know about you. Your feelings are so . . . intense. Being around them was like standing in the path of a firestorm. I felt like it took all my energy just to withstand them."

"I worked so hard to protect you from my feelings. I realize now that that was a mistake, but I wanted to make life easy for you."

"You're kidding. You made sure I knew what your feelings were anyway."

"Your reticence about your feelings was its own kind of warfare. I lightened up whenever you let me know it was safe to do so, but you never wanted me to feel safe for long. My safety threatened you. Maybe even my sanity threatens you."

"This is exactly what I mean by *intense*. Right now, at this stage of my life, I don't want to examine my motives—or yours, or anybody's. All I want right now is to extirpate the anxiety from my heart. Can you understand that?"

Feeling dizzy, she sat down on the sofa he had gotten up from. Shit, she thought, you were supposed to get sick first thing in the morning, not in the middle of the day when you were trying to hold your head up with a man who had broken up with you.

Why was it even necessary for two people to love each other? Wasn't love a form of fiction, a story people told each other just so they could keep each other's attention, everybody playing Scheherazade to everybody else? A story people told so life could keep writing itself into existence, generation after generation? But maybe Claire was a better-told story. Critics preferred Claire. Claire was a bestseller, soon to be a movie! She, Ava, was too experimental, too post-postmodern, a specialized taste, somewhat academic.

"Why have you done this, Ava?" Tony asked. He was looking at his hands. She remembered late-night bull sessions among the girls in the dormitory, how everyone had said that a man's hands are the clue to the size of his penis. He was studying his hands, turning them over as if he needed to find out the size of his own penis. His fingers were educated and enterprising and long. *Let me tell you something*, she thought. Let me tell you something wonderful about yourself.

"I wanted a baby," she said. "You know that. They do artificial insemination on racehorses, but not on single women. Not yet, not here."

"But you didn't have to go to Claire's husband. Do you think this is going to re-involve me with you somehow? Are you sleeping with me vicariously? What the hell is going on in your mind, Ava?"

"I don't know," she mumbled. "It made a kind of sense, that's all. It gave shape to all the stuff that was happening that was stupid and shapeless. It didn't make sense for you to leave me for her."

"She wasn't looking to get something from me. Not even sperm."

"I know you think she's a madonna, but she's a married woman cheating on her husband. By the way, Tony, this is the age of AIDS. Haven't you ever wondered who else she's slept with?"

"And you, on the other hand, achieved conception immaculately. Buchanan never fucked you, he just wished you well and bingo. Now you're going to be a single mother, and you're going to bring into the world a child who won't have a father. I suspect you don't believe that yet. I suspect you have some kind of fantasy that somebody's going to marry you. It won't be me."

She ran to the bathroom to throw up. From her vantage point, she could see that the former tenant had failed to clean underneath the rim of the toilet. Tony was right, she had had that fantasy, yes indeed.

He was standing in the doorway, watching her.

She pulled herself up by the edge of the sink and rinsed out her mouth. Her hair was falling in front of her face, the wet ends, clinging to her cheeks, as stringy as asparagus.

"Have you had amniocentesis?"

"Not yet."

"Do they think you'll be able to carry to term?"

"I don't know. But if it doesn't work, I'll try again."

"Maybe you will, but not with Boyd Buchanan."

"Why not? Who are you to say?"

"I'm nobody to say, but you've forgotten about Claire. Claire is somebody to say."

"You're going to tell her? Why?"

"That's another life in there." He looked pointedly at her stomach. "You can't fuck around with it like this."

Him telling her not to fuck around, that was funny. "That's not why you're going to tell her," she said. "You want to tell her so she'll have a reason to get angry with her husband and ask for a divorce so you can marry her." She turned away from him, back to the sink, and stared into the mirror, but it was his image that held her there, not hers. "Don't you," she said.

Claire

■ IN the Colours Salon Claire sat on a loveseat facing a wide, tall mirror while a part-time actress ("I'm a Winter," she had announced) held swatches of bright-colored fabric up to her face. The Winter woman had pulled Claire's hair back from her face under a triangle of white cloth knotted at the nape, making her look vaguely nunnish. Winter held a peach color and then a pink color next to Claire's skin, whisking each of them away dramatically in turn. "Peach," she said, "you are definitely a peach." *A real peach.* "Now we have to find out whether you're Autumn or Spring."

For the next two hours Winter draped colored cloth around Claire's neck. Claire stared at her bare face in the mirror, thinking, If you have been beautiful, there will come a time when you must realize that not in a long while has anyone called you beautiful. There will be a stretch of time like a desert of unsaying, a desert of waiting for what is never said, during which no one calls you anything, maybe they just don't think of it or maybe they look at you and think, She was beautiful once, and the "once" somehow embarrasses them so they say nothing and then at a still later point men will begin to say things like, You are still a very attractive woman, and this is supposed to be a compliment but it will make you cry in the back of your mind, behind your fading face. You will hate yourself for being self-absorbed, you will accuse yourself of being vain—foolishly vain—and superficial, but that sense of failure, that sense of loss, is how you will feel. A loss of self.

Like someone who used to be someone else.

Like someone who used to be someone.

In the end, it was decided that Claire was a Spring. This meant that she was to wear deep jade rather than cool jade, ranch mink rather than pink-champagne mink, though she never wore any kind of jade, any kind of mink.

Winter told her she should wear gold rather than silver and sold her a gold collar-necklace worked into a bow-tie design. Winter handed her a tiny booklet of color swatches so she could test the colors in stores before buying anything. Winter gave her a card listing the proper neutrals for accessories, the allowable jewels. If you were a Spring, you would be making a dreadful but now thanks to the Colours Salon a correctable mistake to dress out of season.

But sometimes, Claire thought, it was all she could do to remember what season it was. There was a tendency for time to slide out of mind, away from you, toward, for example, the world you grew up in, that world that was so different from the world you lived in now. In that other world, her parents would have been horrified to see her spending money like this. Even her hair pulled back from her face would not compensate for her profligacy. In that other world, her mother and father used to sit at the dining room table late into the night, placemats pushed aside, going grimly over the bills. This was the Rite of Getting Through To the End of the Month. A tension surrounded the house for ten days, a kind of economic version of PMS. Later on her parents had bought an adding machine with their hard-earned savings, so they could work all the harder at keeping track of everything they worked so hard to earn.

She had quickly learned that if that world was to hold together she must shelter her parents from their own sense of responsibility, by which they frequently felt overwhelmed. Her sister had certainly been no help, marrying and moving out as soon as possible.

The intense sun had erased all the shadow from the city of Los Angeles. There were no hiding places left anywhere. The only way to cross the street was out in the open, in front of everybody. Everything, including the street itself, had a slippery, stretched-out feeling to it, as if the world were really one big balloon or a sweet pink bubble, an endless pull of taffy. Claire clutched her package and her briefcase and stepped off the curb.

Boyd

■ IN the Plaza, the Indian market was bright and colorful. The town was packed with people who'd come for the annual opera and chamber music festival. Ava was here too, because he had prevailed upon her to come, but she was subdued. "I don't think this is a good idea," she said, again and again. "We weren't supposed to get involved, remember?"

He had had to telephone her repeatedly. "I miss you," he'd said, feeling guilty about saying it—was he betraying her as well as Claire, leading her to expect what he couldn't proffer?—but he couldn't help it, he did miss her.

He drove her past St. Francis. The shadow-dappled flat-roofed houses were secretive in the late afternoon. Bluebirds sang in the juniper trees. "Have you thought of a name yet?" he asked. When she hesitated, he said, "Buchanan. Name it Buchanan."

"What if it's a girl?"

"It works for a girl, too. Buchanan Martel." He passed the car in front of them. "Little Bucky."

She made a face. "Bucky?"

A picture in his mind of a small girl in a meadow or field somewhere near Arkansas. She was wearing blue jeans and a plaid flannel shirt and she was barefoot sitting on a fence and holding an apple out to a horse. He would have to buy her a pony. "I'm wild about you," he said.

"I think it's a boy," she said. "I just have that feeling."

He thought of how she looked when she got up out of bed and curled up in the pink armchair. It was as if it was a large shell, and she, naked on it, was his Aphrodite, rising from the sea of sex. Oh, he was a romantic at heart, he thought. No question about it. "Are you still in love with your surgeon?"

"He belongs to your wife now." She turned away to look out the side window. "I keep asking myself what I did wrong, and I guess I failed to give him what he wanted."

"He has dishonored himself before you. Don't beat your breast too black and blue. I might want to rest my weary head on it."

That night, when she was asleep under the skylight, he eased out of bed, dressed, and went outside to the stables. Even before he reached the stables, he heard a horse snuffle, switch its tail, shake its mane. The sounds carried clearly in the chill night air. The moonlight on the mountains made them look like they were in 3-D, jutting out in front of the dark sky.

A boy, he thought. "Buck" was a good name for a wheeler-dealer's son, you'd have to say.

He knew a woman screenwriter whose license plate on her Mercedes convertible read I LV BKS. When she pulled into the filling station, the attendant, in overalls and wiping his hands on a much-begrimed towel he kept in his hip pocket, had said to her, "Honey, there's more to life than dollars."

He saddled Paloma, his favorite mare, stroking her neck and talking to her quietly. He walked her out of the corral and around and around, her hooves ringing on the hard earth, in the sharp air. He rode faster and faster, trying to get away from himself. From the gullies and ditches and ravines, he pursued himself, he fled himself. A sense of hurt too ghastly to bear was gaining on him.

Ava

■ THE cyclopean eye of the machine stared at her stomach. Sonar electrodes clung to her stomach as if she were some kind of marsupial. The gynecologist cleansed the puncture site with antiseptic, having already explained the procedure and delivered a local anesthetic, and jabbed her with a needle, drawing fluid from the amniotic sac. They would monitor the fetal heartbeat for a couple of hours, to confirm that the fetus was alive and well, and living in Ava.

Would it be normal? Would it have Down syndrome? Would it have an extra X chromosome, or an extra Y chromosome? Would it love her? Would it hate her for bringing it into the world without a father? Would it run away and get involved with drugs? Would it run away and join a cult, maybe the Moonies, god forbid? Were there still Moonies in the world for it to join? Would it be glad to be alive, or rue the day of its birth? If it had Down syndrome, would she have it anyway?

The only thing she was sure of was that it would be not be black. This made her sad, made her a sad woman, lying there: that one little black boy who might have been, had been decided against. She had meant to do her part in making the world a better place.

Look on the bright side she told herself, she should just be happy she was pregnant even if not with Tony's child and one other nice thing about not having periods, at least there was no little monthly wet string curled up in the crotch of her underpants, like a dead white worm.

Boyd

■ CLAIRE huddled at the far end of the living room couch, blowing her nose. Behind her, framed in the window, the canyon fell away into the distance like perspective in a painting. She balled the used tissue in her fist. "Why did you have to make her *pregnant*?" she asked.

It was a good question, he thought. He thought now that it was not a question he had ever really asked himself. Had he done it out of revenge (revenge was not, he realized, the exclusive prerogative of ditched women)? Loneliness? Because he was horny? Because he liked feeling useful? Or maybe he really did it, as he had said to Ava, out of a sense of urgency, a sense of mortality? *I don't understand why we*—he meant humans—*feel this*, he had said to her, looking at the stars through the skylight. *Dead is dead. To the dead, time is meaningless. Not even that, since something has to have the potential of meaning in order to be meaningless, and when you're dead, time doesn't even exist.* He had liked lying next to her like that, looking up at the night sky. It was a little like being at camp. There was a sense of tribal connection and companionship that protected you physically as you contemplated large and possibly dangerous questions. He wondered if she was feeling the same way. *Soon enough,* he said, *the whole species will be dead. So where does all this ego come from? Is it viral, some essentially viral desire to persist and dominate? Maybe it's simply fear. But maybe it's less a fear of death than of meaninglessness.*

Or maybe, she said, *it's generosity. People just naturally want to give of themselves.*

Nobody believes in altruism anymore.

You do, she said.

He thought now, *I did it because I'm alive, or want to feel alive.* But he couldn't say that to Claire; it would only hurt her more.

"I wish Ferro had kept the hell out of this, that's what I wish," he said. "There was no need for you to know."

Claire was drinking martinis, he didn't know how many, but they were plural. She leaned over to the end table and poured herself another. Light from the brass floorlamp fell on her blond hair and familiar face, her lovely nose, from all the crying she'd done, blossoming bright pink in the cool garden of her face. Her diamond earrings glittered like stars. Sweat beaded on the cool, silver pitcher.

"You could at least say you're sorry," she said, settling back again.

"I'm sorry I broke our rules."

"I don't know what you mean."

"You know you do. We had an understanding." *A misunderstanding? A non-understanding?* It seemed to him that what they had understood was that some things were better not understood too well. "We understood that you would have lovers, and you would not take any of them seriously."

She chased the olive around the bottom of her glass.

He waited until she had speared it with a toothpick. Then he said, "It was a silent understanding, but still."

He expected her to say, Still what? but she didn't. He pushed on. "I guess we should have spoken about this long ago."

"What did you mean, *I* would have lovers? You—"

He shook his head. "Never. Not once." He hated himself for sounding as though he expected a Faithful Spouse award and added, "I've never wanted anyone but you, Claire."

She held a hand to her throat, the manicured nails splayed like a stop sign. "So why now?"

He said, "Ferro scared me, if you want to know the truth." He was not sure Claire wanted to know the truth.

"So you knocked up his ex-girlfriend."

"She asked me to make her pregnant. She wanted a child."

"You expect *me* to feel sorry for her? Do you think *I* didn't want to have a child? Do you think I can convince myself that you didn't deliberately do the thing that would hurt me most?"

He dropped his eyes, unable to look at her. The question put this way had been torn from his throat, put this way it was his question too. He heard her anguish and felt embarrassed for her—twenty-five years of marriage did not eradicate the need for certain kinds of privacy. He hated himself. Everything he touched, he spoiled. He was good for nothing except making profitable shit.

"You left her without a man to father her child, remember?"

"I didn't *steal* him. He's forty-five years old. Jesus God Almighty."

The doorbell rang. He went to get it.

It was the dry cleaners. Boyd paid the man and stood on the steps, holding the bag—someone was always left holding the bag, weren't they, he thought—until the van had turned around and driven past the first tight curve in the road.

His marriage was disappearing out from under him, like the coastline. He didn't understand how this could be happening to him after all these years and at the same time it seemed to him that all along he had just been waiting for the inevitable.

He hung the black plastic bag of dry-cleaned clothes—something slightly ominous about it, like a body bag—on a coat hook in the foyer and went back to the living room in time to watch his wife uncurling her legs, rising from the silk taupe pillows. It seemed to him that she was doing this in slow motion, that everything was happening in slow motion. "Do you love him?" he asked.

She was wearing a skirt with a slit up the side, and an angora sweater, and the diamond earrings danced on her ears like sprites. *Angels on a pinhead*, he thought meanly.

Claire

■ ALL these years and he'd never fallen off the wagon, she had to give him that, she was drinking martinis and he was eating olives—couldn't he do something, have a drink for god's sake, be less himself? She began to cry, astonished to discover that she was capable of crying, and the more she cried the angrier she got at Boyd, thinking he ought to be doing something to stop her from crying, but he just stood there loudly sucking the pimento out of the olives.

She looked down at her hands and saw that the Kleenex was wet and shredded, a thin hard bump in her hands. She dropped it beside her. She sat up straight and crossed her legs, her smooth, waxed legs, and thought with a small warm pleasure of her painted toenails inside her Manolo Blahniks. She poured herself another drink.

"You could at least say you're sorry," she said. Maybe he would get angry with her, it would be better than having him just standing there eating olives. Not even olives! The *pimento*.

"I know you're the one who gets to have affairs!" he shouted. "I'm sorry I broke our rules."

She wondered what rules these were. If there were any rules at all, there must have been one that said flings were one thing but getting a woman pregnant was a betrayal. He was saying that they had had a silent understanding, but if they'd had anything, it was a silent misunderstanding.

"What did you mean, I'm the one—" She let her sentence trail off as the meaning came clear.

From a distance she heard him telling her that he had been faithful to her. That he had never been interested in any woman but her. But, she thought, he *had* been interested in another woman, and if it was the first time in all their life together, that only meant his interest was all the deeper. She didn't want to have this thought, she wanted to protect herself from this thought, and therefore, she realized, it was fortunate for her that somehow her heart had moved up to her throat and become a barricade. She could barely breathe.

"I don't know what you're talking about," she said but of course she did, she hated herself when she got like this, all knotted up in her own rationalizations and defenses, just like the Kleenex. This was what happened when you weren't true to yourself, she could feel the tension in her calves and shoulders, when you were not yourself your body knew it and protested.

"Yes, you do," he countered. "You know damn good and well what I'm talking about. But you broke our contract."

As soon as he said that, she realized he was correct. They had had a contract even though she had never thought of it that way. But why had he been willing to agree to such a contract? Suddenly he seemed to her the most mysterious of men, someone whose motives lay completely outside her ken. She had lived with him for twenty-five years, and he was a stranger.

"Maybe it doesn't matter to you that everything's broken," he said. "It matters to me."

"Then why have you done this?"

"Done what? *I* haven't gotten anyone pregnant!" *Jesus God Almighty.*

Then the doorbell rang, amputating their conversation. Claire stayed where she was while Boyd went to get it. The front window overlooked the driveway that led to the main road, and she could see the dry-cleaning van pulling out.

She felt cold and clasped her arms across her chest, the short-sleeved angora sweater soft against the vulnerable undersides of her wrists. He would leave her. Boyd would leave her. He would not be able to stay away from the child that this insane woman was going to give him. Claire thought he must really hate her, to use against her the one thing she could do nothing about, her childlessness.

She made herself get up from the couch. She had to prepare herself for whatever was going to happen; she wanted to call Tony.

Boyd came back in. "Do you love him?" he asked.

She carried her empty glass to the bar.

Tony

■ SOMETIMES he thought about trying to find Francie. Desirée might know where she was. Likely working as a maid somewhere, unless Norbert took care of her. He wondered how Norbert was doing, a mild, disintegrated man whose general practice had declined into a day here, a day there, using his car as an office: abortions, cough remedies. A sad man; when you were raised in a back room you became very sad. He could not look up Norbert to ask after Francie because it was not possible to quiz your half-brother about his mother when you had slept with her. He wondered how Francie had felt, raising her own child in the back room while he, Tony, was the center of the household. How had his mother felt, having to give up one of her children, visit him like a nephew? How did Ava Martel feel, carrying a child that she had intended to be his? In his mind, Ava's creamy skin poured into Francie's full-breasted darkness, and the blend was like a dream of distance in which he could lose himself, become lost to the world.

Ava

■ WHEN she went to the hospital for her checkups, she tried to hurry past Tony's clinic without him or any of his partners noticing her. She could still do this but in a few months it would start to get more and more difficult not to notice her, her stomach big as a billboard, maybe when that happened she'd put up a sign, a sign that said NOT TONY'S. Sometimes she caught a glimpse of him disappearing into one of the examining rooms, stethoscope dangling from his pocket. And upstairs, she knew, in the locked ward where silence was longed for as a country in which one might at last feel at home, were forgotten women who screamed obscenities ritually as if saying a rosary, nurses who laughed too loudly in the middle of the night, and a TV that never shut up.

Tony

■ HE realized that Ava had succeeded in making him feel that *he* was being cheated on by *her*. She had achieved this even though he was no longer her lover. At the same time, he figured, this wasn't all bad. It brought with it a certain kind of relief, relief he was ashamed of but was glad to feel. Limits had been imposed. Limits Ava had no inkling of were the result of what she had done. For one thing, he did not have to continue revealing himself to Claire as completely as he had been doing, because Claire was no longer purely herself: Now she was also Ava, because Ava was sleeping with Claire's husband, and so both Claire and Ava were, so to speak, divorced from him, both, so to speak, married to Boyd Buchanan, and he, Tony Ferro, was left to himself. And it was better this way. For a while, he had felt trapped, like being in an elevator stalled between floors. Too much closeness made him feel anxious. It made him want to run, made him want to find another woman.

Claire

■ "YES," she said, feeling trapped into it. "I love Tony."

And he would have to marry her, she thought. *Tony would have to marry her.* He had begun pulling away but now he would have to make good on his offer. That was all there was to it. She had lived her life with a man—she had no intention of not living it with one now.

Later, she called Tony. "In a way," she said, "you brought this about, by telling me about Boyd and his child-to-be."

"I don't see how I brought this about. I rather thought you wanted to love us both equally but stay married to Boyd. That was what I understood you to say, Claire." Tony's voice was guarded. *What's the matter, she wanted to say, afraid of me?*

"I rather thought you wanted to live with me," she said.

He didn't answer.

"If you want to live with me, you'll have to marry me. I certainly can't give up my position at UCLA without some measure of security, can I? Would you be willing to find a position out here?"

"I can't. You know that."

"Yes. I'll have to move there, and that's why we'll have to get married. If I'm not going to be tenured, I'm at least going to be married." But of course she couldn't actually give up tenure, she was in love but not crazy in love, not that crazy in love; she would find a way to commute.

Boyd

■ AT night he prowled the house while his wife slept upstairs. In and out of the kitchen, turning the pages of the photo albums in the library with its shaded lights and leather chairs, back to the kitchen for a glass of milk. . . . She was going to leave him, he was sure. He was sure of that, and not sure he could stand it. His heart hurt him, it seemed to be working so hard just to keep pumping blood through his veins. If it had to keep working like this, and it would if she left him, it would wear itself out. For so long, she had been the only thing in his life that had made him feel worthwhile. If she left, he would be nothing. If she left, he'd be an aging con artist with a couple of sunburned bimbos flanking his table at Spago's. He could practically see the two girls nibbling duck sausage grilled over mesquite.

Ava

■ IT was one in the morning when Boyd called; he never paid any attention to the time differential. *That's men for you*, Ava imagined herself saying to Marilyn the next time they saw each other, *when did a man ever pay any attention to the time differential.*

"I made a mistake," he said, whispering into the phone. *Was he in bed, Claire lying next to him?* "A terrible mistake. I don't know why I did it. But we've got to do something about it."

Ava switched on the bedside lamp. She had fallen asleep reading and the book fell off the bed with a clatter. "What do you mean? There's nothing anybody can do about it now."

"Are you sure?"

She wanted to cry. Without quite acknowledging it to herself, she had begun to imagine that at some point the father of her child would want to act like the father of her child. He would show up on the baby's birthdays! He'd teach the kid to throw a baseball! "They called me with the results from the amniocentesis," she said. "They said it's a healthy fetus."

"I never told you," he said. "Claire and I tried, but she couldn't have children."

What could she say? She could say, Tough titty! She could say, That's an excuse for sleeping with a man who's involved with another woman? "I'm sorry," she said. "Is that why you agreed to do this with me?"

"Claire knows about the baby. Your surgeon told her."

"I *wish* you would stop calling him my surgeon. My surgeon is an OB/GYN. His name is Dr. Klimek. It's a good old Polish name. We have a lot of Poles in Chicago."

"How could I have hurt Claire like this? She's in such pain. Ava, I think she's going to leave me."

Her heart was so heavy. It was like a stone that had been tied to her chest. It was like something she had to lug around all day. It was like something she was pregnant with. "Does that mean she's going to marry Tony?"

"She can't do that until she divorces me."

"Would that be so terrible?" she asked. "It doesn't sound like the world's greatest marriage." *But if Claire married Tony, that would be terrible.*

"It's *my* greatest marriage."

"Then work it out, if you have to. But don't ask me to do something I can't do. I am having this baby."

"Oh, Martel, Martel. That's not what I meant! Did you think that's what I meant? But how could you?"

"Then what did you mean by *do something*?"

"I'm going to do whatever I can to save my marriage. I think we need to talk with your friend. The surgeon. Ferro."

"Why?"

"If I'm going to work it out, this is the only way to do it. I have to make him see what he's violating."

"Well, goddammit," she said, getting angry now, "you won't find him here. He hasn't been here since he met your free-spirited wife." *Oh, the TV. There was the time he returned the TV.*

"Talk to him for me, Martel. Tell him I want to talk with him. I think it's better if he has some forewarning from you that I'm going to call."

She was thinking it over.

"What's his number?" Boyd asked.

Tony

■ WHEN the phone rang, it was Ted. "Can I talk to you?" he asked. "Man to man."

"Sure," Tony said, surprised. It was usually Yvonne who called him, not Ted. "I thought you were in the Antarctic or Siberia or someplace."

"Siberia," Ted said. "I don't go to the South Pole until next winter. It's a matter of timing. You have to go when the ice floes will let you in. How well would you say you know Yvonne?"

"Pretty well, I guess." He and Yvonne had been collaborating on their research for two years now. But what did he know about her?

"Do you think you could tell if she was having an affair?"

Tony tried to think how to answer. "You think she's having an affair?" he asked.

"It's hard to say. But I keep having this feeling—"

"You're probably imagining things. This is what happens when you hang out in places where you have to worry about the ice floes. You start imagining things." Tony laughed into the receiver, because it seemed to him that a laugh was called for. Then he said, "You mean you haven't been having an affair?"

"What? Me? Why would I have an affair?"

Tony said, "I just figured, all those months in the middle of nowhere."

"With who, Santa Claus?"

"Claire was convinced."

"Shit. I hope she didn't say something like that to Yvonne. Maybe that's why. Maybe she thinks she's getting back at me."

"But you don't know if she's having an affair."

Tony thought Ted must be spending too much time at base camp. It was lonely, despite the state-of-art heating system, the hydroponic experiments, the satellite phone.

"That's true," Ted said. "But I know. A person always knows, don't they?"

"Not always," Tony said, remembering how Ava had not known. "Sometimes a person doesn't want to know. So maybe sometimes a person thinks they know something when they don't. It can work both ways."

"What can?"

"Self-delusion," Tony said.

"You think I'm deluding myself? I mean, please, Ferro! I'd really *like* to be deluding myself, I really would."

"Join the club," Tony said.

"I know I talk big," Ted said, "but I'm just an ordinary guy, you know. You know me, I snap up a ticket to a Bulls game whenever I get the chance. In the summer I take a week and go fishing up north. You and Boyd Buchanan, you're the swingers. I wouldn't know what to do with myself if I were single again."

"I remind you that Buchanan is not single."

"Well hell, he's a movie producer, right? And you're shtupping his wife, right?"

Boyd

■ THE sun played the scales on the backs of fish as if practicing the piano. Arpeggios of bream, chords of bass. Buford glanced at his uncle, asleep under the cottonwood, his line tied to a pole jammed into the ground. It was strange to realize that his uncle was in some other state of consciousness, a state as far from Arkansas as New York, maybe. As far as just about anywhere. Buford looked up at the sky. Poplar leaves flashed like miniature green train signals while small white clouds chugged across the blue, blue afternoon. He tried to stare straight into the sun but it was too bright, and without meaning to, he jerked his eyes back down to the ground. An ant was idling its way across his sock and he brushed it off. It landed on its feet and resumed its journey. Buford's line remained inert. Water whispered seductively to the pier. His uncle's face, under the hat, was as blank as a blank cartridge, as empty as an empty pocket. Buford squirmed on his buttocks, seeking softer grass. He reeled in his line, checked the worm, and tossed it into the water again, liking the soft splash of it. Dreamily, he thought that God could be a big fish, a trout or even a sailfish, and that He swam through the sky the way other fish swam in the river. As soon as he thought this, his thinking it astonished him. He sat up straighter. It was so quiet he could hear himself thinking—it seemed to him that his brain made a low, insistent hum, like a power saw in the distance. Amazed, he went on thinking. When you were bad, he thought, God swallowed you, like the whale swallowing Jonah, or else, how about this? God made you eat worms, worms a thousand times bigger than the ones in his jar with the holes punched in the top. With a single dorsal fin, the fish that was God could cut the world in half. Was he being stupid to think this? No one had ever seen God, so no one could say He wasn't a fish. But God had created man in His own image. Buford carefully examined his uncle, snoring away under his shapeless canvas hat, his mouth puckering with each contented breath as if he were blowing bubbles.

Ava

■ ON her way to meet Marilyn at the school cafeteria, she was startled to see a poster, tacked to a kiosk, headlined: WHY WASPS ARE NOT SOCIAL. It took her a moment to realize that this was the title of a lecture to be given by a visiting entomologist.

Marilyn was already there, seated at a table near the wall of windows that overlooked the lake. A few years ago the graduating class for its gift to the University had paid to have the lawn paved, and now there were painted metal tables and chairs scattered over the terrace, with students and professors lined up at the short-order grill, loading their bratwursts with sauerkraut, and then hauling chairs from under trees into the sun as if to soak up a supply to get through the coming winter. On a beautiful summer day in Chicago, they bared as much skin as the Midwest would allow. When the waves kicked up and hit the seawall, students felt the spray on their legs. It was not yet September, but summer was serving notice. A few leaves had begun to change, and every now and again one would fly down onto a table like a sparrow taking time out on its journey south. In just a minute or two, it would rise off the table and fly away again. It would! Ava missed the grass, the actual dirt, nature, but the view from inside the cafeteria, looking out, reminded her of her favorite painting, Monet's *Terrace at Sainte-Adresse* and she told Marilyn that. Sailboats scudded over the lake like small white clouds.

"Why is that your favorite painting?" Marilyn asked.

"I don't know," Ava said. "It just is. I'm not an art historian, you know. Unlike what seem to be a great many other women."

Marilyn snorted. "Two. You know two of us."

Actually, Ava did know why it was her favorite painting. There was such tension and balance in it, a sense of violence controlled, a sense of contradictory impulses holding each other in abeyance and of opposites conjoined. The first time she'd seen it, she had not liked it. It had seemed too simple to her, too easy. But something lured her back, and back again, and each time she saw something she had failed to see before. It was a painting that had opened her eyes, *that* was why she loved it.

"I had something I wanted to tell you," Ava said, "but I don't remember what it was." She sighed. "I've been working on my syllabi for the fall."

"How on earth do you think you're going to teach in the fall? And what about second semester? Who's going to look after the baby?"

"I don't know. Isn't it unreal that there's no such thing as paid family leave, here at the dawn of the new millennium?"

"You didn't answer my question. Who's going to look after the baby?"

"Of course, even if there was," Ava said, "it wouldn't cover single women. We're not supposed to have families. We're just supposed to grow old and die without getting in anyone's way."

"Answer me."

"Why don't we live in a civilized country? Maybe we should emigrate. Go someplace kinder, gentler."

"Answer me."

"It's a very good question," Ava said. "It really is. Who is going to take care of the baby?"

Claire

■ CLAIRE thought of the baby. Who would take care of it? What would Boyd's responsibilities to it be? Did she have any responsibilities to it? Why was it not *hers*?

It was difficult not to see it as her own.

She and Boyd might have enlisted a surrogate. A birth mother. If Martel—

Drawing up reading lists for her courses in the fall, choosing and arranging slides—because she still had to perform these tasks, had to be prepared, not knowing whether Tony would ask her to marry him or if she would really say yes if he did and leave L.A., leave the department she'd been in for a decade now, no, she wouldn't, she would work something out, a leave of absence—going over her lecture notes, she found herself thinking about the baby. She thought about how it would come out of this madwoman's (she had to be) body, this body that both her husband and her lover had entered.

Ava

■ "IT'S a question you don't have an answer for."

"Well, I do. And the answer's obvious. I hesitate to state it only because I know you're determined to be skeptical. I'm going to take care of the baby. And teach. I'll take the baby to class with me. I'm going to get one of those slings that let you carry the baby in front so he can hear your heartbeat. It won't hurt the students to see a little bit of real life. It'll help them to understand their required reading."

"Humppff," said Marilyn.

"What was that?" Ava asked, laughing. "I didn't quite catch what you said."

"Humppff. I said humppff."

"If you're such a big believer in having a man around the house, why don't you marry Gordon?"

"It would kill my father."

"What?"

"You heard me." Marilyn's eyes slid away to the picture-perfect view. She seemed to be studying it, as if it and she were in a museum.

"My father would be deeply disappointed in me if he knew I was going with a white man."

"Did you really say that? No," Ava said, "I refuse to believe you could say such a thing. How old *are* you, anyway?"

"Old enough to know I'd regret needlessly hurting an old man."

"What about Gordon?"

"Oh, him," she said. "*Him*."

"You're letting prejudice rule your life. I would never have thought that you'd do that."

"Gordon will still be around after my father dies. Maybe I'll marry him then."

"And offend your father's ghost?"

"My father's ghost will be white," Marilyn said. "There are no black ghosts."

"You don't know that for sure. There could be black ghosts all around, but we just can't see them when they come around at night."

"Those aren't ghosts," Marilyn said. "Those are bogeymen. Besides, you are in no position to throw stones. You have such a glorious relationship with your patriarch. When was the last time you even talked with him?"

"That's not fair. It's not like I haven't tried."

"Me too. So did you get your syllabi done?"

"I guess so," Ava said. "Not that there's that much leeway. There's a canon in Women's Studies already, you know, even though we're not supposed to call it a *canon*. But it's there, and you can't deviate from it without getting into trouble."

"Everything in this world has rules. Just like my father."

"You know what, Marilyn, this is a whole new millennium. It's too late to be thinking in terms of race."

"Oh, girlfriend," Marilyn said. "Don't you know that people have only just begun to think in those terms? Up till now, they've been thinking in terms of *whiteness*, not race. There hasn't even *been* any race to be thought of, in the eyes of the rulers of the world, until a few years ago. Now we've got their eyes open, and they see that there are other colors besides white, and we've got to make them know what these colors *mean*. I mean, a man like Tony makes me mad because he's black and he *still* doesn't know what that means."

"WASPs are not social."

"I don't know about that," Marilyn said. "Gordon's pretty social."

Ava looked at Marilyn, the bracelets on both arms, the earrings that were made of some cloudlike stuff, soft and fluffy but blue, light blue, her meticulous, complex cornrows braided like grillework on a mosque, some coded, iconic design. How we ornament ourselves, she thought.

"What are you thinking about now?" Marilyn asked. "Deracination? Deconstruction? I don't think you can be a deconstructionist and a mother at the same time."

"What kind of beads are those?" Ava asked, for Marilyn was wearing multi-loops of trading beads around her neck.

"These are cowhorn beads from Kenya," Marilyn said, picking up one strand, "and these," she said, lifting another draped across her breast, "are Ethiopian glass beads, and these," she said, fingering a third, "are Venetian glass millefiori trade beads from the Ashanti tribe in Ghana."

"Oh my," Ava said. "My."

"I think of these beads as a kind of self-valorization," Marilyn said.

"What you can do about a canon, though, is you can sometimes come at things from a different angle," said Ava. "You can do that, sometimes."

Claire

■ NEVER had she had any desire to paint or to sculpt. She found this interesting, in a vaguely inauspicious sort of way—that one could spend one's life commenting on what other people had done and be content with that, but she had been content, and convinced she was making a contribution. Still, she thought she might once have had a desire to create, in a time before her memory began, but that it had been driven out of her, like a demon perhaps: yes, her family would have thought of it as a demon. Or an evil godmother had come to the christening and put a spell on her, binding all her creativity into a fisted heart of anxiety. She had been afraid, that was it, and the fear came from seeing how her parents fretted about money, about what she and her sister would make of their lives: would it be something more, something better than they had made of their own lives, their lives with which they were so displeased.

Only, who was not afraid? Boyd was afraid. Boyd had always been afraid. His being afraid had drawn her to him, pushed her away from him. And she had always counted on it, hadn't she, counted on his fear to keep him with her?

Tony, too, was afraid, without understanding that he was afraid.

But maybe Ava Martel was not afraid. Or did Ava Martel think that rescue or protection was available for her somewhere in all this? Oh, that was surely it, or else she'd never have done it! This vengeful woman thought Boyd would marry her. This was some bizarre way of getting back at Claire for Tony's falling in love with her! But she was not responsible for Tony's falling in love with her. She couldn't help it that Tony had fallen in love with her. She had been as surprised as anyone, when you came right down to it. That was so, when you really came right down to it!

Ava

■ THERE was an idea she was trying to come at from a new angle, and she thought about it as she prepared her lectures for the fall semester.

For as long as she could remember, she had been assuring herself that no one ever got used. That we are the perpetrators of our own psychic crimes. That we have no one to blame but ourselves. And she had so stated, speaking on the subject the previous year when Sylvia Plath came up on the syllabus in her Women in Lit class, which, as a woman in Women's Studies, she was obliged to take her turn teaching although it was not her field, her field was theory and history of feminism.

Twenty very serious young female students and one man scribbled in their spiral notebooks as she talked.

Plath—Professor Martel had diligently maintained to the students, a year ago—aggrandized her own troubles by identifying herself as a victim. And this—lamented Professor Martel, a year ago—was a literary shame, maybe even a literary tragedy, because the more interesting thing, the transcendent thing, would have been for Plath to recognize the fascist in herself, her share of responsibility for the huge basin of sorrow that inundates and bathes the world. The poet Plath—

argued Professor Martel, last year—was her own murderer long before she took her life, because her failure to accept responsibility throttled any opportunity for her talent to grow.

Now Ava's respect for Plath shot up overnight, following Boyd's phone call. If it sprang from Ava's own obsessions, from the realization—it was so clear now—that her year-long abnegation of self (*dating* being the preferred term for that) had brought her nothing but Tony's collaborative dismissal of her—he actually wanted to marry Claire!—her new position, delivered in class, nevertheless went like this: "As everybody knows, we have slaughtered ourselves and our planet"—she waited for the chatting to stop, the page-turning to cease, the eyes to focus—"but a truth less broadly acknowledged, perhaps because it seems self-pitying to particularize it, although I am talking about a general reality, is that we are victims as well. Victims of circumstance, of tyranny, of mismanagement, of genetic confusion, and of course of our own ignorance."

Especially, she wanted to say, looking at this year's crop, of our own ignorance. But she remembered how personally she used to take everything her own teachers had said in class, and she held her tongue.

"The two principles are almost corollaries. If we fail to remember that *both* of these statements are true—that we are the users but we are also the used—we will fail to draw necessary distinctions, and in consequence of that, we will have Jews ecstatically leaping into box cars bound for Auschwitz (as Bruno Bettelheim might have fancied), Russian peasants childlike and happy in their servility (as some historians have claimed), African Americans in need of paternal guidance (as, not so long ago, they were thought to be), 'Untouchables' pleased with their caste because it affords them an opportunity to expiate past errors, and women who serve society best by sacrificing themselves to it. We will say: Everyone is complicit with history. It is, that is, on occasion important—important to *history*—to say, 'I have suffered, and that other person is the cause of my suffering.' This was Plath's landmark discovery. Like all landmark discoveries, it's one that requires time before it can become a part of the map of consciousness."

People do despise a claim of suffering, she thought. They call it "a victim mentality" and equate it with sloth, greed, helplessness. Someone confesses, "I am a murderer," and a thrill runs through the crowd (and there is a crowd), but if someone else, such as Sylvia Plath, says, "I was the victim," people turn the other way, ashamed to be associated with failure. Yet it is just this breach of politeness, this violation of convention both liberal and conservative, this apparent—though not real—assault on the idea of original sin that is essential if the world is to be saved. The victim who refuses to recognize that she is a victim, whose pride insists on bearing the burden of responsibility—however much more attractive personally she may be (because she makes no demands on the world) than the victim who confesses she is a victim (as—ah!—Christ did on the cross)—will in the end do no more than her duty toward the world. She will never learn to love it. And the merely dutiful cannot be trusted forever, even if they succeed in performing their duties forever. At any moment, the work of duty may become too great, leaving them to collapse under pressure of it, hysterical, erratic, resentful, angry, and, in short, absent. Plath, without fully knowing it perhaps, must have been trying to find her way from duty to love.

But after class, at home, propped on pillows to watch the television at the foot of the bed, a softly sullen rain banging its head methodically against the windows, Ava felt hysterical, erratic, resentful, angry, and, finally, absent. Absent from the world. Why should she call Tony to let him know Boyd was going to call? Why should she do anything, ever again? She turned her head into the pillows and sobbed, feeling sorry for herself, feeling guilty about feeling sorry for herself, feeling angry about feeling guilty. Angry, angry, angry!

And slothful, and greedy, and helpless.

After an hour she made herself get up, wash her face, comb her hair, fill out a form for placing books on reserve at the library. In the past, she thought, her mistake had been to tell people too much: if she cried for an hour, she told them she had been crying for an hour. But all you had to do to be considered as sane as anyone else, she was beginning to see, was just keep quiet.

Tony

■ BUCHANAN was suggesting that they all "take a meeting." Buchanan and himself and Claire and Ava. In Los Angeles. He said he would have tickets waiting for Tony and Ava at the counter at O'Hare.

Tony wished he could say, You've reached the wrong number. He wished he could say, This is a recording, Buchanan. He wished he could say, Fuck off, please. Why the hell hadn't Claire or Ava warned him?

"I don't think this is such a good idea," Tony said.

"I think I have a right to do what I can to save my marriage."

"You should be talking to Claire. You should be talking to Ava Martel. There's no need for you and me to talk."

"Cut me some slack," Buchanan said. "My life is talk. I would like us to have an opportunity to negotiate, or at least come to an understanding of the situation." He laughed nervously. Tony could imagine eyes darting, an Adam's-apple jerking up and down, sweat darkening shirtsleeves. Everybody had the same symptoms. "This is what producers do, Ferro."

"Why don't you and Claire come out here after the kid's born? That's not so far off, you know." He had made arrangements for Griff

Klimek to notify him when Ava went into labor; Klimek had told him the child was due in January. There was a winter chill in the air already. Lake-effect snow flurried past his windows. The down comforter was already on the bed. It would be January before you knew it.

"We have to talk now. You must see that," Boyd said.

If Ava had warned him maybe he could have thought of a way out of this, she and Buchanan must have cooked this up together.

Unless it was Claire's idea. But if Claire had already told Buchanan that she wanted a divorce, why would Buchanan pursue a meeting unless he hoped to stop her, but if she had not told Buchanan, did that mean she was vacillating and Buchanan had thought up this meeting as a way of making a grandstand play for his wife? Wouldn't Claire have called with the news if she had already asked for a divorce? Why was she putting it off?

Was she falling out of love with him?

"No, I don't think I do see that. I think it might be better for all concerned if a certain distance were maintained." Had Buchanan said he was going to pay for his ticket? What was this, largess? Did Buchanan imagine he was Howard Fucking Hughes? Orson Fucking Welles? Michael Fucking Eisner?

That exhausted Tony's list of Hollywood producer names

"Distance," Buchanan echoed. "What distance. This is a dance. Do-si-do. We're partners in this, like it or not."

Tony thought about hanging up. But what would that accomplish, besides making Claire feel insignificant, Ava furious, Buchanan shitty.

"Look," Buchanan said, and a suppliant tone had entered his voice, a beggar had taken up a spot on the sidewalk in his throat, a panhandler had found a street corner in his larynx and was holding out a palm. "Maybe a meeting won't change anything. It will make me feel better, is all. We can just sit around and have a civilized discussion and if nothing else, we'll all understand one another a bit better. There can't be anything wrong with that. It's not as if we haven't all helped to create the situation."

It was two in the morning. Claire's husband certainly didn't give a damn about waking people up, Tony thought. Movie producers must think everyone lived on their schedule. Tony had rounds in a few hours, a lecture to deliver immediately after, a tennis tournament that night. And Ry wanted him to drive up to Marshfield for their son's twenty-first birthday celebration on Saturday. He had promised Yvonne he would go over her tabulations before she drafted their new proposal to the National Institutes for Health.

He would do all these things. He could not bring himself not to do the things he was asked or expected to do, so he was, he supposed, still the same person he had always been, he would even take a meeting.

Tony sighed. "If you try to pay for my ticket, I'll beat you to a pulp."

"Fine," Buchanan said. "That's fine. I understand."

"I doubt it."

"Then you'll make it clear to me when you get here."

"So," said Tony, "this is what you do as a producer? Wheedle?"

Boyd

■ HE downed a Quaalude and slid into the tub, letting the hot jets of water stream over him, stretching his neck back on the rim to get rid of the kinks. He tried to keep his mind on work. He had had the idea that the time was right for a revival of romantic comedy. A comedy kind of thing where you have two men, two women. *And a certain light-heartedness, a certain astringency, an unexpected, American frankness, headlong narrative passion, and poetry, heard in Hollywood for the first time since the forties.* The wrong couple get pregnant. A child is born—a star is born. A child is born—not in Bethlehem. The wife and the doctor ride off into the sunset together, on horses stabled in Santa Fe. The girlfriend keeps her baby *and* her job, thanks to modern morality and also tenure. The producer . . . the producer takes a nosedive into despair. In the lexicon of psychological determinism, despair is a river that runs through Little Rock. The producer takes a dive into it and he comes up dripping, a male Ophelia, river grass and black-willow leaves clinging like leeches to his naked body, his balls his only bouquet.

Tony

■ HE wandered out to the kitchen, his bachelor kitchen, to start the coffee. Taking the white bag of Mocha Java from the freezer and shutting the door, he leaned forward against the refrigerator, closing his eyes and pressing his forehead against the cool, noncommittal, lustrous steel.

Ava

■ ON the plane, next to Tony: "I'm sorry this is awkward for you," she said. They looked like a married couple, child on the way. Everyone could tell now.

Tony just looked at her. He didn't pretend that he hadn't heard her, but he didn't say anything. She started to tell him he could do her the courtesy of replying. He could give her credit for recognizing his situation and trying to help him be comfortable in it. Then she castigated herself for her sudden burst of anger, even if it had been a silent burst, and even though it was less anger than annoyance. She remembered that he hadn't *had* to take time off from work to come with her to L.A. and was doing it only because, even if he was a cheat and a louse, he was a decent cheat and a decent louse and not, what, an ax murderer. He must really love Claire—at least enough to realize that Boyd loved her too and to respect him for that. Clearly, he had been unwilling to say no to Boyd. But maybe guilt had been a part of the reason for his acquiescence, too.

When she shifted in her seat, the small hard white pillow behind her back slid to the side, and Tony caught it and slipped it back into position.

A married couple, child on the way. This was what she had not so long ago envisioned: she and Tony, together. Now, sitting next to him—each of them (she could tell it was true of him, too), avoiding using the armrest for fear of accidentally touching the other's arm—she could see close up, once again, the way the outside corners of his eyes seemed to leak into a vanishing point. He bent down to get a book out of his briefcase. His back muscles moved under the cashmere pullover. The hardness of men's bodies was like mechanical engineering, something she wanted to understand, a kind of knowledge.

She would have pulled down the shade but he might think she objected to his reading. She closed her eyes against the glare but then snapped them open again, afraid she might drift and doze. Her mouth would fall open. She might snore a little. She tried to see what he was reading, but he was holding the book at an angle that hid the running heads, and he had removed the jacket from the book. Maybe he wasn't actually reading; maybe the book was just a prop, an excuse for not talking.

Then she would not talk.

Then, sitting next to him while he read, or pretended to read, she found herself feeling as if she had kidnapped the baby and by bringing it along had made him an accomplice, and the worst part was not the stealing but that she had made him an accomplice. "Look," she blurted, "I can't account for anything. I don't understand how things turned out like this any more than you do."

"Don't you? You had something to do with how they turned out."

"So did you."

He slapped his thigh with the book. "I didn't make you pregnant."

"Correction," she said. "You did." She saw him blush, a glow beneath the dark complexion like a coal fire.

"I never intended for you to get pregnant."

"I know," she agreed, thinking she could have reminded him how there had been a time when he had not quite *not* intended for her to get pregnant.

"And I for damn sure did not make you pregnant with Buchanan's child."

"That's true," she conceded. "Buchanan did that. Although he probably wouldn't have if you weren't having an affair with his wife."

"Am I hearing this right? You're blaming Claire and me for what you and Buchanan did?"

She knew she couldn't make a legitimate case for what she was saying, even though what he said she was saying was not what she had thought she was saying. She had thought she was reminding him of her miscarriage. She stammered, "Well, it's partly why things have turned out like this."

"You cannot make me responsible for your actions."

I never even made you responsible for *your* actions, she thought. "No," she said, "I can't do that. And I wouldn't try."

At that, he seemed to relax, reclined his seat, and returned to his book.

She wanted to ask him if he ever missed her, but she knew he would say no. Even if he did miss her—and stupid as she knew she was being, she still hoped he did, at least now and then—he would say no, because he would want her to understand that there was no going back, there would never be any going back. And she understood that, didn't she? She was having a baby. She was entering the future. She had no illusions about going back, ever. If her heart had illusions—well, those were hearts for you. Hearts were weak, fragile, accident-prone. Hearts were like children, needing care and guidance. He should know that.

But a man who broke your heart once had already shown he would break it again, given half a chance. She would not ask him if there were moments (and that was all she hoped for now) when he remembered and regretted that she was not in his life anymore.

She held a short debate in her mind about whether to ask him what she thought of next, but she couldn't see any real reason not to. "You said she made you feel free. Do you still feel that way?"

And truthfully, she wanted him to say yes. She thought it would be wonderful if he could feel a kind of emancipation from all the restrictions and expectations with which he had surrounded himself.

She turned her face toward him. They were so close, with their heads on their headrests, that they could have kissed.

He faced front and said, "It's a long flight. I'm going to grab a nap." Then he closed his eyes and turned his head toward the aisle.

Tony

■ *HE must have lost his mind what was he doing flying with Ava Martel to Los Angeles to take—take!—a fucking meeting with Claire and her husband how had he let himself be talked into this. He had had enough of sitting next to a pregnant woman (but was it awkward for him? no, of course not, unless she meant awkward for him to have to acknowledge her existence, but what did it matter whether strangers took him for her husband) who by the way was wearing the tennis sunglasses he'd given her did she mean to make some kind of point wearing them he wondered. He and Ry had traveled quite a bit when she was pregnant with their son this was a rerun except for the sunglasses, he had not given Ry any sunglasses shaped like tennis rackets but otherwise it was a rerun and he did not need reruns in his life of all people Boyd Buchanan should understand what he meant.*

God, he had not fully grasped how diabolical a scheme Buchanan's insisting on a meeting had been. It was Machiavellian. What were the politics here? What was the hidden agenda? Were he and Ava to rediscover each other, embrace in a slow dissolve? Maybe he was meant to reflect on the error of his ways, see redemption in her third trimester. But he couldn't forget Buchanan's pleading on the phone, the voice faintly off-colored by a tincture of melancholic mania, as if the fellow were about to leap to his death from a high building but in good spirits, the leap of a man convinced that something better had to be awaiting him at the bottom. Tony imagined that people about to commit suicide might smile, quicken their step, that their faces might brighten at the prospect of escape. It was possible, then, that for Boyd Buchanan this meeting of the four of them was not an attempt to seize power but the opposite—a planned crisis, a way of strapping a grenade on himself.

Although Tony barely knew him, he was saddened by the man's pain, of which he was becoming more aware with each in-flight mile. He got a book out of his briefcase and tried to read it, but he wasn't concentrating very well; he could feel Ava's gaze intent upon him, could almost hear what she was thinking—but not quite, and that was what was maddening, the almost-but-not-quite knowing what was going on in her mind.

"Look," she said, "I don't understand how things turned out like this any more than you do."

He couldn't believe it when she said that—who did she think had been responsible for the way things turned out if it wasn't her, would she please answer that?

"It wasn't just me," she said. "You could have behaved differently too. There's something called free will."

He wondered how free anybody really was. The so-called butterfly effect, for instance. You were born and that set in motion a ripple not just in space but in time—or you were the ripple itself—and the next thing you knew you were on a plane to the City of Angels, in coach with your ex-lover who was carrying the child of the husband of the woman you expected to marry.

"You said once that she made you feel free," Ava said. "Do you still feel that?"

He turned his head away from her, facing the aisle and reclining his seat. The stale air, the packed seats—he was getting a headache. He felt crowded in more ways than one. Why was it so difficult to enjoy life? He was in the business of saving it; he believed it was worth saving, but why was it so difficult to enjoy? He kept his head turned so Ava wouldn't see that tears had formed in his eyes, surfacing from God knew where.

Ava

■ "DO you feel all right?" Phaedra asked. "The trip didn't upset you?"

Phaedra asked her this in the green and gray condominium on Wilshire. The mini-Levolor blinds sliced the glare, which seemed to spin off the Lalique vase, its clear glass circled with wide white stripes.

"I'm fine. Did I tell you Boyd's place in Santa Fe is gray and green too? Is that a coincidence, or is that a coincidence?"

"What are you going to do now?"

Phaedra had on eye makeup. Her eyelids were like small gold hinges and whenever she blinked she seemed to be a jewelry box opening and shutting.

"I'm going to wait a while longer," Ava said, "and then give birth."

"And then what are you going to do with the baby? With yourself? Would Boyd Buchanan marry you?"

"I don't think so," she said. "For one thing, he's already got a wife."

"Surely divorce between the Buchanans is imminent."

"I wonder if that subject will come up." They were meeting that evening: she and Tony and both of "the Buchanans." All very civilized.

Or: perfectly savage, looked at another way.

"I kind of doubt it," she added. "I don't think Boyd can conceive of life without Claire."

"He's conceived *a* life without her. That might revise his thinking."

"Green and gray," Ava said. "The combination suggests serenity but life, too."

"Caspar and I will come with you, if you want."

"Oh, I don't think so. I think these people"—she was surprised to hear that phrase in her sentence: *these people*. And she had slept with two of them! What did this mean?—"I think these people are way too uptight for that." It was true, she thought; they were much more tightly wound than she was. She guessed that was why she was the one with a history of coming apart. She had never been put together all that successfully to begin with. Her childhood had scattered pieces about the room, a screw was left loose, essential gizmos had rolled under the couch and never been retrieved. From the beginning she had been patchwork: make-do and jerry-rigged. She had done the best she could with what she had, but for most of her life her father had just been looking in the other direction. But this meant she knew how to scrape by, and she didn't think any of the others did. "They're pretty private, you know, in their own ways. Not like me."

"What's like you?" Phaedra asked, smiling.

"My life is a tabloid," Ava said. "Or would be, if anybody wanted to pay me for an interview. I'm the original tell-all girl."

"No," said Phaedra. "I think you'd like to think that, but will you tell Boyd that you're falling in love with him? Will you tell Claire that you want her husband to be a father to his child? Will you admit to yourself that you are no longer in love with Tony?"

"Who told you these things?" Ava said. "What makes you think even one of them is true!"

For a moment, Ava felt the floor tilting upward; it seemed to be levitating.

She gripped Phaedra's hand.

"Are you all right?" Phaedra asked again.

Ava waited while the floor straightened out, the windows returned to eye level.

"I'm okay," she said, taking her hand back. Then she laughed. "But speaking of pregnancy, let me tell you, it's a good thing Tony isn't trying to drive up the old Hershey Highway now. I have hemorrhoids."

"You couldn't pay me to go through another pregnancy," Phaedra said. "Not on your life."

"I offered her money," Caspar said, materializing from the study, where he had been working on a brief. He stood behind his wife, his hands on her shoulders. "She wouldn't take it. I had to spend it on a forty-foot sloop instead."

Phaedra reached for Caspar's hand and held it to her cheek before letting it drop. "The old Hershey Highway? Ava Martel, really!"

Boyd

■ FERRO arrived first, at eight o'clock prompt. "Please be seated," Boyd said. Like an usher, I'm talking like an idiot usher, he thought. A drink, he could use a drink. Though he had never admitted it to anyone, not even himself really, he still told himself his abstinence was temporary, a decade or two of hanging tough and staying dry and then they'd invent something that would let him drink again.

Claire had put out paté, goat cheese, a pitcher of martinis. Then she had disappeared.

Had said she had changed her mind and preferred not to be a part of this. And left him holding the body bag.

Had simply walked out. After everything was arranged. After Ferro and Ava had made the trip out here. He should have called Ferro and Ava to tell them Claire was not going to be here, but then they wouldn't have come to the meeting either. And anyway, he had thought maybe Claire would go straight to where Ferro was staying, and if so Ferro would already know Claire planned not to be here and maybe Ferro would talk her into coming back to the house.

But no, it was just he and Ferro in the living room. In the movies there were always women present to smooth these moments. Ladies, not just women; ladies with high-heeled shoes and pearl necklaces and dresses that flared into full skirts, accentuating their small waists. Dresses with darts under their bosoms. Ladies made the repartee happen, provided motivation and character analysis. Ladies passed the paté. So how was he supposed to act with Ferro?

He poured him a drink.

Ferro was wearing a cashmere sweater. Boyd couldn't help wondering if Claire had bought it for him.

"Where's Claire?" Ferro asked.

The doorbell rang. Boyd went to answer it. As he opened the door, a taxi was pulling away, down the canyon in the direction of the ocean, behind Ava's back. It was drizzling, and Ava looked as though she had been crying but when she smiled he saw that the tears on her face were raindrops. She took off the scarf she'd draped over her hair and showed him how wet it was, the scarf, still smiling, before she stuffed it into her coat pocket. He hung her coat for her and held her for a minute, feeling the softness of her breasts and the firmness of her belly against him like forgiveness, and then led her into the living room. She wasn't wearing pearls or high-heeled shoes, and her waist was definitely not what he remembered his aunt calling a "wasp-waist," but she had a scarf, and, he didn't know why, just because she had a scarf he wanted to sing hymns of praise in her honor, he wanted to fill her arms with dozens and dozens of long-stemmed roses, he wanted to do anything that would let her know how glad he was that she was here.

He led Ava into the living room.

"Claire's not here," he said, at last.

"Fuck," said Ferro.

"Pardon?"

"I rescheduled clinic appointments to come out here."

"I'm sorry," Boyd said.

Ava had taken a seat on the couch opposite the Queen Anne chair Ferro was occupying and piled the silk taupe pillows behind her back. Boyd could not look at her without remembering what it had been like to sleep with her under the stars in Santa Fe, and the memory of his desire for her was bittersweet.

"What do we do now?" Ferro asked.

"You must think I have a script in hand," Boyd said. "I don't." The script was still in development. Final cut in January. "I just thought it would be a good idea to talk things out." He looked at Ferro, trying to figure out how to address him. "Tony? Do you mind if I ask what your objectives are, as you see them? Once we know what it is each of us hopes for in the way of an outcome, we may be able to prioritize, compromise. It may be possible to work things out to everyone's satisfaction." For example, he thought, I might excuse myself and go into the bathroom and blow my brains out and thereby cease babbling like a complete moron.

"Objectives? I don't have any objectives," Ferro said.

"He's free," Ava said. "Not tied to objectives."

Boyd saw the look Ferro shot Ava, a killing glance. What was I thinking, he thought, to ask everyone to come out here so we could sit around and wish each other dead? Have I lost my mind? I used to be reasonably intelligent, an ept or at least not inept guy, calm on a set, goddamn charming at black-tie affairs, and now I'm a loose cannon.

Ferro was explaining himself. "I don't have objectives because I think you owe it to Claire to find out from her, first, what it is she wants. I don't want to impose my wishes on her," Ferro said. "Where is she?"

Where was she?

"Do you have mineral water?" Ava asked, and Boyd thought that she meant for this question to be a secret between them, a reference to that meeting in that place on Wilshire, when she'd offered him alcohol and he had made it clear that he was in recovery. A way of letting him know that she, too, remembered everything that had passed between them. Her heart-shaped mouth looked so friendly, it always did, even when she was serious or sad or upset.

"I guess," Boyd said to Ferro, "that what I want to know is whether you intend to get married." *To my wife*, he meant.

Ferro seemed to be focusing on the floor. As if he were trying to convince himself that this conversation was not taking place. Maybe Ferro didn't want to marry Claire after all, maybe he had just been screwing around. Well, he had better want to marry her! What a callous fucker the man was. Boyd was not going to let him toy with Claire's emotions, he was not going to allow his own life for that matter to be invalidated for no good reason. If Ferro and Claire weren't going to get married they had had no business falling in love and fucking up what had been a perfectly good, going concern.

Boyd put the heel of his palm to his own forehead, confused to discover where his emotions had taken him. He felt baffled, befuddled, like a middle-aged king on the verge of becoming an old fool. He glanced quickly at Ferro and Ava, hoping neither had followed his thoughts. Ava looked undisturbed, even cheerful. Ferro was still staring at the floor as if hypnotized by the grain of the wood.

"Intentions," said Ava, still smiling. "They're a lot like objectives. Can you be free if you have intentions?"

"That's enough, Ava," Ferro said.

Boyd bent down to hand Ferro a refill. He felt he was walking a fine line—between being a butler and grilling the guy his daughter had brought home for permission to date. Will you treat my wife right, will you promise not to hurt her and, er, by the way, if your intentions are less than honorable I'll kill you.

Ferro reclaimed his gaze from the floor. "Are you going to marry Ava?"

Boyd could hear that Ava's breathing had stopped.

"I am married," Boyd said, seized by an urge to laugh. It wasn't that anything was funny, it was just that the situation seemed to provoke him to laughter, a reflex action, like too much sunlight making you sneeze.

"You feel no responsibility for the child? No compunction?" Ferro asked.

"I promised I wouldn't interfere," Boyd said, now carefully not looking at Ava.

"I can handle everything myself," Ava said. "Really, I can, Tony."

"Right. You're so strong and independent. A woman of steel. This is why you were in the loony bin," Ferro said.

"What loony bin?" Boyd asked.

"It doesn't matter." Ava kept her face in profile.

"We're going to have a kid and you think it doesn't matter whether the mother is fit to raise it?"

He was attacking Ava now, and he didn't know why.

And why, although she had surely resumed breathing, did he have the sense that she had not, that she had moved from one plane of existence to another—as if the first, which required breathing, had become suddenly unbearable to continue upon?

"I'm fit," she said. "You know what? I am going to be a great mother. I am going to be a *much better mother* than either of you two. I might even turn out to be a better father than either of you."

Boyd's heart was as heavy as a tombstone. He felt as though he had already died inside. He sat down on the piano bench. They had a Steinway in the living room, though he didn't know why they had a Steinway in the living room. They had art on the walls, and that made a bit more sense, given Claire's profession. But why did they have a Steinway?

"I'm sorry," Ava said, biting her lip, that lip he found so sexy, looking at Boyd at last. "I didn't mean that. I just got carried away, you know?"

"I feel responsibility," he said. "I feel compunction." He clasped his hands together and let them dangle between his legs. He was wearing jeans. And his own cashmere sweater from Claire.

Ferro was leaning over the platter of goat cheese, as if deciding whether he was up to it. He fixed himself a cracker. A little blizzard of crumbs fell from his lips and dropped onto his front.

"Have a martini," Boyd said, waving at the pitcher and glasses.

"No thanks."

"It was my business," Ava said. "Not yours. It's never been anybody's business but mine."

"Maybe Boyd would welcome an opportunity to express his sense of responsibility," Ferro said. "Maybe he even *intends* to."

This time, when Boyd looked at Ava, he caught her eyes directly, and he could see hope in them. She could deny it, but he could see it the same way he used to be able to see right through the water—if the angle of the sun was right—to tell if a bass was finning just off the bottom.

Ferro stood up, brushing crumbs off onto the floor. His fixity had given way to agitation, as if he'd just done a line. He began to pace and swing his outstretched arms back and forth, as if exercising. "Claire should be here," he said. "What's the point of this, if she's not here."

Boyd was recalling the flicker of hope in Ava's eyes. It must be hard, he was thinking, to listen to the men in your life bemoan the absence of another woman.

Hope for what? he also thought. Have I led her to hope where I told her there was no hope? She said she wouldn't, but when do we ever know what we hope for until we find ourselves hoping for it. I have sinned.

"I have sinned," he said.

Which brought Ferro to a sharp stop.

Ava rested her hands on her stomach. Perhaps she thought he meant the baby, too, was a sin, but he didn't mean that. How could anyone ever mean that? He meant that he had hurt so many people—Ava as well as Claire, the child, of course the child, even Tony Ferro.

Now Ferro was leaning over him. They had swapped positions.

"You've sinned," Ferro said. "That's great. What else? You've repented? You want to be absolved? I absolve you. Of everything except not telling us that Claire wouldn't be here. If you had told us, we could have saved ourselves a trip."

"She didn't decide this until five minutes before you arrived."

"*Why* did she decide this?"

"She decided she didn't want to meet Ava." Claire didn't want to look at Ava and realize that his child was inside her. She said it would be different after the child was born. It would be a separate being then.

"And I was so looking forward to meeting her," Ava said, her voice as creamy as a cat's purr.

"So what do we do now?"

"I don't know, Tony. I guess nothing. The next trip will be ours, if it's okay with Ava. Claire and I would like to come out when the baby's born."

"What?" said Ava. "What are you *saying*?"

"It's my child, too, Ava. Even if you plan to raise it yourself, I would like at least to set eyes on my child, just once."

"Didn't I hear earlier that you were not going to interfere?"

"Not interfere. Just—this is important to me. I don't know if anything has ever been this important to me. Tony said he thought it would be okay."

"Tony said—! Good Christ, who gave you any rights in the matter, Tony?"

"When I called him to set up the meeting," Boyd said, "Tony mentioned that the birth will take place at his hospital."

"It's not *his* hospital. So did you think you'd be there too, Tony?"

Ferro spread his arms as if he were going to say something that required a great deal of space, but then he let them fall back to his sides.

Come on, man, Boyd wanted to say, *I can't do this all myself! Be present!* But he didn't know exactly what he meant by *this*.

"And Claire? Claire, who can't stand to be in my presence, is going to be present at the birth of my child? I don't think so," Ava said.

"No, she wants to be," Boyd said. "She really does. We talked about this. As difficult as it is for her, she wants the child to feel wanted by everyone."

"As difficult as it is for *her*," Ava noted.

"We *should* be there, Ava," Boyd said. "One of the reasons I wanted to have this meeting is to let you know that I've had my will rewritten. To include the kid."

"Did Claire agree to that?" Ferro asked.

"Did I agree to that?" Ava asked.

"Certainly Claire agreed. How could she not? There are some things in all this that are perfectly obvious, you know."

"Yes," said Ava. "But which ones are they, exactly?"

Ava

■ SHE had dried her face on her scarf and followed Boyd into the living room—tracked his boots, anyway, not yet ready to look up. When she did lift her head, she saw Tony seated on a chair next to a coffee table with a silver pitcher on it. *He was wearing that sweater.*

Maybe she should have brought Phaedra and Caspar, she thought, feeling a need for reinforcements. Where was Claire? In the kitchen, probably. Even in the new millennium, wives would be found in the kitchen. She was disgusted by this—had she not spent her life educating younger women toward a greater sense of entitlement?—and yet part of her envied Claire for having that defined role, that purpose, that value.

She sat down on the couch—with Boyd's help—and while Boyd and Tony were talking, she sneaked the pillows behind her back.

Boyd announced that there were martinis in the silver pitcher.

It was so swank, she thought, the way the silver gleamed, beads of sweat glistening on the pitcher's sides as if sewn into the silver.

As Boyd and Tony talked—or as, mostly, Boyd talked and Tony glared at the floor as if he were angered by it—she rested against the pillows and waited for Claire to appear. She felt like Jean Simmons in an old movie, or Anjelica Huston in a less-old one. Of course she looked more like Jean Simmons. Not that she looked all that much like Jean Simmons.

Ava wondered what it was with men that made everything a contest. A push-pull, tug-of-war, arm-wrestling match. Jockeying for position. She let them lob their balls back and forth. But then suddenly—it seemed sudden to her, since she had not thought anything important was taking place or would take place until Claire came into the room, she heard Boyd say, "Claire's not here," and then he asked Tony what his intentions were regarding Claire and then Tony said, "I don't know. Are you going to marry Ava?"

The question suddenly right there, too soon, or not soon enough.

She had the sensation that Ava was someone else. Who was she?

Oh, yes! That's me! I'm Ava.

Please, Tony, she thought, her throat closing against an impulse to burst into sobs, take back that question I don't want to hear the answer.

Her heart stopped. Came to a screeching halt as if a traffic light had just turned red.

"I *am* married," Boyd said.

It started again. She returned to the land of the living. Perhaps a part of her heart stayed dead. A corner, not a space so big a person couldn't walk around it.

"Do you have mineral water?" she asked Boyd. "Or tonic?" She had been careful not even to let a bottle of wine breathe near her for eight months.

Tony could be such a prig. A beautiful, sexy, son-of-a-bitch prig. Listen to him, she thought, Mr. Righteous: "You don't feel any responsibility for this child that you conceived to spite your wife?"

"That's not why he—I mean we—conceived it," Ava offered. "Let me explain. Boyd was haunted by a growing awareness of his own mortality." She was being only half-facetious.

Trying to be droll, she discovered an edge of sarcasm to her voice that, she realized, she had not allowed herself to reveal to Boyd before. But it was time he recognized that she was not weak or vague.

"I promised not to interfere," Boyd answered Tony.

As he said this, Ava saw a new desperation drive through Boyd's blue eyes, something fast and dangerous, something that could cross a dividing line. She realized that he no longer understood why he had promised not to interfere. Perhaps he had begun to feel that he had been wrong, done the wrong thing for the child, by promising not to interfere. But surely it was the right thing?

"This baby is nobody's business but my own," Ava said. "There's no law that says I have to have a man in my life."

"Sure," Tony said. "You are fantastically strong and independent, a veritable woman of steel."

"I promised, but— We're going to have a kid," Boyd said.

"I'm going to have a kid," Ava said.

"Ava, Claire and I would like to come out to Chicago when the baby is born."

"What is this, why are you two giving me the third degree? Boyd, you are not pregnant! Tony, you are not pregnant! Get this straight." And Claire? Boyd had just explained that Claire, who was not in the kitchen, had ducked out on the meeting specifically in order to avoid her. Why would she even consider allowing Claire to see the baby?

"We want to help. We want to provide for the child. We've talked about this, about rewriting our wills—"

Shit, now her heart had gone into hyperdrive, she had to keep her face smooth, untroubled, show no signs of the fact that her heart was speeding through outer space and time warps.

"Would you please stop pacing?" Ava said to Tony. "You're making me nervous."

"I wish Claire were here," Tony said.

I'll bet you do, Ava thought, I'll bet you wish she were here to take the heat.

"She was going to be. At the last minute she felt she just wasn't ready for this, you know? But we'll be there for the birth."

"What! Says who?" Her shrill cry reminded her of the peacocks in the Memphis zoo.

"Only with your permission, Ava, that goes without saying—"

"No, it does not. And now that you've said it, you do not have my permission."

"Please think about it, Ava. Tony said he'd let us know when it's time."

"He did? Tony said that? He said he'll let you know when it's time?"

It seemed to her that Boyd answered her in slow motion. His voice came to her through a tunnel. "Yes," he said.

"Tony thought he had a right to say that?" Ava tried to absorb this information. "Maybe I don't want you there," she said. "Maybe I'm having a baby, not throwing a party. Maybe WASPs are not social."

Claire

■ THEY were going to think she was antisocial. They were going to think she was a coward. They were right on both counts.

She was in her office at school, standing by the window while she waited for her computer to boot up, letting herself dream—daydream, evening-dream—as she observed the glow of the city at night. The screeching, wounded sound of the city—the last gasp that it took every night—was mercifully muted by the closed window, the maze of stone in the garden below. She was trying to think of some reason for being here, but of course there was no reason for her to be here. Except that she did not want to be *there*. At the last minute, it had come to her that she did not have to be *there* if she didn't want to be there.

She made herself a pot of tea. Then, sitting down at her desk, she leaned forward on her elbows, the tea still standing unpoured, resting her chin on a double fist. She kept thinking of all the people she'd known who were now dead. Her parents; her mentor, who had died unexpectedly two months ago, before the festschrift could be completed, so now the volume would be a tribute, but not something that could be placed in his hands at a banquet. And so many others, for you could walk through a cemetery now and find all kinds of people you used to know. AIDS had claimed many of them, young artists and art historians. Or else accidents. Or just time.

One of the things about somebody dying was how it brought you back to the present. Not the past, but the *present*. Ordinarily you walked around thinking that all those people in your past were really still there. Your parents were still sitting at the table writing checks and worrying. Your first lover—not counting Boyd—was still flying an airplane in Kashmir. And you were still the girl or the young woman you were, you were lovely and energetic and well-intentioned toward everyone and you had plans, a lot of plans. Then someone died and you realized that the girl or young woman you had been when you had known that person was dead also. That was reincarnation—the new self you became when the old self died, which it did again and again, countless anguished times.

Not long ago, a friend had said to her, "We must begin to prepare ourselves for many, many losses now. For you see, we are going to lose so much, and not only friends. We are going to begin to lose ourselves, now. All this time, we have remained more or less who we were, but in the next ten or fifteen years we will become unrecognizable, even to each other, even to ourselves." They would hardly know their own faces in their own mirrors.

"Then we'd better have something to put in the place of ourselves," Claire had said.

How odd, to think that her place would be taken by a child conceived by her husband and Tony's former girlfriend. It was an idea to which she was beginning to accustom herself. As painful as it was to realize that this was the best she could do, she also understood that fate or fortune was giving her a second chance: not a biological destiny, but nevertheless a new life that her own had somehow—inadvertently, unwillingly, even farcically; but none of that mattered, did it, not in the least—helped to create. She wondered if Ava Martel were capable of grasping this reality. Presumably, Ava Martel thought of herself as Sole Mother and Proprietor. But whether Martel was aware of it or not, she had given Claire something to put in the place of herself. And I, thought Claire, have given her something to put in the place of ourselves.

Tony

■ IT was not that he had been handing out invitations to the birth of Ava Martel's child. It was that Buchanan had seemed so much to need something from him. He didn't even know what, exactly, and how could he? But: some kind of consent, or recognition. So he had said to him, "I'll let you know when the baby's born." That was all! It was not as if the advent of a baby was a secret. But, he thought, it was quite a lot as if Buchanan were a wounded bird.

Ava

■ THEY called it an *arrival date*, as if it were coming in on a certain flight. They called it a *due date*, as if it were a bill that had to be paid at a certain time. She marked the days off on her calendar.

She had refused to let them tell her whether it was a boy or a girl, but she was sure it would be a boy and so she bought things for a boy baby, ignoring everything she'd ever read about the adverse effects of cultural reinforcement of gender differences. She bought blue blankets. Phaedra sent her a cradle that she and Caspar had stored in their condo's storage unit, and Marilyn presented her with a chest to keep baby clothes in, and Ava painted both items blue—but then the fumes began to make her sick and she had to give up painting anything.

She gave exams and graded them, and she ate dinner on Christmas day with Marilyn and Gordon, and a week later, having already experienced false labor, she timed new contractions by the watch she kept on her nightstand and in the evening called Klimek. When he asked how far apart the contractions were she told him they were indeed the thirty minutes apart he had said they should be when she called, and he asked how long they'd been going on, and then he said it was time for her to go to the hospital. "I'll meet you there," he said.

"The last time a man told me that," she said, "he stood me up."

He laughed warily. He knew about her history, that she'd met Tony while she was in the hospital psych ward. "I don't want Tony to know," she told him.

"Now, now," he said, "Tony's just concerned about your welfare. And after all, he's my colleague."

"Oh *well,"* she said, "since he's your *colleague."*

"You're in labor," he said, gently, as if this were an excuse for her gibe.

"I've been supporting myself all my life," she said. "I've been in *labor* since I was sixteen. What I'm in now is *pain*."

She called a cab and picked up the bag she'd packed and placed by her front door and waited for the cab to come. And later, much, much later—she had a good idea, now, of how long an eon was!—when the baby, a boy, was swaddled and handed to her, she wanted to apologize to Klimek, to Tony, to every doctor who'd ever existed, and every nurse, except, always excepting, those who monitored the hallways in the locked ward upstairs as if it were a sinister high school, because it was clear to her now, so clear, that doctors and nurses were messengers of God's grace, since it was they who brought beautiful babies into hospital rooms and laid them in one's arms. It was they who said things like, "He's perfect." It was they who said, "Ten fingers, ten toes." She touched the back of her fingers to his small cheek, still fiery red as if he had been working out, and she supposed in a way he had, and his skin was so soft she was afraid even a single tap of her fingertip might bruise him. *I'm in love*, she thought, the nurse taking him away again, and fell asleep.

She dreamed this dream: A giant female wasp floated down from the ceiling, segmented antennae waving in the stark, winter sunshine, mouthparts thick with longing and satiation, covering Ava's arms with shimmery membranous wings, Ava's face with her dull black head, Ava's body with six enwrapping legs and an attenuated thorax and abdomen attached by a thin stalk. She pinned Ava to the bed as if Ava were prey that had been paralyzed and then she tenderly inserted her ovipositor, transferring a delicate egg to Ava's own protective nest. And Ava woke with her nerves buzzing, her vagina as alive as a hive.

Boyd

■ HE and Claire waited in the lobby, or whatever the room they were in was called. Claire had brought sandwiches up from the cafeteria, and there was coffee from a vending machine. He did not know how Ava would feel about their being there. She had never come right out and said definitively no. Or had she? He could no longer remember. But she could still say no. All he wanted was a glimpse of his child. He didn't even know if she would put his name on the birth certificate. Claire was pale, she needed lipstick. He could not believe he had done this to her. It made him wonder what other harm he was capable of. But he tried not to think about that now. He didn't want to think about anything except his child.

Ava

■ WHEN she woke, they brought the baby back to her. With the equipment stowed, the delivery room now looked like a hotel room, or more precisely, a room in a bed-and-breakfast, vaguely Victorian, the kind of room that had woven straw baskets filled with potpourri petals and, on the pseudo-mantel, crocheted dolls, and a sampler over the mantel, but no fireplace. She thought she would have been content in a cave, on a bed of pine needles and maple leaves, with her son beside her.

"You have company," the nurse said.

Her first thought was Marilyn.

"Lots of folks," the nurse said.

"I don't believe it!" Ava said.

The nurse stopped doing what she was doing and looked at Ava. "What a strange thing to say," she said. "Why wouldn't you believe your friends and family are here to see the new baby?"

"I don't have any family."

She thought of her father. She wished he had come, but of course, he wouldn't.

"And no friends, either?" The nurse wore white pants but her top was black, long-sleeved cotton decorated with three felt flowers, one pink, one blue, and one yellow. The petals and leaves were sewn to the top but the stems were loose loops of yarn. She had a broad face and wore glasses and earrings, and her spongy shoe soles seemed to put a spring in her step.

"I didn't invite them."

"Then they must be *really* good friends. People who show up even when they're not invited really want to be there."

"Are you a Sophist?"

"No, ma'am, I'm not Lesbian, but I can tell you've got folks out there who really care about you, irregardless of their sexual orientation."

Ava frowned. Had anyone ever truly loved her? Marilyn, Phaedra—she believed in sorority, but after all, she was not a Sophist either. Didn't she always say her father had always been looking in the wrong direction whenever she did something special—swished two in a row from the foul line, got asked out for the first time, gave the valedictory speech? He hadn't cared.

The nurse chucked the baby under his chin. "You just brought a new life into the world. You don't think that's special, something to celebrate?"

Ava bent her head over her baby boy, wrapped in his blue receiving blanket.

"Why else do you think those three duded-up wise guys went all that way to see the Christ child?"

"I'm no virgin," Ava muttered.

"That's a relief," the nurse said. "I've never known exactly what it is Sophists do in bed."

And then Ava looked up and caught the nurse's eye and they both started to laugh, both women, and Ava realized she had never in all her life been so happy, and she realized that, having given birth to the most miraculous being there had ever been, she could not possibly deny the world acquaintance with her son.

Boyd

■ IN the hospital room—*birthing room*, they called it these days, it was fixed up just like somebody's room at home, you'd hardly know you were in a hospital—he stared at Ava Martel and her child, *his child*, and the child seemed to him so closely connected to him that it was a secret agony not to be able to hold it and touch it, a secret ecstatic agony like Christian self-flagellation. He felt faint from the onslaught of feeling and had to sit down. In an icy voice, Claire said to Ava, "Would you mind if Boyd held the baby?"

"I shouldn't—" Boyd said, getting halfway up again.

But Ava had handed his son over to his wife—without hesitation, as if she had already made up her mind even before the question was asked—and Claire was passing him along, and now he was holding his son, holding him, this vested share in the future, this dream.

He saw how cold Claire's face was and knew it was not the coldness of contempt or hatred but the coldness of having to control the passion of despair. He felt ashamed of himself for being so elated and tried not to let her see how elated he was. "Please," he said to his wife, "maybe you'd like to hold—"

She turned away quickly. Stepped over to where Ferro was standing, watching. Ferro was in his greens, wearing a hairnet. He had come from surgery.

"I wanted to be sure everything was all right," Ferro said.

"I told you everything was going to be all right," Ava said.

"You're the doctor," Ferro said.

"Tony—" Claire said, and Boyd recognized the way plea, warning, and embarrassment came together in her single spoken word, the tone of it, like a confluence of tributaries.

Boyd heard these voices but there was a muffled, underwater quality to them. He seemed to himself to be swimming in the blue ocean of his son's eyes.

The telephone rang and Ava answered it. He recognized the names of the people she had stayed with in L.A. "Phaedra!" she cried with a pleasure that was like sex. "Caspar!"

"*Caspar?*" said a new voice, jovial with skepticism. It was Ted, entering the room with Yvonne. "Well, well, well," Ted said. "Well, well, well."

"That's my husband," Yvonne said, holding his arm. "Never at a loss for words." They had brought champagne, and plastic cups appeared, and the sound of the cork popping was like a firecracker. "Think of it," Yvonne said, "it's almost still New Year's. Hello, Claire," she added.

"Hello, Ted," a black woman with dreadlocks said quietly from the doorway. "Shouldn't you be in Tibet or somewhere?"

"South Pole," Ted said. "Changed my mind." Boyd saw him squeeze Yvonne's elbow. Yvonne had put on a little weight, and it gave her a smoother sort of look, as if hungry, empty places had been filled in.

The bald man with the black woman said, "Oh my God. The Frequent Flyer miles lost!"

Ava was whispering into the telephone.

"Christ, Marilyn, you can do that, you know," Ted said defensively to the black woman. "You can change your mind about a trip."

"Hi, Mom," Marilyn the black woman hailed Ava. "Hi, cutie," she said to the baby—his baby, who was, he smiled to himself, a cutie. He decided he liked Marilyn Whatever-Her-Last-Name-Was immensely.

She was outfitted in a dashiki and a parka and mountain-climbing boots. "Take off your coat," Boyd said to her, feeling it was right that Ava should have all her friends with her. It was *meet.* He felt he had just learned the true meaning of *meet.* It meant that this was good: people who had been on the planet for a period of time and had gotten acclimated to its weathers and varied topography welcoming a new person in their midst. He thought Ava deserved it, too, the attention and care, a moment of stardom. He wanted to tell her how proud of her he was. But how could he say such a thing, with Claire here. And Marilyn Whoever was still standing next to him, him with his son in his arms, and hadn't he been saying something to her . . . oh yes, "Stay a while."

She ignored him. "'lo, Tony," she said, nodding at Ferro. "Nothing new in this for you, is there. You already know what it feels like to be a father."

"What do you mean by that?" Ferro asked, and even though she had acted as if he didn't exist, Boyd felt another surge of affection for this small, fierce woman, whoever she was, who could stand up to anyone, even surgeons.

"Nothing in particular," she said. "Whatever you want it to mean. Four percent of all black men in this country are in jail. Maybe you can think of this white child as a form of crime prevention. Is that how you think of it?"

Before Ferro could manage a response or retort Boyd heard Claire say, cool as air conditioning, "And how's your curriculum vitae these days, Marilyn?" He realized his wife must have met Marilyn on one of the trips she'd made here to tryst with Ferro.

Marilyn shrugged.

"Don't worry about it," Claire said. "Everyone hits a dry spell."

"Not with Ted and me around, they don't," Yvonne said, pouring the champagne into the plastic cups.

"I decided this would be a good year to stay home," Ted said, to nobody in particular.

"Phaedra says hello to everyone," Ava said, hanging up.

"Who the hell is Phaedra?" asked the bald guy, whose name was apparently Gordon Something.

"A friend," Ava said. "A friend who says hello."

"Always to be preferred," Gordon Something said, "to a friend who says good-bye."

"Things aren't always so simple," Tony said. "Sometimes the real test of a friend is whether they can say good-bye."

Ava was sitting up, her back against the raised head of the bed. Her face looked paler than usual, which made her brows darker, a deep sable, as if they were wild, swift, minklike creatures that might flee at any moment. There was a look of alarm on her face, as she surveyed the room. "Boyd?" she asked, and it seemed to him that she was reaching for him to save her.

"It's okay," he assured her. "It's okay."

He had tried to speak softly, but Claire heard him, and he saw her take yet another step in Ferro's direction.

He didn't know what to do. He didn't know where he belonged. Each time he moved toward his wife, she moved closer to Ferro. He didn't understand how just by moving toward somebody you could drive them away. He had this child in his arms and he wasn't even sure what he was supposed to do with it. He held it out, like an offering, and said, "But hey, is this kid going to be a studio head, or what?" And when nobody said anything, he said, "I mean, is this kid going to be a major player, or what?"

Tony

■ GRIFF Klimek had beeped him, as he said he would, the beeper going off on the middle of the bedroom floor, the floor of the bedroom that was like a secret, the windows so high, the walls so close-mouthed. He had rolled out of bed, arrived at the hospital in plenty of time. The baby had been born about 2 A.M. Tony had gone back home, slept a bit more, gotten up again to do rounds. The day started with a defective valve, and then there'd been an infant, an infant like this one except it had been a girl and its heart had been on the wrong side of the chest. She died. Then he did a bypass.

He was here on his lunch break, except it was already three in the afternoon.

Even looking tired as she did, her hair pushed behind her ears, her face almost as pale as that of someone in shock, Ava was very pretty, sitting up in bed—it made him remember how gentle he'd felt toward her when he first met her, wanting just to hang out with her all the time and look at her mobile face, her big eyes and her mouth that was a lot like a valentine when she smiled. She was beaming, clearly euphoric, and he had to give her credit, she had done what she set out to do even if was a crazy thing to have done. *Crazy like a fox. Crazy like a very foxy lady.* She had her arms outstretched, the white nylony sleeves falling away from her narrow wrists, handing her child to Claire. And it was Claire who had asked for it, Claire who had said do you mind if my husband holds it and Tony respected the classiness in that, a disciplined strength of generosity only Desirée could ever have matched—regal Desirée, who, like Claire, could have no children. Claire passed the child along to Buchanan, who accepted it with a disconcerting humility, taking it into his arms as if it were something he didn't quite deserve.

The room was blue with blue chintz curtains, and the January sunshine seemed trapped in the curtains.

The telephone rang, and Ava chattered happily into the receiver. Then Yvonne and Ted came into the room, Ted going Well well well and Yvonne threatening to drench everyone in a shower of champagne. Claire was standing next to Tony and moved a little in his direction, and Tony wanted to put his arm around her, pull her closer, but he would not be rude.

"Hello, Claire," Yvonne said, and it seemed to Tony that a signal had passed between the two women but he had no idea what message had been sent. Women were like Morse code, their bodies always tapping out cryptic messages that you had to know how to decipher before you could understand.

Marilyn came into the room. She had abandoned her cornrows for Rastafarian dreadlocks. This was the Midwest, for crying out loud. Did she think she was going to turn Chicago into a third-world country? Did she think she was going to start a revolution? Marilyn spoke first to Ted. "Aren't you supposed to be at the South Pole?" she asked, as if unready to forgive Ted for not being where he had said he would be, though Jesus Christ if you had decided the South Pole was not where you wanted to go should you be strung up and quartered for that?

Ted blinked as if, unconsciously, to prevent Marilyn's dreadlocks from turning him to stone.

Gordon appeared at Marilyn's shoulder. How had he avoided being turned to stone? But then again, Tony thought, maybe he hadn't. Gordon, Tony thought, might indeed be stone—stony-hearted, a stone for a soul.

Marilyn was wearing kinte cloth like a flag of allegiance, and a parka and mountain-climbing boots. She nodded at Tony. "Well, Tony," she said, "you're familiar with what this is all about, aren't you. Being a father."

He did not know what she was driving at. "What do you mean by that?" he asked as neutrally as possible, but he felt the flutter of anxiety.

"Whatever you want it to mean," she said.

Oh yes, now he saw! She was telling him it had been his duty to father Ava's child, a duty not to Ava but to his race. It was his obligation, as she saw it, to sire and raise more black children. He almost laughed. He had not sired and raised a son with Ry out of a sense of duty but because love mandated itself, it required expression. He did know what it meant to be a father, and what Boyd Buchanan must be feeling, and he appreciated the depth of both the joy and the fear that a father felt and under other circumstances could have imagined himself in a sort of communion with Buchanan, but Marilyn, with her notion that people could be assigned responsibilities, would never have a clue, not a clue, regarding that. Besides, who in this room could talk of duty? Didn't they understand what had transpired among them, how they had all used one another to get what they wanted? That was the way of the world and nothing either to magnify or expect to change. Ava had used Buchanan, the poor sucker, to get her child. Buchanan had used her to strike at Claire. And he himself—he and Ava had used each other, hadn't they, first to escape their separate lives that had come to seem boring and restricted, and then it had been necessary, for him at any rate, to escape a future as limited and choking as the past they had created. So he had used Claire, and Claire him. And what about the child?

A dark thought occurred to Tony then, a thought so dark he could not tolerate it for long. Suppose the child had used them—not the child, exactly, but the idea of the child. Suppose biology had its own ambition—an intent if not a purpose—which it would realize no matter what. And it used them the way parasites use hosts, to live. For that was all its ambition—to live, live, live.

He felt sick. He had been on his feet for too long, the baby girl had died. Before he could think of how to respond to Marilyn, he heard Claire ask, as if inquiring after a spouse or lover, how her c.v. was looking. Chalk one up for Claire, he thought. This is how you play hardball in the groves of academe, and he was glad to see Claire holding her own, this had to be a hell of a situation for her to be in.

Someone uncorked a magnum and Yvonne began pouring champagne into plastic cups.

"You think I like always having to go off to weird places?" Ted asked, seemingly addressing the room in general. "Sometimes I'd just as soon go to, I don't know, France. Nobody ever asks me to go to France."

"Phaedra says hello to everyone," Ava reported.

"Who's Phaedra?" asked Gordon. "How's this for serendipity, Ted? Ava has a direct line to *Phaedra*."

"I've never read Racine," Ted said.

"You've never read anything," Yvonne said.

"Phaedra's a friend," Ava said. "She says hello to everybody."

"There's Racine, Wisconsin, of course," Gordon said. "But it's very dairy."

So suppose life just had to keep finding ways of coming into existence and people thought they knew what they were doing but really all they were doing was making more of themselves and pretty soon you wouldn't be able to breathe, the whole world would be like one big body, a huge heart, the thick, pulsing muscle of itself, systole and diastole.

Ava was sitting up, her legs outstretched under the bedclothes. Without makeup, she still looked like a kid. She had a way of turning her head, keeping it high, that articulated the long line of her neck, as if her whole body was a word, a sentence speaking itself. She surveyed the room. "Boyd?" she asked, and when Tony heard her say *Boyd* and not *Tony*, he felt a combination of relief and regret that was like walking between mirrors, making him feel lost among a multitude of himself.

Buchanan responded by moving toward Ava, toward the three of them because Tony and Claire were standing by the head of the bed, and Claire took one more step in Tony's direction, leaning into him.

In the quickest, subtlest way he could manage, he put his arm around Claire's shoulders. I'm here, I'm standing by you, he wanted to say.

Buchanan had the child in his arms and was holding it out, like an offering or was it a sacrifice? "But hey, is this kid going to be a studio head, or what?" Buchanan said, as if maybe he'd gone stupid with shock. Nobody knew what to say. And when nobody said anything, Buchanan said, "I mean, is this kid going to be a major player, or what?"

Somebody has to say something, Tony caught himself thinking, with a clarity that was like foresight, or Buchanan'll go over some kind of edge.

Claire

■ IT was called *a birthing room* but she was thinking it was also a dying room, for her, because she felt as if she were dying. *I wish I were dead*, Claire thought. *I wish I could just die and not go through this*. There was Ava Martel, sitting up in the bed, looking marvelously fragile and in command at the same time, with everyone paying court. It was as if they were gathered around a manger, having come here from far off, even if it was via O'Hare and not caravan. And there was the baby, looking the way babies look, vaguely larval and amazingly unsurprised. Shouldn't they enter the world stunned and blinking, perhaps horrified? But perhaps that came later. And there, directly across from her, was her husband, enraptured by the sight of his child in its mother's arms.

She realized that she didn't really have very many options when it came to playing this scene. There was no room here for self-indulgence or even for righting wrongs that had been done to her. And some had been done. By this woman who was getting away with acting like the Holy Virgin and that was a pretty cute trick when the father of your child was the husband of the woman standing by your bedside. How had Ava Martel claimed this high moral ground when she was just one more desperate female, like the rest of them—like herself, Claire certainly admitted that, but she knew where she stood, while the girl was, alas, politically correct and aesthetically confused, born and bred in a climate of intellectual relativism, ready to believe that everything is a matter of taste or point of view. Ava Martel had no dignity, not even a concept of dignity. Claire had had her own affairs, yes, but she had never interfered with a marriage, she had never brought an illegitimate baby into the world, she had never brought a baby into the world. She had to play everything straight, straight from the heart. Thank God Tony was here. She felt his presence next to her, quiet and contained, like a refuge, a place she could retreat to if she had to but knowing it was there would be enough, would see her through.

But her husband—there was something wrong, emotion was pushing against his face from the inside as if it would burst through, scatter his features every which way. His face was like a stock market that had climbed too high, was teetering dizzily, and would crash. He was like a man on the edge of something, balancing precariously. Somebody has to say something, she said to herself, or Boyd'll go over the edge, she felt so sorry for him, in spite of herself, he was staring at the baby as if it were not just a new life but a new life form. "Would you mind if Boyd held him?" she asked Martel.

"I probably shouldn't," Boyd said, getting halfway up again from the vinyl wing chair he'd been sitting in, a chair that despite the blue walls and blue chintz curtains was the pukey green of morning sickness.

Martel handed the baby to her, and for the fraction of a second, as she passed it along to her husband, it was like touching fire, the child a small flame, blue blanket burning her fingers. Walking on coals? Now her heart caught fire, became a live coal split and spitting.

And Boyd said to *her*, to *Claire*, "Maybe you'd like to hold—"

She turned away quickly and stepped over to where Tony was standing, watching. Tony was in his greens, and he was wearing a hairnet.

He had come from surgery. A coronary bypass, he had told her, is called a CABG, pronounced *cabbage*. She stood next to him, and he stood near the head of the bed, and it felt to her almost as if they were the parents of the woman in the bed and that woman had just given birth to their grandchild. This was how confused things had become!

"I had to be sure everything was all right," Tony said to the woman whose mother she almost felt like *but how could she feel this way*.

"Why wouldn't everything be all right?" said Martel. The long sleeves of her nylon nightgown fell back to the elbows as she raised her arms behind her head, running her hands through her short hair in a show-stopping gesture of—what? Just youthful femininity? Or was it more calculated that that? Claire remembered when she had been that thirtyish age thirtysomething was now the phrase and oh yes, let me tell you Miss or Ms., I put you in the shade by a mile I had you beat I was something, let me tell you.

But she had never had a baby.

The telephone rang. "Phaedra!" Martel cried into the receiver, and again it seemed to Claire that it was unfair, that how the hell many women get to answer a telephone, having just had a baby, and say, "It's my friends Phaedra and Caspar!" Give me a break, she thought but of course as soon as the words appeared in her mind she was disgusted with herself for thinking them. It occurred to her that it was possible that this whole thing was a kind of karmic test, something she had to pass or pass through in order to reach a higher plane or, what the hell, maybe it was just a good old old-fashioned test of character.

"*Caspar?*" said Ted, entering the room. "Well, well, well," Ted said. "Well, well, well."

"That's my husband." Yvonne was holding onto her husband's arm as if she had just discovered that he had one. They had brought champagne, and the sound of the cork popping was like a firecracker or a car backfiring. "Hey," Yvonne said, "it's practically still New Year's. Hello, Claire."

Before Claire could answer her, she heard another voice from the doorway. It was Marilyn Henegar, the black woman who'd been at Yvonne's dinner party that night. "Hello, Ted," Marilyn said. "Shouldn't you be someplace like the Bering Strait?"

"I decided not to go," Ted said. Claire saw him squeeze, protectively, Yvonne's elbow. Yvonne had put on a little weight, and it gave her a smoother sort of look, skin pulled tighter over the mattress of her body.

"It's so sad," Gordon said, drawing the syllables out like taffy, something phallically extensible and self-congratulatory in the way he said it, "so many Frequent Flyer miles foregone."

Ava Martel was still whispering into the telephone.

"It is possible, Marilyn," Ted said, "to change one's mind about a trip."

"You don't say," Marilyn said. She was wearing a dashiki of kinte cloth, and a parka and mountain-climbing boots though there was no mountain in Chicago. There were a lot of tall buildings, but no mountain. "And how are mother and child?" Marilyn asked, leaning over to Ava to kiss her cheek.

"Take off your coat," Boyd said. Always the gracious host Claire thought, trying to be sarcastic at least to herself, at least to protect herself, but it didn't work, she wanted to cry, because it was true, her husband was always a gracious host, a well-meaning person, a kind-hearted, lovely man. "Stay a while."

Claire felt herself go cold inside, as if she could will herself into a state of suspended animation, her body temperature lowered, all her feelings in hibernation. Perhaps she would wake up to the rushing tunes of meltwater in spring, grass reaching its green fingers upward to shake hands with the sky. She would thaw into an attitude of forgiveness that for now she could only simulate.

As if from a distance, as if she were standing far off in the center of a field, a lonely field, Claire heard Marilyn telling Tony that she had read that four percent of all black men in the U.S. were in jail. "Maybe you can think of this child," she said to Tony, "as a form of crime prevention."

"What do you mean by that?" Tony asked.

What *did* she mean by that?

Maybe she meant: Not only should Tony have fathered a second black child but Boyd had no right to be a father. Could she mean that? Could anyone really mean that? No, Henegar was merely as confused as they all were, had not yet sorted her thoughts into a logical sequence. She was speaking unthinkingly, from a passionate belief in the crucial contributions of her own race to human life. Because if she meant that Boyd did not deserve or have the right to be the father of a child and wanted Boyd to pick up on that, Claire could, in all good conscience, kill her.

But instead of killing her, Claire asked, "How's your curriculum vitae coming along, Marilyn?"

What a ridiculous thing to have said, Claire thought. *Why did I say that?*

Marilyn shrugged.

"Don't worry about it," Claire said. "Everyone hits a dry spell."

That's why I said that. So I could say, Everyone hits a dry spell.

Yvonne rescued the occasion by pouring the champagne into plastic cups.

"I decided this would be a good year to stay home," Ted said, apparently waiting for someone to ask why.

"Phaedra says hello to everyone," Ava Martel said.

"And Phaedra would be—?" said Henegar's boyfriend.

"A friend who says hello," Ava Martel said.

"Always to be preferred," Gordon said, "to a friend who says goodbye." Claire wished he would shut up.

"Not always," Tony said, so earnestly that it embarrassed Claire, almost like bad manners, like revealing a secret that should have stayed secret. Although he was a surgeon, he was not particularly sophisticated. But she was irritated with herself for even noticing that. What mattered was his seriousness, wasn't it? (And yet, she had begun to feel a need to drift away from all this seriousness, the seriousness that stood at the edge of this celebration like the witch who comes to the wedding or christening or, nowadays, equity hearing, to make life difficult for everyone present.) "Sometimes the real test of a friend is whether they can say good-bye."

Ava Martel was sitting up, her back against the raised head of the bed. Her face was pale, her brows dark, her hair short. Pretty, but not beautiful. All at once a look of alarm invaded her face. At first Claire thought something was wrong, Martel was having some drastic reaction to the birth or medication, maybe. "Boyd?" Ava Martel asked, and it seemed to Claire as if Ava Martel was reaching for Boyd to save her. Then she realized that Martel was responding to the extreme emotions that had been playing themselves out on Boyd's face, that Martel meant to be expressing her concern for Boyd.

But Boyd had failed to understand. "It's okay," he said, and Claire could tell he thought Martel was asking him for reassurance. "It's okay."

Instinctively, Claire moved still closer to Tony.

Yet when she did so, Boyd seemed to follow her. For one moment she thought, irrationally, that he was coming after her. He had the child in his arms and was holding it out as if he'd gotten confused about which woman it belonged to, as if he might be about to present it to her. I don't want it, she almost said. *It's not mine, keep it, it's yours*. And she leaned into Tony, thinking *He is my sanctuary*, and Boyd said, "But hey, is this kid going to be a studio head, or what?" And when nobody said anything, her husband added, "I mean, is this kid going to be a major player, or what?"

And still nobody said anything.

Ava

■ In the hospital room—*the birthing room* it was called as if the room, not she, had done the birthing—Ava looked at the child that her body had made and could hardly believe that she had done this, had set this life in motion like a chain of events. Even with the medical bustle going on around her, it had been a secret ecstasy to be able to hold him and touch him, a secret ecstasy like self-love. Now Boyd and Tony and Claire Buchanan were watching her and she knew she had to be careful not to let her face show everything she felt, because what she felt was something pure that could be contaminated if it became public—a mountain stream, a place in the woods, a place in the desert.

"Would you mind if Boyd held him?"

With a start, she looked up and realized that Claire Buchanan had spoken to her. "Of course not," she said. She held out the small bundle.

"I shouldn't—" Boyd said, but he was already halfway out of his chair.

Claire handed Ava's son to Boyd, and now Boyd was holding him, awkwardly, like a football.

Your father, she thought, talking to the baby in her mind. She saw the emotion on Boyd's face and knew it must mirror hers and it seemed to her that this shared emotion was rude, a kind of bad manners as if they'd been making love in front of the others. Tony's face had gone dark the way it did when he retreated, as if he'd turned off a light and retired somewhere inside himself for the night. Claire's had flattened, as if under the pressure of all the emotion in the room. "Claire," Boyd said to his wife, "maybe you'd like to hold—"

Claire turned away quickly, stepped over to where Tony was standing. Tony had come from surgery and was in his greens, the loose pants with a drawstring, the V-necked pullover shirt. Ava had always thought he looked so sexy in his greens but now he just looked like someone who cut into people for a living.

"I wanted to be sure everything was all right," he said to her, in that medical way he could adopt.

"I told you everything was going to be all right," Ava said.

Boyd was cradling her child, having an unspoken conversation with her child. All at once she was scared, she wanted her son back.

The telephone on her night table rang. It was Phaedra and Caspar. "Caspar, hi!" she said, hearing for herself how her voice rose and flew into the telephone, escaping from the cage of the room.

She heard a new voice in the room. Still talking into the phone, Ava looked up. Ted and Yvonne had turned up. She felt a bit like a tabloid celebrity trying to have an outdoor wedding and being buzzed by paparazzi with zoom lenses in helicopters. This was not what she had had in mind when she had joked with Phaedra about her life being an open book! There were passages that should stay private, but everyone seemed to think she *required* their presence, that because she was single she would not be able to function without their help, could not manage life on her own. Hey, she wanted to say, you want to help? Teach my classes! Bring my filing up to date! Change the oil in my car! Of course, it didn't help that Tony felt free to discuss her life with everyone. Well, of course Yvonne would know, even if Tony hadn't gotten around to telling her yet, and maybe he had. The medical world was small, Ava knew. When she'd been in the psych ward upstairs, everyone had known everything about her. Why shouldn't they know everything about her now?

"Well, well, well," Ted said. "Well, well, well."

"That's my husband," Yvonne said. "Never at a loss for words." They had brought champagne and plastic cups, and the sound of the cork popping was like a firecracker.

"We heard that cork all the way out here," Phaedra said on the extension. "Unless Tony Ferro finally farted."

Ava hunched closer over the phone. "I can't believe I told you that," she said.

"You tell me everything," Phaedra said. "You tell everybody everything. It's all right. It's the way you are. You even *told* me it's the way you are, remember?"

"Do you tell Ava everything?" Caspar asked Phaedra, from his extension. "Phaedra never tells me anything," he complained to Ava.

"Oh, my friends Marilyn and Gordon just came in," Ava said. "It's a party. A birthday party. Oh, I wish you were here!"

"But we are," Phaedra said.

And Caspar said, "I'd have followed the North Star, but you don't earn any Frequent Flyer miles for following the North Star."

Smiling at Ted and Yvonne from the phone, Ava saw him squeeze her elbow. Yvonne had put on a little weight, and it gave her a smoother, rested sort of look. And Ava thought—*knew*—Yvonne was pregnant. It was pushing it—she was how old?—older, anyway—but she was pregnant and she was far enough along to know it was going to be okay. Well, good for her! Wouldn't everyone be surprised when they found out what Yvonne had managed to pull off at the last minute!

"No, Marilyn," Ted said. "I'm *not* supposed to be in Tierra del Fuego."

"You and Caspar," Ava said to Gordon, cupping a hand over the mouthpiece. "Great minds."

"What's that?" Caspar asked from L.A. "I have a great mind?"

"Ava," Phaedra said, "tell us about the baby."

Ava whispered into the telephone—weight (seven pounds, four ounces), length, the baby's blue eyes. Would they stay blue? All she wanted to do for the rest of her life was babble about her perfect baby, his hands and feet and fingers and toes. Phaedra asked her about the birth; Caspar wanted Ava to enroll him in Harvard Law.

"Take off your coat," she heard Boyd saying to Marilyn, and Ava looked up again and tried to tell him with her eyes how grateful to him she was for the way he was handling everything, looking after everyone. "Stay a while."

Marilyn had gone and done something weird with her hair and Ava felt an upwelling of affection for her friend who had such a bad hairdo.

As she continued her conversation with Phaedra and Caspar, Ava could feel tension building in the room. She heard words—*father*, *jail*, *white*, *child*. "I'm trying to keep up with two conversations at once," she explained to Los Angeles.

She could never understand why Marilyn was so angry with Tony. It even offended her, a little, as if Marilyn were trying to usurp the anger Ava had every right, far more right, she reminded herself, to feel toward Tony. What did color have to do with any of this? Race, she thought, was an outmoded concept. It was as worthless as nineteenth-century nationalism. And gender itself—like everything else, an accident of birth. All these forms—race, gender, nationality—were merely the impulses of particularity, and only life itself was not an accident but an intention, the intention to realize itself in every possible particular.

She felt herself a vehicle for something beyond herself, motivated by something beyond her control. She had planned to have a child, but perhaps it was also true that something had planned for her to have it.

She shuddered as she thought this, not from fear, exactly, but—from fear inexactly, and it seemed to her that the late-afternoon light of winter, timidly broaching the blue curtains, was like a messenger bringing news no one wanted to hear—news of death and disaster, news of a great calamity that had occurred somewhere else but which would have repercussions for the rest of your life.

"We'll let you go," Phaedra and Caspar said, simultaneously, and Phaedra added, "Say hello to everyone." They hung up, and suddenly Ava found herself tossed back into the room again, having to face all these people who knew too much about her.

"Phaedra says hello to everyone," Ava said, replacing the receiver.

"You've been reading Racine again, haven't you," said Gordon, mock-chiding her. "Well, who is Phaedra?"

"A friend," Ava said. "A friend who says hello."

"Always to be preferred," he said, "to a friend who says good-bye."

Tony said, "Sometimes the real test of a friendship is whether you can say good-bye."

Just like Tony to say something pregnant with meaning, as if he were competing with her. If she weren't aware that it would embarrass him in front of the crowd, she would tell him to stop trying to justify himself.

She was sitting up, her back against the raised head of the bed. Her legs hurt, and she had not had a chance to put on makeup. For a moment, while everyone stared at her, she felt self-conscious. She had succeeded in keeping Claire's attendance peripheral, something not to be focused on, but she couldn't do this forever. She had heard her saying something to Marilyn about a c.v. They were all professional women, degreed and independent, savvy about both the pleasures and the demands of the life of the mind: that ought to count for something. "You probably don't know," she said to Claire, "that I did my dissertation on the role of women in labor unions in the early twentieth century?" She laughed at her own joke, and while everyone joined in, she thought about Claire. At first, she had been relieved to find out that Claire Buchanan was not, after all, beautiful. Maybe she had been beautiful once, but no more. But now Ava wished she had had a chance to do her own tricks with eyeshadow, mascara, blush-on. Then she looked at Boyd. He was coming toward her, and carrying the baby with him, but there was a look on his face that frightened her. "Boyd?" she asked, and it seemed to her as if she was calling for him from a long way off. He had the look of a man who was falling over the edge of a cliff, only the cliff was inside himself. She knew what it was like to fall into a pit inside yourself and know that you were going to go on falling into it forever, with nothing to stop you except death.

"It's okay," he said. "It's okay."

But she had no idea whom he was talking to, and she did not think he did either.

He took yet another step in her direction.

She felt rather than saw Boyd's wife move toward Tony, lean into Tony. Boyd held out her baby, like an offering, his arms extended, and said—something—something about a movie studio or the baby being—something—she couldn't hear, and this time it was not because everyone was talking or because she was trying to keep up with simultaneous conversations or because of anything except the loudness of her heart, its rushing like a waterfall into an enormous unmodulated tumult.

Like an offering or a sacrifice, the child raised and held out.

Please, she thought, *let me have my baby back.*

Boyd

■ THE moment had passed, and Boyd tried now to reconstruct it, but every time he felt himself on the verge of remembering all the materials that had gone into the making of that moment, a black wall would rise up in front of him and he could remember nothing. There had been a moment when the child was held in his hands like a gift or a prize, perhaps even a taunt, and he had been about to— But he did not know what he had been about to do. Maybe he had merely been waiting, waiting for something to be done, something to happen that would explain his premonition of doom, his sense that even his elation was predicated on a murderous error.

Even in the taxi on the way back to the airport, he had recognized a bitter darkness bursting out of his heart and flooding his soul, and by the time he and Claire were on the airplane he was thinking and feeling in a cloud of anxiety. They were in first class. When the flight attendant asked what he would like to drink, he said champagne. Claire hissed, "What's got into you? Are you crazy?" and he wondered who she was, this blond woman in a beige suit and silk shirt with a gold necklace worked into the shape of a bow-tie. She was sleek, all right, but she was no one he knew.

"It's a day for drinking champagne. Everyone else has been drinking champagne."

"Boyd! Please!"

He was surprised by the look of helplessness on her face, the way her face lost control of its features so that they seemed to be roaming around, loose and untamed.

Why was he so determined to ignore her? It would hurt her—she would feel sorry—he could not bear to stay sober one moment longer, after all these years—everyone thought he was a fool, anyway—but perhaps most of all, he thought that if he infantilized himself, she would not leave him. She would realize how much he needed her. "If ever there was a day when I was entitled to a drink, today's it. I want to toast my son, even if it's only here on the airplane."

The flight attendant had turned away at the first sign of altercation. Now she returned with the champagne. "My wife will have one too," he said to her, taking the glass. The heat of stupidity rose in his face, and he knew he was behaving like an idiot, but it had become a point of honor: he had to be just as stupid as he really was, he would not go on presenting himself to the world as anything other than himself.

"No, thank you," Claire said to the flight attendant. She didn't look at him. "I think I'll try to get some sleep." She propped a pillow against the window and leaned sideways, closing her eyes. The setting sun slipped in at the bottom of the plastic window shade and made the gold bow-tie gleam.

"They tell you that on an airplane," Claire pronounced slowly, her eyelids still closed, "one drink is equal to two on the ground."

The champagne went to his head in a flash. He ordered another, and then another.

How had that moment taken shape, how had it been put together?

He unfastened his seat belt and stretched out his legs. There was only one other passenger forward of the coach curtain, a young woman in skin-tight black leggings under a tight red Spandex mini-dress with a wide black belt. Her high heels were red. She had her seat tray up and was riffling frantically through a formidable attaché case.

The bitter darkness was in him like a kind of death, a night that would never end.

Martel! he thought—and he glanced guiltily around the cabin, half-convinced that he had not remained silent, he had called out her name. But Claire was asleep; the Spandexed executive, her head bent, earrings falling forward, was scanning a spread sheet; the flight attendant smiled at him but he could tell she was also keeping an eye on him to make sure he didn't get out of line.

Martel! he thought again, and this time her name seemed to him a wilderness of syllables. He'd gotten lost in that wilderness and he knew it was not too much to say he would die out here.

He meant to deplore the compassion he'd felt for her, the affection he'd felt for her, to will himself to an angry numbness. He had let her use him. That she had been candid about what she wanted him for only threw into high relief his own stupidity, because in spite of everything, he had thought that he knew what he was doing. But he had never known what he was doing, and compassion and affection withstood his assault and grew stronger in spite of him.

The champagne and the bitter darkness flowed together, and the moment fragmented, and he felt himself lost in a place that was so barren it did not even bear a name.

Lost in an unnamed place, how could he be found? No one would know where to look for him. No, he had to do something to bring himself back to himself. And drinking—he remembered now, he had forgotten it had been so long, but now his glass was magically full no matter how much he drank from it—was like saying hello to the deepest part of yourself, it put you in touch with whatever part of yourself you had had to set aside in order to get along in the world.

But he felt such disgust with himself. After all these years to have succumbed like this—maybe that was the part of himself he had gotten in touch with, the part that was so disgusting, that wasn't worth a shit, really, when you got right down to it. This part that was underneath everything else and spoiled everything else.

He had been willing to conspire against everything he valued: willing to father a child who would have no father; willing to hurt Claire so deeply that she would never, really, get over it. Whatever of evil had gone on here—or of supreme disregard, a kind of hardheartedness—he had been complicitous with it. Oh, he had done things he had never suspected he would do, and these things might not have violated national security but they had had consequences, they would have more!

So he thought, sinking deeper and deeper into the bitter darkness that was bursting and flooding inside him. . . .

For a time it looked as though they might fly faster than night, but when they landed in L.A., it was dark. On the ground at LAX, he kept bumping into people. He was heading straight for the parking lot but people kept coming right up to him and bumping into him.

"We'll have to take a cab," Claire said.

"What for?" he asked.

"You're drunk. You're too drunk to drive."

"Not," he said, admiring his pithiness.

"Darling, let's catch a cab. We can come back for the car tomorrow."

"Tomorrow!" he shouted. "Tomorrow, and tomorrow, and tomorrow creeps in this petty pace from day to day, to the last syllable of recorded time; and all our yesterdays have lighted fools the way to dusty death. Out, out, brief candle! Life's but a walking shadow, a poor player that struts and frets his hour upon the stage, and then is heard no more: it is a tale told by an idiot, full of sound and fury, signifying nothing."

Claire was staring at him. But she should have been applauding! Why wasn't she applauding!

"I mean," he said, "what the fuck are we going to do tomorrow? I have a son and you have a lover and they are both miles from here. Are you prepared to live with that?" he asked, but his words slurred and he knew that what he had actually said was, "Are you *prepped* to live with that?" It was Ferro's influence, he thought, everything in his head mixed up and insanely surgical because of Ferro. "Don't you know what you mean to me?" he begged, looking at his lovely wife in her expensive, understated clothes, the champagne blouse, that gold bow-tie. "Don't you understand anything?" he cried, amazed by her immense stupidity, and fled from her through the needle-sharp rain, the dark night, the bitter, bitter darkness, to the car.

Claire

■ FOR months after it happened she kept trying to reconstruct that moment, but it always collapsed into darkness. She remembered his question, hurled at her like a stone, and the way he'd run from her before she could answer. She remembered him disappearing into the crowd. She remembered herself standing there and refusing to think, refusing to have any thoughts at all, and then at some point getting into a cab.

A thin, chilly drizzle started up, spitting against the windows of the cab, and thunder tolled in the distance. The driver turned his wipers on, but the rubber backing had come off of one of them and it scraped across the windshield like a fingernail.

Even if she had looked, she would have seen nothing. It was too dark.

When she got home and found he wasn't there, she called the highway patrol. It could have taken him longer to get out of the parking lot, she told herself. He'll walk in any minute, she promised herself, but she called the highway patrol anyway.

She had fixed herself a martini after she made the call, and when they called back a little while later, she spilled her drink on her skirt.

She ran outdoors, into the rain, and she remembered now that her skirt had been soaked with rain and gin. She took off her heels and threw them down on the lawn.

She was standing on something sharp, it had cut her stockinged foot and she was bleeding. She was standing on the side of the road, in Queen Anne's lace, shooting stars, and dandelions. People were swimming down below, it was like a day at the beach, a night at the beach. A cop was holding her back and saying something but she had no idea what, it was as if he was talking in a language she had never studied. Then she heard someone say, "Let's get this woman to the Santa Monica Hospital Medical Center," and she realized, with relief, that she understood the words, she was not in a foreign country.

They reconstructed the accident, not the moment: He accelerated too fast for the curve and started to go off the side of the road. He slammed the brakes down too hard, causing the wheels to lock up as he turned the steering wheel to the left. He turned the steering wheel some more. The Jaguar slid over the edge.

She kept trying to reconstruct the moment, but it kept coming apart in her hands, there was the taste of bitter darkness on her hands, her fingers smelled of bitter darkness. She washed her hands but that smoky odor still clung to them, and she dabbed perfume on her wrists to disguise it.

She kept trying to reconstruct the moment, but she could not look over the edge. She could not look down at the heap of smashed steel and rubber, leather and chrome, the violent slide of mud and torn bushes.

Looking back, she thought she had known as soon as he left her at the airport that he was headed for this edge. She thought she had known this, but it was hard to say for sure. Anything that happened took on the cast of inevitability. It had been an accident—was not an accident, by definition, something not inevitable? But she recalled the emptiness she had felt when he fled from her, and it seemed to her that that emptiness was a foreknowledge of life without him and that she had recognized it as foreknowledge at that moment, even though she had not, could not have, acknowledged it as foreknowledge until now, after the fact.

So she should have done something.

She should have called the police from the airport—but would police have responded to her request? "My husband is drunk for the first time in years and upset and I'm afraid he might have an accident on the way home." Who knows; maybe they would have, and maybe they'd have stopped him in time.

Boyd was dead because she had let it happen.

She could not understand how she could have failed to protect the one man who had always protected her. She had let him drink, drive into the rain, had recognized herself as a figure in a tragedy, doom looming and herself doing nothing to prevent it.

And was this blood on her hands all for the sake of Tony?

She had not even thought to call Tony until the next day, and then, of course, she realized that Ava Martel would have to be told too. She would let Tony tell her. *A surgeon could do that, a surgeon could convey news of death.* There would be no funeral. A memorial service, maybe, later on for the people her husband had worked with over the years. Hollywood always liked a memorial service, which was like a retrospective.

■

She put the house up for sale and moved into a bungalow closer to work. By the time Tony came out to see her, so much had changed that it was hard to know what to say to him. And she worried that she was getting farther and farther away from that moment and would not be able to make her way back to it.

He went out and bought the *Los Angeles Times*, bagels, cream cheese, fresh orange juice. He kissed her on her cheek and spread cream cheese on a split bagel and set it in front of her, and poured her a glass of orange juice, and then he sat down and began to read the paper. She wanted to scream at him.

He must have felt it, her desire to scream, because he looked up from the paper and said, "Things don't stop. You have to understand that. They just don't stop."

"We do," she said. "We stop right here."

He put his elbows on the paper. He was wearing a white sweater, not the sweater she had given him, and he would get newsprint ink all over the sleeves but she said nothing about this. She had said everything she had to say. Her heart was like a cliff she was falling from, but she had said everything she had to say.

"Why?" he asked.

"Why? You have to ask why?"

He waited a long time before answering. "I don't have to ask why," he said. "I want to ask why."

"Because."

He stood up and reached for the jar of orange juice and threw it across the room. She went into the kitchen and tore paper towels off a roll and came back and began cleaning up the mess. "I'm sorry," he said. "That was childish."

She shrugged.

"I'll call you next week," he said. "This can still be worked out."

At night, waiting for the sedative to take effect, she tried to see how it could still be worked out, and sometimes she fell into a dream that was like a solution, but when she woke up she realized it was no solution at all, only a denial. So when he came back to see her, a second and third time, she was on guard against him, not wanting to be tricked by the dream of him.

"You're punishing yourself," he told her, "that's all." Of course, he didn't know how he had begun to irritate her. His quiet arrogance, his secret insecurities, the way he entered her as if he were doing her a favor—these things were getting on her nerves.

She thought that, if truth be told, it wouldn't be out of place for him to punish himself a little. It was not as if he bore no responsibility at all. At least, when they first became involved, she was acting within the bounds of the marriage she and Boyd had defined for themselves. At least as she had understood them to be. Or misunderstood them to be. She was not wittingly breaking a contract or violating the conditions of their life together. But Tony had still been involved with Ava Martel, so that Martel still held expectations and when she learned about Claire had been angry and frightened, and why wouldn't she have been? I would have been, Claire thought, imagining the way her own heart would have contracted, the claustrophobia of blood with no room to circulate, the sickening anxiety. She caught herself wanting to say to Tony, "I am beginning to see how Martel might have felt about us," or *you*, what she really wanted to tell him was that she was beginning to see how callous he had been to Martel, why she had felt cheated and owed, and if she had not felt something was due her would it not never have occurred to her to seek out Boyd, and if she had not sought out Boyd would he not be alive today? Because there would have been no child, no champagne, no argument on an airplane, no curve too tricky to negotiate, at night, while drunk, while hating your wife, the windshield wipers sweeping a speckling, glinting rain back and forth, back and forth—and sitting in the back of her own cab she had traveled right past the spot where he had gone over the edge, right past *him*.

Perhaps this had all been there for her to see before, but she had not been in a position to see it. She had achieved a new perspective.

From this perspective, she saw that Tony had been at least a co-conspirator. She did not wish to absolve herself of responsibility, but she thought how much more becoming of him it would be if he would accept his share of it. Her respect for him—for his profession, his competence in it, his unobtrusive good manners and willingness to help whoever needed help, his way of living in quiet harmony in a society that was still divisively racist—this respect, which had been, she would now say, to her something like a silver chalice, was tarnished. She began to think he was not the man she had thought he was and, even if he was, that he was not the man for her. When she looked at him reading the newspaper, with the air conditioning going on and off, and the sunlight through the window over the kitchen sink on the breakfast table like a glaze, he was a reminder of what she had lost—and she could not bear it, this bad trade she had made, and she blamed him for forcing her into this trade, because had she ever intended more than the sweetest, most exhilarating of love affairs, rejuvenation, something life-giving and not life-taking? She had never, no never, intended a trade! How she hated Tony now. How she resented him for being alive. Yet still she did not say to him *I hate you, get out*, because had she not invited him into her life? He had not led her on, she could not pretend to herself that it had ever been like that.

Oh no, she thought, *I* led; I led Tony on not knowing that for him everything would be, is always, life and death and now it is death not life—but here she thought of the baby, and did not know what to do with the thought. She went to bed earlier and earlier, so she could take her sleeping pill earlier.

In her dream, time was restored to itself, but when she woke she realized that the odor on her fingers was rather obscene, and she held her hands up to her face and smelled the bitterness rubbed into the fingertips, the smoky flavor of her palms.

Why couldn't she remember? Her weakness, her inability to remember, tore at her like a harsh wind. This was what she had to do, she thought, even if it took the rest of her life. She had to remember.

Tony

■ BETWEEN them was a wall that got higher every day, a wall as black as a plague.

When he kissed her, he felt her tongue against his like a burst of bitterness, a sophisticated sensation that flooded his mouth and left him hungry for more.

Afterward, she raged like a fire. She seemed to hate herself for the way her body still responded to his.

He thought she would understand what was happening but she didn't want to. She wanted to build a wall to protect herself. And he hesitated to interfere, because he knew how vulnerable she felt.

But sometimes when she touched him, a flame seemed to shudder through the length of his body, like a wildfire, and afterward, when the fire had been extinguished, he was surprised to find the wall still there, higher than ever.

It seemed to him that he, too, was slow to understand what was happening. Exactly how the wall was being built, what materials went into its construction. He didn't recognize the resentment until later, for example. At first he was conscious only of the guilt—the omnipresent guilt that he and Claire both felt and that had become the source of a series of small embarrassments between them. Like viruses, these embarrassments were barely discernible but multitudinous and consequential. They infected everything. He was not immune. If he made love to her, he found himself almost saying, Excuse me. If he held her close, he wanted to apologize for being alive, for having a body for her to lie next to. He sometimes thought the last time they had looked each other in the eye had been even before the accident, even before . . . well, even before almost everything.

"You have nothing to feel guilty about," he said, speaking to himself as much as to her. "An accident is—an accident. It's something you don't *expect*. An accident changes everything," he continued, thinking of the many times he had conferred with family members, telling them, always, that there was hope, at least hope of a kind. "But not necessarily for the worse."

The contempt on her face when she looked at him was scalding. It made her face red and he backed away as if it might burn him. "Boyd is dead," she said. "That's a change for the better? Is that what you're saying?"

"No. That's not what I'm saying." He sighed, but he tried not to let her hear him sighing—she would take offense at his sighing, too.

"I let him drink. I watched him drive into the rain," she said.

"There was nothing you could do. You couldn't have stopped him."

He wished she could understand that it was the dead man she was angry with, not him. A deep slow resentment was building in her, layer by layer, but when he tried to warn her against it, she accused him of underestimating her. "You don't think very highly of women, do you," she said, and though previously he would have resisted this characterization of himself whole-heartedly, as soon as she said it he became aware of how deeply her self-involvement dismayed him.

As did her complete misunderstanding of her own motives.

As did her thinking that she knew him better than he knew himself.

She was living in a bungalow on a side street, between two other bungalows, the kind of street where the lawn sprinklers run all day and half the night. If you stepped off the sidewalk your shoes got waterlogged. She was here to do penance, and perhaps she realized that, but he did not think she realized that her doing penance was just another way of thinking about herself.

As were all her romances, including her romance with the East, with Indian art, Japanese flower-arranging, Chinese poetry. With a delusional philosophy of detachment.

He had thought that if he could simply be patient she would come back to herself, but that was not what happened. What happened was that the resentment began to build, and each layer that was laid down had to be covered over with something that would keep her from recognizing it. So as the resentment grew, so did the drama, and the drama removed her farther and farther from herself—and him.

This despite the fact that he had come out here when he could, a weekend here, a weekend there, but it wasn't easy, juggling schedules. And there were clinic, operating, teaching, and research schedules. What he had hoped would be a wonderful partnership, two people sharing their busy professional lives, the traffic of it, and a central park where there could be rest and privacy before returning to work, had devolved to mere show, performance in place of life.

He leaned over the newspaper, which he had spread on the table before him, putting his head in his hands. He felt, he thought, run over.

Claire was careening out of control. He kept trying to anticipate her turns, but he was not a psychiatrist. Hadn't he already learned that with Ava Martel?

A surgeon is an auto mechanic, he often told his residents. Sometimes he said, *A surgeon is like an athlete. What counts is how long you can last on your feet.* He was good with his hands; he was capable of great physical concentration. But he was not a psychiatrist, and he hated scenes. He hated the repartee, the cutting comments and psychic surgery of scenes. A touch of flamboyance could be entertaining in a woman, even exciting, but he was essentially a quiet man, not someone who could swap the serious work of repairing bodies for a bit part in someone's passion play. He was not a Philistine: He knew how labyrinthine the mind could be, how a human being could be a test subject caught in the maze of her own mind; he knew that the practical plane was only one dimension, not coextensive with life as it is lived; he knew he himself must be driven by forces of which he was unaware, or not fully aware. But it was a kind of mythologizing that Claire was engaged in, as ritual and false as theater, though she believed in it, thought she was forcing herself to face the truth. She had placed a scrim between herself and him, and she was disappearing into shadow.

He felt sad when he thought about this, thinking about what he had lost. It seemed to him that he had, after all, loved her very much. He had changed his life, broken off with Ava because of her; he had brought her into his circle of friends and colleagues; he had felt such passionate sympathy for her and he still did, despite the resentment building, he admitted, in him.

When the accident happened, his first impulse had been to go to her, but she said *Wait. Not yet. In a little while.* That was when he began to realize that she had not given herself over to him as unreservedly as he had given himself to her. She had never stopped being Buchanan's wife. It had made him uncomfortable to realize this—he was not accustomed to taking a back seat, and it was when he realized that was where he'd been relegated that the resentment began to build in him.

A wall like segregation. A wall like racial intolerance.

Sometimes he thought about Buchanan. He wondered if it had really been an accident, or if Buchanan had driven over the cliff deliberately. Maybe he had thought he wanted to do it and at the last minute had second thoughts. But no—the man had just become a father. Surely a sense of responsibility would have stopped him from considering such a maneuver seriously.

Unless he'd thought the child would be better off with him out of the picture.

Out of the picture.

He conveyed none of these speculations about the accident to Claire, and after a while he began to be able to put them out of his own mind. They were of no use, and if they had occurred to Claire, she had found a way to keep them hidden. He certainly did not wish to introduce them to her. Lying next to her in bed, she on her side with her back turned toward him like a wall, he thought how ironic it was that as a wife she had had no compunction about beginning an affair with him but as a widow, she was afraid to be emotionally accessible, she had closed herself off from him. The back porch light next door had been left on, and it threw into the room a golden oblong, a bullion of light, that reached across the bed and made her hair gleam. He reached out to touch her hair and then pulled back, hand hovering like a faith-healer's for a second of indecision. The numbers of his digital travel alarm pulsed and soundlessly changed.

When she said *We stop here*, what he felt, first of all, was relief. Then that sadness, it was true, because how could there not be sadness over the loss of what you have treasured, but he also felt cheated. She had ruled him out of her life, as if love could ever be unilateral. This made him angry, and yet he was grateful to her for doing it, because it meant he would not have to hurt her. There had never been, he could see, any hope of continuing. They, and what they had together, were casualties too. And since to go on would have been to live in a dead relationship, he felt relief and sadness and anger and gratitude and was eager, yes, eager, to return to his own life, which was both so demanding and so rewarding. Life was pulling at him—Buchanan's was not the only son in the world; he had his own son, who'd announced he would like to drop out of school and go to Africa for a year. "I think we should let him," Ry had said, her face like a balance sheet that read *You owe me*. There was work he had to tend to: conferences, committee assignments, clinical diagnosis, surgery. People needed bypass operations and pacemakers. People had heart congestion. They had angina.

They didn't always drive over cliffs. They sometimes had rupture of the atrium or the interventricular septum instead. They got posttraumatic ventricular aneurysms. They had heart attacks.

You couldn't put these things on hold. You had to be there to take care of them. If you could; and one thing no one understood about his life, not Claire or Ava or Ry, not any of his friends, certainly not his son, was that a surgeon lives in terror. Even the most confident son-of-a-bitch surgeon there is—and he did not claim to be that—lives in terror of making a mistake. You had to focus and not get sidetracked. You did your best and hoped for the best and you did not forget what was important. If you were concerned for anybody at all besides yourself, you couldn't forever keep trying to tear down a black wall that someone was trying to put in your way.

Ava

■ IF she had been awake to the world she would have remembered him—she told herself this—but for months after it happened she had lived in a dream of exhaustion, tiredness in her brain like a room with the light turned off, and it was sweet, this dream, it was not bitter, it was a place of rest. A place where she could go to forget.

When Tony called to tell her, she was still in the hospital but she was getting ready to go home. They turned you out of the hospital almost immediately now. Medically speaking, having a baby was not much more of an event than going to the dentist or getting your hair done! She was packing her small suitcase, and a nurse was in the room, holding the baby whose father was dead, just like that, but then there was a sense, she saw, in which he'd never been real, not really a part of her life anyway, or the baby's. He had never been cold enough to survive, she thought, after Tony had hung up and while she was replacing the receiver in its cradle, you had to have a certain degree of coldness in you to get through certain things that was one thing she had learned from her earlier stay in the hospital, upstairs where the women were like a

Greek chorus, their gibberish a runic text unscrolling itself through a library of tragic nights.

For months afterward, she was so busy with the baby and work that she had to put on hold all questions of meaning, though sometimes it seemed to her that there *was* a meaning, something of depth, a sign like the sign of a fish, say, and it might suddenly burst to the surface and reveal itself, but it never did because she was too busy. Then, too, she wasn't eager to think about him—her instinct, when she heard the news, had been to protect her son, as if thinking too much about the past could imperil his future. She did not want to be reminded of accidents, contingencies, uncertain or dangerous conditions of life. . . . In the blue and white nursery, she blew on the mobile of brightly colored cardboard stars and hedgehogs to make it turn above her baby's crib, the stars a promise of brilliance, the flat little hedgehogs helpless creatures in need of love.

She was so tired, working, and caring for her child, that she was never fully awake, but it was a sweet grogginess, not bitter, it was a kind of forgetting, like drinking from a river from which no sign ever surfaced. It was a kind of forgetting, this darkness that carried you away from yourself, this dream.

There had been a moment—a moment of—a moment in which, or during which—a moment of terror so pure that all thought of herself had been filtered out of it, leaving only the fear itself, numinous and sheer, fear like nothing else, like itself only—there had been this moment, and then it had been succeeded by another moment, and that by another, and the simple thought of all these moments made her so tired that she nearly fell asleep, reading her students' term papers and taking care of her baby. Sometimes something seemed about to burst to the surface, a sign or memory, but she was asleep, asleep to the world, and it never did. Marilyn came over to talk now and then, and the students were touchingly considerate, not complaining when Ava came to class with the baby strapped to her chest ("My little drum," she called him, doing a drumroll on his back; "my companion-in-arms"; "my kangaroo"). She carried him to faculty meetings, stepping out of the room only if he began to fuss or cry. This was a world where you could do anything you wanted to—you could have a child without a husband, you could take your child to faculty meetings—if you could get pregnant, and find someone to get you pregnant, and didn't mind being poor and didn't mind being tired all the time. As long as none of this interfered with her work, no one objected. Sometimes it would half-cross her mind to go up to someone and tell everyone what she'd done—all of it, every last crazy trifling bit of it—and see if they minded then, but she never did crazy things like that anymore.

Though once in a while, exactly when she was trying hardest to say and do the appropriate thing, the fissure that had always existed between herself and the world would open up again, the way a crack in the wall will reappear as a house settles on its foundation.

As when she turned to Gordon during a meeting and said brightly, "At the faculty meetings in Memphis they served lemonade and cookies!" And he simply smiled at her, as if he thought she was daffy but was fond of her anyway.

But would lemonade and cookies be so terrible? Was there a law that said you could not eat a cookie and be a scholar too?

At Midland U., apparently, there was such a law.

And as when, at a reception for a visiting sociologist, a dean who was, clearly, unaware of her existence as a member of his faculty, said, "And who are you?" instead of saying, as she knew she should have, "I am in Women's Studies, and next year I will deliver the keynote address at the International Conference on Women in Academia, which will be meeting in Reykjavik," she answered him:

"I'm a woman who when she comes makes little mewing sounds."

The dean stared at her.

"So sue me," she said. And she turned and walked away.

But she had not violated the Midland U. Speech Act!

She had not done anything she could be locked up for!

She couldn't help thinking, *Boyd would have appreciated that.*

But for the most part she kept her mouth shut, too exhausted to open it. When Marilyn's father died, and Marilyn married Gordon in a small ceremony in the landmark synagogue no longer used for Sabbath services but rentable for weddings of any faith, the couple with their faces shining like a pair of candles lighting the early dark of a cloudy day, the lake choppy, the clear, tall windows featuring compositions of wind-tossed trees, their leaves kaleidoscopic and as richly green as emeralds, Ava did not bring up the old subject of Marilyn's father and how she had avoided confronting him. Marilyn's peau de soie gown was straight and slimming, columnar as a lily, and her brown arms gleamed in the lake-light of late afternoon. She wore sprinkles of tiny stars in her newly short, curly hair. Gordon, who had grown a beard, was sleek in a bespoke suit from Savile Row. Ava looked at them admiringly, as if they were art, something one might encounter in a museum or gallery, but not a part of life as she now knew it. (She did not know marriage. She did not know life with a man. She knew motherhood.)

She received a letter from a lawyer in California informing her that probate of Boyd Buchanan's estate had been completed and that he had left her and her son the house in Santa Fe. She called the lawyer, and while he explained procedures to her, she imagined Boyd signing the codicil, his Mark Cross pen a flash of light in the shaded office as he scrawled his name, oddly embarrassed by his own signature.

She didn't need to remember, she thought. A child was more than a memory.

Something cold drove through her heart, fast as a Jaguar.

"What am I going to do with a ranch?" she asked the lawyer. "I'll have to sell it."

"Mrs. Buchanan hopes you will accept the gift," the lawyer said. "She has asked me to say that she's prepared to help make the gift feasible for you." Claire had offered to pay for taxes and caretaking. Boyd had wanted his child to know this place that had been so special to him.

As she knew it now, life was a hurrying to do this task and that chore, to shop and cook and clean, and prepare lectures—and that keynote speech!—and grade papers and serve on committees and write recommendations, and somehow find time to be a mother.

There were regular checkups for the baby. There was the night he developed a high fever and an earache. There was the week the water heater stopped working and the water got colder and colder, and she was desperate to get it fixed but every other water heater in Chicago, evidently, had quit the same week. There was the time the baby peed in her face while she was changing his diaper. But there were also his smiles, his gurgles, his delight when she sang to him.

Although the pediatrician was in the same hospital as Tony, he was in a different part of the hospital, and she never ran into Tony when she took her son for his checkups.

On a few occasions, she saw Tony at a distance—on campus, at the grocery store, at a gallery opening she went to with Marilyn, leaving the baby at home with a sitter for the first time. She turned her back in his direction, examining the lithograph furiously, willing him to leave, and he did. Marilyn jabbed her in the ribs when the coast was clear. She wondered if he was still with Claire, but she wouldn't ask. She wouldn't! And she didn't. He was not a part of her life, not now anyway, and would never be a part of her baby's life, which was happening so rapidly. Already the trees were unfurling their green flags and the lake had metamorphosed from still photography into a motion picture with sailboats and windsurfers gliding from blue frame to blue frame, and her baby boy was pulling himself up on the bars of the crib, and before very long it would be registration week for the fall semester and time to do a new syllabus.

Yet, though Tony made no effort to get in touch with her, she began to hear from Claire: the simplest, shortest notes, nearly always accompanying a gift for the baby. A toy duck, soft and cuddly and almost as big as he was. A scrub mitt with a puppet face on each finger. A silver baby spoon. Should she return the gifts? They had been sent to her baby, and belonged to him, not to her. She imagined someone returning a gift she had sent to a newborn; she couldn't think of many gestures that would be crueler. So she found herself writing thank-you notes to Claire Buchanan, who was after all in some sense a part of the baby's family. There was even the occasional phone call, and since Claire always wanted to hear about the baby, it was not hard to fill up the conversation, and after a while, Ava didn't even stop to feel awkward. "Like all new mothers," she told Marilyn, justifying the conversations with Claire, "I just want to talk about my child endlessly. And," she added quickly, "you're a good enough friend not to say you noticed that!"

Married Marilyn asked her how she was going to manage the trip to Reykjavik.

Ava didn't know.

One day Claire Buchanan called and said she had arranged for a memorial service for Boyd. "I hope you can come," she said. "I hope you will want to bring Chase."

Ava talked with Claire from the living room while keeping an eye on her son in his portable playpen. He had the toy duck's beak in his mouth. She had not yet put the storms in and the weather was warm enough to crack a window. A modest breeze crossed the room and ruffled her son's silklike hair. "Why now?" Ava asked.

"I feel ready," Claire said. "That's all."

"I have classes—"

"Please. Boyd would want you to be here. We both know that. He'd want Chase to be here, too, I think."

"I don't know—"

"I know how taken up your time must be. I know this doesn't mean as much to you as it does to me. But it means so much, so very much, to me. Maybe to Chase, too, someday."

Ava said nothing.

"Please—"

"I'll see if I can manage it," Ava said.

How can I not go? she asked herself, buying strained peaches and bananas for Chase. *How can I not go and take him.*

Part of her wanted to flee. She was ready to fly to Reykjavik right now! Part of her, the part that was sensitive to her own guilt, so sensitive that she avoided feeling it, the way someone who'd gotten sunburned would avoid touching her own skin, was moved by Claire's plea. Part of her wanted to honor Boyd.

Time had passed. She could begin to remember him now.

All of her wanted her son to have been at his father's memorial. Chase should be able to say to himself, when he grew up, *I attended my father's memorial.*

She would have to go. Even Marilyn and Phaedra agreed she would have to go.

Phaedra said, "This is not about you or Claire. It's about Boyd." Marilyn, back from her deferred honeymoon in Mauritania, said, "You didn't clone Chase. He has a heritage. Would you want to deprive him of it?"

Claire

■ FOR the service Claire has chosen a chapel in the canyons. The chapel sits on a wooded slope from which one can see other, distant slopes, the soft green haze of them stretching to the horizon as if moss could grow on the north side of the sky. The sky itself is almost turquoise with the California light that is like the light of a semi-precious stone and is found more often in Big Sur country. Perhaps it is a sky with a sense of occasion.

Private, discreet. Those were words Claire had emphasized when describing for the minister her own sense of what the occasion should be. By Hollywood standards *private* and *discreet* are probably what it is. And yet half of Hollywood seems to have wended its way here.

So many closeups, but oddly small, as if seen through the wrong end of a telescope; as if on a movie screen the size of a postage stamp. She was familiar with this phenomenon but is disconcerted by it anyway, because so many of the famous are here: The singer/dancer whose last picture bombed but whose videos still top the charts. Eric Harrold, out of rehab and giving interviews about the virtues of court-ordered community service. Sally Darlington, Boyd's secretary, her face blotchy, and tight as if Ziplocked to keep it from being spoiled by exposure to despondency, in a back pew.

A-listees. B-listees who had been on the A list for a time but whose careers had been reduced to cameo appearances and infomercials, or to serving as parade meisters; or maybe they had always been on the B-list, negotiating their lives with one foot still in the wings or the orchestra pit, and perhaps, often enough, the whole show had depended on them—the character actors, the stunt doubles, the prop men and film cutters and set designers, the writers. When had Boyd met all these people? How was it they had wanted to come, months after her husband's death, to this out-of-the-way chapel in the woods where not a single reporter from *Entertainment Tonight* ran interference with a microphone and a cameraman?

There are a few of her own friends, academics and artists who scoff at lists but certainly have their own. She sees the Wylders, now elderly, the couple who had mentored Boyd in the beginning—guiding him toward success, which he'd had, even if he failed to perceive it as such—being ushered to their pew, and they seem to be growing older even as they take their seats, their backs burdened by the loss of their younger friend, who should have outlived them.

Inevitably, there is the aging actress whose face lifts can no longer hold her features up, so that they seem to have clustered in the lower half of a narrow frontal plane. There is the middle-aged actress whose face lifts have stretched her features out from the center, elongating eyes and mouth and giving her a fish-face flattened by unseen pressures, with an eye on each side of her compressed skull. It was Picassoesque, the way women in Hollywood disassembled the geometry of their bones in the name of art. She half expects to see a woman with a head facing front and sideways at the same time.

A woman constructed of cubes and depthless surfaces, every inch of her painted.

They pull at her, these people, reach for her, hands stroking her hair, patting her arms. The air around her trembles with the small, tenuous kisses they deposit an inch or two away from her face, quick, phantom smooches.

She feels like a bank teller, knowing these kisses are supposed to go on account, be returned someday.

But for now she has the use of them.

There are no flowers in the vestibule or main room but she ordered ferns for the front of the room, palm fronds for the entrances to the two aisles, cedar boughs to be placed just inside the door, and the green fragrance wanders through the chapel like a guest hosted by a slight breeze, which lifts a collar here, stirs a sleeve there, animating people with its bemusing reminder of a real world. People grow restive, and they are only just finding their seats.

Ava Martel arrives. She climbs out of a cab. She pays the driver and he sets a large carryall, a stroller, and a car seat on the grass beside her. She has Boyd's son in her arms. Claire watches as Ava looks around to see where, exactly, her life has brought her now.

Claire approaches her. She says hello. Ava shakes Claire's hand.

They both look at the boy. "Hello, Chase," Claire says. He regards her for a brief moment, then turns his face upward to his mother's.

"He's getting so big," Claire says to Ava, picking up the diaper bag and stroller and car seat, though the truth is he seems to her so precariously small that the whole process of how an infant grows into a man suddenly seems to her the most mysterious of all mysteries. She invites Ava to sit next to her, up front.

The gray stone chapel, with its simple, un-ironic spire, awaits them. They follow the flagstone walk to the oak door with its impressive handle and flanged hinges.

An usher seizes the carryall and car seat and stroller and leads the way.

Claire had run a public announcement in *Variety*, in addition to the invitation she mailed, and so many people have responded to it that the door has to be left open, and the crowd fills the vestibule and spills onto the lawn. Claire and Ava take seats side by side. Ava holds Chase in her lap. Claire says to Ava, "He won't be here."

Ava

■ *WHO won't be here?* Ava wonders, and all she can think is: *Boyd*. Then she realizes that Claire is referring to Tony. Did he decline Claire's invitation? Did Claire decline to invite him? She wants to know the answers to these questions but she doesn't want to ask them, so she's relieved when someone gets up and steps to the front and begins to talk about Boyd. "He's talking about your daddy," she whispers to Chase, receiving the same unblinking regard that he gave Claire.

There ensue tributes, anecdotes, a poem, a song, a reading, a dramatic monologue (and how could there not be dramatic monologues, given all these actors, she thinks). Sometimes people move to the front, sometimes they simply stand. Eric Harrold, whom she has seen on screen, tells the story of a lunch he had with Boyd. "He looked at me over the water glasses and bread-and-butter plates and said, 'You think you're exploring an edge, when you're young you do and often it's okay, okay to think that, because thinking it can jumpstart a career, but it's merely going to devastate yours because, fact is, you're about a hundred years behind the times. In this century, you don't get to be a feckless Edwardian dandy. In this country, nobody bankrolls a loser for long. I know you don't think of yourself as a loser—you think of yourself as investigating self and reality, as contemptuous of convention, or it could be you're just stupid—but if you're losing the heads' money, you're what they think of as a loser. It's all right with me,' he said, 'if you want to cut your own throat, but somehow I don't think that's what you want to do.' He was a truth-teller, and there are not a lot of those in this industry. I owe him—man, do I owe him. He said he liked movies and horses and that he cried at funerals. Now I'm crying at his. Boyd, I miss you, buddy."

She remembers that she and Marilyn saw Harrold in a movie about corporate spies from outer space. He had played a double agent. With the secret formula on a micro-disk implanted in one of his molars like a filling, he had made his getaway from Altarion-X back to Earth via a worm hole.

Chase cried most of the way from Chicago to Los Angeles, and now exhaustion is proving victorious over curiosity. He slumps in her lap, his head lolling against her breasts. There's a tiny pool of drool at the corner of his mouth, and she wipes it away with her sleeve. When she presses her palm to his cheek, she is amazed, as she is at least a dozen times a day (when she has time to think of it, when she is not simply so busy that she has no time to be amazed at anything), at how soft his skin is, how fresh and new, a pale rose. It is like touching rose petals, the surface as slick as satin, tremulous as a raindrop on a window pane. She feels his sleeping breath on her fingertips. His chin is a sort of radar blip, his forehead is expressive, his lashes are long and surprisingly dark, and as she looks at him, she realizes that he is the great love of her life. No other love could begin to compare with this.

She, who has always felt her life was unnecessary and worked so hard to try to make it mean something at least professionally, must now acknowledge that existence and individuality are intrinsically meaningful. She and her son, both, are nothing to history and the solar system, but because she cannot say that he is nothing, she cannot say that she is nothing.

He is more than history and more than the solar system.

Thinking these thoughts, she is aware that Claire has risen and is walking toward the lectern. Is it a lectern or a pulpit? She doesn't know. She also doesn't know if she wants to hear what Claire says, because it is bound to make her reflect on her own actions. She will have to pay attention to Claire's suffering and her part in it, and she frankly can't see what good that will do anyone. She refrains from looking in Claire's direction and tries to remember the name of that movie, the one with Eric Harrold in it. When she hears Claire saying her name, she realizes she is hearing it for the second time.

"I would like to introduce to you my late husband's son, Chase Buchanan Martel," Claire says, "and his mother, Ava Martel."

She is motioning for Ava to stand up.

Ava stands up, turning to face the gathering.

Does anybody have a clue how to behave here? No. But Claire starts to clap, and others recognize it as a prompt and then everyone is clapping. Chase acknowledges the applause by opening his eyes. Ava catches his wrist—his fat little wrist with its sweet-smelling folds of flesh—and helps him to give a little wave. People smile in spite of themselves. (Who is she? they must be thinking. What kind of marriage had the Buchanans had, anyway? With their bicoastal confusion about the middle of America, they were, perhaps, asking themselves if they had misplaced all the Mormons: was that Tabernacle and the choir in Arkansas and not, after all, Utah?)

People come up to say good-bye to Claire; they miss Boyd, they say, and wish her well. They stop to chuck Chase under the chin or let him grasp their index finger for a moment, then they look at Ava quizzically, shrug, and turn away. Eric Harrold is one of these people. "Nice to meet you," he says to Ava. "Hey, slugger," he says to Chase.

As the crowd thins, Ava sets Chase down on the floor. He is wide awake now, and scrambles speedily on all fours toward Claire, as if he can't get to her fast enough. He grabs her skirt, gripping it with both tiny fists, and hauls himself up, tottering face first into her. She laughs and gets down on the floor with him. Ava drops down beside them. It is almost like having a picnic on the chapel floor.

"Why didn't he come?" she asks.

"I didn't invite him."

Ava nods. Again, she would like to know whether they still see each other but does not want to ask. She is, however, as ever, determined and adroit when it comes to finding out what she needs to know, and canny about the routes of talk, its main roads and underpasses, dead-ends and detours. "I've tried to figure out," she says, "what the source of his power was. His power over us."

"Don't you know?"

Claire has caught her off guard. Ava was not expecting an answer, nor such confidence. Claire knows something that she does not. This humbles her.

She bows her head. "Not really."

"His seriousness," Claire says.

Chase has crawled into Claire's lap. Ava retrieves his toys from the diaper bag and places them on the floor. She thinks back to Tony; she remembers that she couldn't get enough of looking at him. She thinks the source of his power over her may have been his profile. But his profile articulated strength and humanity.

Claire is playing peekaboo with Chase.

Ava is finding it difficult to recall Tony's profile, even though she easily recalls how she once felt about it.

In between boos Claire says, "I've thought about this, about what made him so attractive. It's that he has devoted his life to work that's important, and he does it well."

"It's true," Ava says. "I admired him so much for doing something real. Those of us in academia—well, it's all academic, what we do." She says *academia* because she does not want to say *and the entertainment industry*, but she knows Claire must have the entertainment industry in mind as well as academia. "He may be a selfish son of a bitch, but he's also one of the most generous men I ever met. How can that be? But it is. I guess that's what seriousness is: a form of generosity, a devotion of attention."

"That's what I mean. We can still admire him for that," Claire says. "We can always admire him for that." She takes her hand away from her eyes and says, "Boo," and Chase is filling up with hilarity as if with helium, as if he is a balloon about to float up to the ceiling.

Perhaps it's because they are in a church, but Claire's gold hair looks somehow angelic. Especially with Chase in her arms, gazing up at her as if he's enchanted. "I'd like to see more of him," she says, and Ava knows that this time Claire means Chase. If she didn't know, the look on Claire's face would tell her. There's no sign of confidence there now. Briefly, Claire looks like someone handing over a gun with which she fully assumes she will be shot. "I've been hoping you might let me visit sometime." Ava doesn't know what to say, and Claire stammers, "I have a lot of free time now—"

"I'm so sorry," Ava says, whispering, for she, Ava, is, she thinks, the guilty cause of all that free time. But what can she do about it now? The past is so insistent about remaining past. Confronted with the present, it becomes balky. Becomes downright mulish.

She is turning a soft, fat, toy block over in her hands, over and over. It is made of felt and feels rather spongy. "This is a block that needs to exercise more," she says, looking at it hard. "This is a block that needs to take up weight-lifting, watch its cholesterol. If it weren't for me, Boyd might still be alive."

"Maybe," Claire says. "Maybe not. He always drove like a daredevil. But without you, Boyd's son wouldn't be here."

"*Futures*," Ava says.

"What?"

"That's the name of the movie Eric Harrold was in. I've been trying to think of it. He came up to me. I was surprised he was so polite."

"A lot of actors are like that," Claire said. "When they're not on, they tend to be reserved and mannerly. I was even thinking— I had been thinking of returning to Chicago anyway—"

Ava looks up.

"No, not to see him." Ava has no trouble following Claire; she knows Claire is referring to Tony. "All I mean is, moving to Chicago is not a new idea for me."

"You'd move?"

"Not permanently. I'd take a leave of absence for a year. I could help you with Chase."

Ava drops the block on the tower she has been building for Chase and that makes all the blocks fall, a Babel of colored blocks. Chase picks up his Raggedy Andy and starts chewing on it.

Buildings can topple. Cities can crumble. He has his father's accepting temperament.

When he is not crying.

Then again, Boyd sometimes cried too. As Eric Harrold said in his encomium.

"Are you saying—" She can hardly say it herself, because she doesn't want to be caught in an awkward misunderstanding. "Are you saying, you want to come live with me?"

Chase looks at Claire as if he, too, wants to know what she is going to say.

"Do I want to live with you?"

Claire erases emotion from her face, but it's a hurried job, and Ava can see the traces. "Darling, no," Claire says, the way, Ava thinks, she might have said it to Boyd or Tony. "I would have to have my own place, of course. The idea is that I could—"

But here, emotion returns, and when Claire says the next word, it is less like speaking and more like she is praying.

"—babysit for you, look after Chase when you're working—"

Ava remembers how much she used to want a child, how she would have done anything for a child. How she did do anything for one.

Ava remembers Reykjavik, thinks of trying to give a keynote address while her son sleeps in a hotel room minded by, well, by an Icelander, whoever it was.

"There's the ranch," Claire says, her voice broken and throaty with supplication. "It might be a place for the three of us to spend holidays together, without our actually living together. I don't want to impose."

Ava thinks it is interesting that the word *angelic* came to her mind, and even more interesting that she is surprised it did. Does that mean, she asks herself, that I saw her as demonic? Who did I think she was? She's a woman, a chic, professional woman, a woman who would have had to chip away at the glass ceiling, a woman for whom a kind of countdown is about to begin, a woman I may be someday.

"It's just a proposition," Claire says. "An idea." Claire's voice catches, and Ava is embarrassed, no, she thinks, ashamed, to see tears lining up on Claire's carefully tinted lashes. She fusses with her son's toys.

"He's Boyd's son," Claire says, simply.

"And mine."

"I haven't forgotten. Believe me."

There is room here for something harsh or cynical or mean, but Ava doesn't say it, and neither does Claire.

"A year," Ava says.

"I'll be returning to my job. I do have one, you know."

"Yes," Ava can't help saying, her scholastic research her hobbyhorse with or without a ranch in Santa Fe, and anyhow, equal pay for equal work seems, just now, something like comic relief, "but I bet you're compensated less than your male colleagues. Most of us are." She wants to add, "Especially women of your generation," because she knows it's true, but doesn't. She does say, "If you and Tony pick up where you left off, my ex-boyfriend's lover will be my babysitter! This would be too much like a puzzle where you get tripped up by your assumptions about the doctor's gender."

"I wouldn't have invited him anyway," Claire responds, "but you should know he's seeing someone else now."

There. What she had thought she wanted to know.

And now, she discovers, she has to feign interest, because she has no real interest in Tony anymore. She only needed to locate him in the world, figure out where to place him on her mental map of it. Geography: it says so much about who we are.

"Oh!" Ava exclaims. "Who told you that?"

"Marilyn."

"Marilyn didn't tell me she was in touch with you."

"I called her to see if she thought it would be okay for me to make this suggestion to you."

"I guess she thought it would be okay."

"She said she thought it was a great idea."

Ava is a past master by now of the art of keeping an eye on her son while doing anything else she might be doing, and she has been watching him while she and Claire converse. He has begun to scrinch his eyes, and his cheeks are heating up like two turnips set to boil, and she knows that in about two seconds he is going to give Claire a reason to reconsider her babysitting idea. She checks, but he's dry. "I should feed him before we leave. Do you mind?"

Claire shakes her head, and Ava reclaims Chase and opens her blouse to him.

There's a lull like recess. Ava realizes that she has not given Claire an answer and that Claire is unsure of where to go next. Of where it is safe to go.

"Do your parents mind that you're a single mother?" Claire asks, the one question Ava would never have anticipated.

"My parents?"

"How do they feel about Chase?"

"There's just my father. My mother's dead."

"I didn't know—"

"It was a long time ago." Chase is sucking greedily. Softly she says: "She needed chemo. She refused to do it because she was pregnant with me. She died a couple of months after I was born."

"I'm sorry."

She seems to mean it, and Ava says, and she thinks it is as if Claire has found the switch that opens the hidden door to the secret room, "My father never forgave me."

She is horrified that she has said this. She recognizes that she has presented Claire with information that Claire should never have had to deal with. She doesn't know why she's done this. Possibly because Claire is cool and accessorized, older and capable.

Possibly because Claire's concern is both feelingful and brilliantly composed, something like a Japanese flower arrangement of concern. Ava feels that Claire cares and also that Claire will not punish her for causing her to care.

The room is so silent that Ava can hear the torpid ticking of the fronds and ferns, can almost hear the sunshine brush against the hymnals and Holy Bibles, the envelopes tucked in the backs of pews, awaiting tithes.

Why did she say that? What can Claire say to it?

"He was probably afraid. Afraid that if he got too close to you, you would leave him too."

"Do you think so? I've always figured he just hated me." She practically chokes as she says that. She never said that before, either.

She feels panicky. Her throat is tight. She feels as if she has swallowed a tear.

It has lodged in her esophagus.

It has been a tenant there for her entire life.

Once they put a tube down her throat. The doctors. They wanted to know how many pills she'd taken, but she had not counted. She had not gotten out a scratch pad and made a vertical line for each pill and drawn through every four vertical pencil lines with a horizontal pencil line for the fifth and then started a new set of lines for the next five pills.

She had not gone out and bought an abacus and brought it home and set it down on the table beside the pill bottle and pushed a bead across the wire for each pill swallowed.

She had not looked for the calculator on the top shelf of the hall closet and fetched it down and recorded how many pills were in the bottle to begin with and entered the number and subtracted them one by one.

She had forgotten to do the math.

The minister emerges from a door off to the side and sees them sitting on the floor. "You are welcome to use my office," he says, lifting his eyebrows. "Mrs. Buchanan?"

"Yes?"

"I was going to say that you might like to take some of the greenery home with you."

"No," she says. "The church can keep it."

"People sometimes like to take it home." He waits.

"We won't be long," she assures him.

He recedes into the chapel's hidden chambers.

"The greenery?" Ava says. "Take home the fucking greenery?" They laugh, and the tear that has lived forever in her throat loosens and bursts out in a sob, a sob that shakes her. Will this mar Chase for life, is he imbibing more than her milk, her woe, her grief?

A month ago, Chase would not have noticed anything wrong. Then, his world was her nipple; he wouldn't have noticed that her nose is running and she can't blow it because she is holding him, but now, even with his mouth clamped to her breast, his eyes turn toward Claire, and Ava understands that her son has begun to register that there is a world beyond her, a world of others. There is no telling what he may notice from here on. He may notice anything.

It will be a process, she understands that, too. He will notice and be drawn to and frightened by, and he'll return to her but then he will be pulled away again, and although it will take years, one day he will not come back. What she must do is help him to be ready for that day so that he will enter it confidently, knowing himself strong enough, loved enough, to take a chance on the world.

Can he see that Claire is grieving too? It does not bother Ava that she does not know whether Claire is crying out of sympathy for her or on her own behalf. For Ava's son, or his father.

How can such distinctions matter, when Claire enfolds Ava and Chase in her arms, cradling them both.

After a few moments, the storm is over and the women swipe at lingering tears with their fingers and dab at the moist corners of their eyes with the fingernail side of their forefingers so they won't make their mascara run worse than it already has. They ask each other if their mascara is smeared and reassure each other that it isn't, and they pull away from each other, but not too quickly, they especially take care not to pull away too quickly, because neither wants to hurt or offend the other. Ava takes Chase and puts him in his stroller. She buttons her blouse. She begins collecting the squishy blocks and pacifier and Raggedy Andy, dropping them into a cloth pouch with a drawstring and then dropping the pouch into her copious carryall. The light from outside has dimmed. Shadows are seeping under the pews, down the aisles.

"Getting late," Claire says. "No wonder the minister was trying to get us to leave."

Claire is still waiting for an answer, and now Ava has an answer for Claire.

"It's not such a bad idea," she says.

The camera pulls back into the flooding night as she and Claire leave the chapel with Chase and pans in a leisurely manner down the hillside, the flagstone walk falling away, the woods falling away, the minister closing up the chapel, and Ava settling her plump baby boy in his safety seat and then getting into the limousine with Claire. Between them is a certain lightheartedness, a certain astringency, an unexpected, American frankness, and narrative passion and poetry.

And there is nothing to guide us. And if everything is so nebulous about a matter so elementary as the morals of sex, what is there to guide us in the more subtle morality of all other personal contacts, associations, and activities? Or are we meant to act on impulse alone? It is all a darkness.

—Ford Madox Ford, *The Good Soldier*